Mr. Hudson:
New York City Billionaires Book 1
by Mary Jennings

Table of Contents

GET **"*The Billionaire's Secret Wife*"** FOR FREE

To sign up for my free author newsletter and get your **free copy of the novella *The Billionaire's Secret Wife***, visit maryjenningsauthor.com/secrets

Prologue

The sun was setting in London.

Prior to that weekend, Emilie had never been to Europe, let alone one of its biggest cities. However, given that she didn't live under a rock, she knew London was known for being rainy and cloudy. Therefore, she was naturally surprised to find the sky was clear and sunny upon her arrival and throughout the entirety of the weekend.

She figured if anyone deserved to have the rare English sun shine on their wedding day, it was her friend Lena.

"Can I please get a vodka?" she asked the old man working the deserted bar of the hotel. Everyone else was inside the ballroom where the newlyweds hosted an open bar, but Emilie wanted to be alone.

"Straight vodka, madam?" he asked, eyeing her with concern. His posh accent would have been amusing if Emilie was in the mood to smile.

"Yes, please."

"Aren't you one of the wedding guests? There's an open bar inside—"

"I'm well aware, thank you," Emilie interrupted, staring down the man on the other side of the counter. "Regardless, I would like to order a vodka out here, if you don't mind."

The bartender bowed his head and busied himself with preparing Emilie's drink. His politeness was endearing. Back in New York, her request wouldn't have been second-guessed. What did they care if she was dumb enough to pay for a drink when there was free liquor down the hall? *Mind your business* was the first rule of survival in New York City.

When a short glass with two fingers' worth of vodka was placed on an expensive cloth napkin in front of Emilie, she forced a grateful smile onto her face and took a healthy gulp. The alcohol was smooth and expensive, but that didn't stop it from burning its way down her throat and settling like smoldering coals in the pit of her stomach.

After that, the bartender left her alone.

Emilie felt like a terrible person. There she was, a guest at her friend's beautiful wedding, feeling too sorry for herself to join in on the celebration. The dull thump of the music could be heard from her perch on the barstool, coupled with various shouts and cheers of the reception crowd. Thankfully, Lena wouldn't mind that Emilie had stepped away for a few moments. She knew that Emilie, though a vibrant extrovert like her, was having a difficult time.

In short, Emilie had been stood up by her wedding date.

She'd only been dating Ben Wang for a couple of months and, even though he was a dashing investment banker with wealth and charm by the boatload, the couple had been taking it very slow. Yet, when Emilie bit the bullet and asked him to join her in London for Lena's wedding, he had wholeheartedly agreed. Given that he was a very busy man, the plan was for Ben to take a later flight than Emilie and arrive the morning of the wedding.

However, when Emilie had landed at Heathrow Airport two days earlier, and over the course of the day and evening had not received a single response from her texts and calls to Ben, she understood without question that he wasn't going to show up. Sure enough, when the morning of Lena's wedding day dawned on the bustling city of London, Emilie had no choice but to go stag.

Had he forgotten? Had he died? Had he decided that the best way to end things was to wait for her to go abroad and never speak a word to her ever again?

Emilie didn't know. Nor did she care.

At least, that's what she told herself. The reality was that she was sitting alone at a luxury hotel bar on a Saturday evening, dressed in a stunning red jumpsuit and expensive red lingerie—both of which she had purchased because red was Ben's favorite color—and nursing a glass of vodka like a middle-aged divorcee. The black stilettos she wore had been kicked off the second she sat down on the barstool, abandoned several inches below her on the marble floor, above which her bare feet dangled childishly due to her petite stature.

This wasn't supposed to be happening to her. Emilie was twenty-eight years old. She was beautiful, witty, and usually didn't have trouble earning the affection of men. She should have been drunk off a liter of Prosecco and jumping around on the dance floor with her newly married friend. Instead, here she was, pathetic, sad, and alone.

Emilie was jealous of Lena. In college, they had been thick as thieves. Lena had majored in history and Emilie had majored in studio art, so they had initially bonded over the utter uselessness of their chosen academic paths. But it didn't take long for them to realize that they had a lot of other things in common. For example, they were both spontaneous, loud, and ambitious. They had always planned to graduate and together take the world by storm.

The first part of that plan had gone off without a hitch. They graduated, both at the top of their class. Then Lena had gotten an offer she couldn't refuse from the British Museum to join their curatorial team, moved across the ocean, met the love of her life, and impressed everyone with every breath she took.

Emilie, on the other hand, got a job as a barista at a café on the lower east side, bounced around in various other minimum wage positions over the years, dated a slew of disappointing men, and had become yet another warning to all youth who dreamed of entering a creative yet impractical career field.

It wasn't that Emilie resented Lena for her success. She was happy for her friend. She was so happy for her that she felt as though her heart would burst. Envy is a funny thing, though. It can thrive anywhere, even amongst joy.

Screw Ben, Emilie thought to herself. *Screw Ben and his stupid Soho loft and his ugly Rolex watch and his ridiculously impeccable manners. Screw him. When I get back to Manhattan, I'm going to—*

Emilie was so caught up in her thoughts that she didn't notice the man who sat down on the stool next to her at the quiet bar. That is, not until he leaned over and tapped the side of her empty glass with his index finger.

"If I correctly guess what was in there, can I buy you another?" he asked, his voice deep and velvety. He had an American accent.

Emilie blinked. "Sorry?"

"It wasn't whiskey," continued the stranger, leaning closer to peer into Emilie's glass. "It looks like it was a clear liquor. You don't seem like a tequila girl, and I don't think I've ever met anyone who drinks straight rum. Was it vodka?"

Not knowing what to say to the conversational man, she merely nodded. She could smell alcohol on his breath, but he didn't appear drunk.

The man motioned for the bartender, who was already looking in their direction. They were the only two customers, after all.

"Two vodkas," he requested. "Straight, apparently."

Emilie stared at him. Whoever this man was, he was… *hot*. Like, stupidly hot. The kind of gorgeous that modeling agencies gobbled up. Not too masculine, but not too soft. His skin was light with a flawless golden hue and his black hair was gleaming under the crystal chandeliers.

Maybe it was the effects of the vodka, but all thoughts of Ben immediately dissolved from Emilie's mind.

"It was water, actually," she lied, allowing a smirk to melt onto her lips.

"Oh, shit—" he cursed, quickly turning away to call the bartender back and correct their drink orders, but Emilie giggled and placed a hand on his forearm to stop him.

"I'm just kidding," she said. "You were right. It was vodka."

"You know they've got free vodka inside the ballroom, right?"

"And yet you're also out here ordering not-free drinks."

"Touché," he grinned. "I'm Ezra, by the way. I'm assuming you're here for the wedding, right? Bride or groom?"

"I'm Emilie," she replied, shaking his hand. "And yes… Lena—the bride— and I were friends in college. We were randomly sorted together as roommates freshman year and the rest was history."

"That's sweet," Ezra said with a smile. "I'm here for the groom. Pierre and I have known each other since we were teenagers. We met when my dad was stationed here in England for a couple of years."

Pierre was Lena's new husband. Despite the French name, he was incurably British, down to the blond hair, shy demeanor, and strong opinions on tea versus coffee.

"I see. A military brat," Emilie responded, pursing her lips.

Ezra thanked the bartender when he arrived with their drinks, and turned to raise his eyebrows at Emilie. There was a mischievous glimmer in his eye that was somehow both innocently playful and wickedly daring. Emilie was drawn to him, simultaneously pulled in by his looks and his energy.

"I'm hardly a brat," he quipped, smiling crookedly. "But, yes, my father was in the army. We've lived all over the place. Germany, Korea, Egypt… but I've mostly stayed in one spot since I started college. What about you?"

"What about me?"

"Where are you from?"

"I was born and raised in Queens," Emilie replied. "Other than a field trip to Montreal when I was in high school, this is my first time out of the United States."

"No way! How do you like London?"

Emilie shrugged. "I wasn't expecting the sun to shine, but it's nice. It's a lot different than New York."

"Definitely," Ezra agreed. Emilie wanted to ask him how he knew what New York was like, if he lived there or was merely a tourist at one point, but he carried on speaking without pause. "What's a girl like you doing at wedding by herself, though?"

"A girl like me?"

Ezra took a sip of his drink and flinched, but didn't make any commentary about Emilie's odd choice of beverage.

"Gorgeous, of course," he answered. "It's hard to believe you're here alone."

Emilie raised a single eyebrow at him. The alcohol made her feel bold—bolder than she already was. "The same could be said for you."

Ezra grinned. "I haven't had much time for dating recently. Plus, I kind of like coming to weddings without a date. There's a certain sense of drama to it that I can't resist. What's your excuse?"

"My date bailed," Emilie deadpanned. "He didn't even get on the plane."

"Oh," breathed Ezra. "Sorry. Did he at least have a good excuse?"

"He hasn't said a word to me since I got in the cab to LaGuardia," she admitted. "I mean, it's not like we were a couple or anything. We've only been seeing each other for a couple of months. Maybe asking him to come with me to a destination wedding in London was a mistake, you know? Like, maybe I was asking for too much too soon?"

Ezra frowned at Emilie. "I'm going to be completely honest with you, Emilie. If you asked me to board a flight to Siberia with you right now, I'd do it."

She laughed, warmth rising to her cheeks at his flirtation. Was it just her or was he suddenly sitting a lot closer than before? His presence was so intoxicating that it was difficult for her to maintain awareness of her surroundings, but she'd be lying if she said she didn't like it.

"Well, you're a kinder man than he is, Ezra," she sighed. "It's really no big deal, though. There wasn't much of a spark."

"That's always important," Ezra replied. "A spark. You've got to have chemistry. Otherwise, what's the point?"

Ezra was *definitely* looking down at her lips. God, what was happening? Who was this guy? Where did he come from? Why did she want to drown in his hazel eyes for the rest of her life?

Tearing her gaze away from his, Emilie cleared her throat and downed the rest of her glass.

"I should get back to Lena—" she began, but Ezra placed his hand lightly on top of hers. She froze instantly.

"She's currently six or seven cherry bombs deep and in the middle of a conga line," Ezra laughed. "I don't think she'll mind that you're sitting this one out."

"I can't spend all night out here," she protested. "The bartender already feels bad for me."

Ezra bit his lip. When he did so, Emilie wished she was the one biting down playfully on that plump bottom lip. It was a fleeting thought, but one that made her knees feel like jelly, nonetheless.

"What if we got out of here?" he murmured. Their hands were still touching, the smooth pads of his fingertips resting on top of her knuckles. "I'm staying at a hotel in Kensington. It's not far from here. We could walk."

Emilie spent a grand total of two seconds feeling shocked at his suggestion. She was neither modest nor proper, so Ezra's question didn't sound scandalous. She was an artist. Her most strongly held belief was that inspiration came from treating life like an endless series of adventures. Even if risks didn't work out; in the end, at least she would have a story to tell.

On top of that, Emilie was jilted, bored, and drunk on foreign soil. She didn't know Ezra's surname nor did she know what city he called home, but that was part of the appeal. He was a sexy stranger and she had nothing to lose.

But instead of standing up and following Ezra out of the ritzy hotel that was located right across the street from the stunning chapel where Lena and Pierre had been married hours ago, she shook her head.

"There's no need to go anywhere," Emilie told him. "I've got a room here. Come upstairs with me."

"You don't have to tell me twice," Ezra whispered.

He slipped a large bill across the counter while Emilie stopped to collect her shoes. Giggling and grinning like fools, they dashed toward the elevators and made their way up to the fourth floor. Heart racing, she fumbled with the keycard a few times before the electronic knob finally unlocked with a little *ding*. She pushed the door open a few inches, then paused and stared up at Ezra.

"Wait," she whispered. "This isn't all part of some elaborate plan to kidnap me and force me into an international sex trafficking ring, is it?"

"I was just about to ask you the same question," he joked.

Emilie snorted, then clapped a hand over her mouth in embarrassment.

"Do I look like a kidnapper?" she giggled.

Ezra held up his hands in surrender. "Do I?"

As if she was genuinely thinking about his question, Emilie eyed Ezra up and down. He was tall, broad, and looked incredible in the suit he was wearing. His body was relaxed in the ensemble, as if he was used to formalwear. She knew it was irresponsible to judge someone based on looks alone, but nothing about Ezra suggested that he had ill intentions. From the dark, hungry look in his eyes, he was interested in only one thing that evening.

Emilie's stomach swooped.

She led Ezra into her hotel room. Both Lena and Pierre had buckets of generational wealth, so the luxurious suite was hers for the weekend with no strings attached. Emilie didn't care much for fancy things, but she appreciated the plush mattress and the luxurious French windows that overlooked the courtyard gardens.

"How long have you been here?" Ezra asked once the door closed behind them. Emilie turned around, confused by the question until she remembered that her organizational habits were subpar.

In short, the room was a mess. Her suitcase looked as though it had exploded onto every available surface. Emilie couldn't help that she was a visual person, though. She needed to see every available option in front of her when she was getting dressed for important events.

"A couple of days," she replied.

Ezra smirked. "Looks like you've made yourself at home."

"What are you, my mother?" Emilie chuckled. "Now, add that suit and tie to the pile, pretty boy."

"Pretty boy?" Ezra gasped, reaching up and loosening his tie. "I'm *not* pretty."

"Fragile masculinity isn't sexy nowadays," she giggled, stepping up close to him and pushing his jacket off his shoulders. He tossed it aside onto the chaise by the window.

"In that case, you're right," he crooned, grabbing her waist and holding her tight against his body. "I'm very pretty. However, this pretty boy prefers to be the one in charge in the bedroom."

"Sounds like this pretty boy has his work cut out for him, then," Emilie smirked, pulling down the zipper of her jumpsuit and letting the silky fabric slip off her smooth skin and pool at her feet. "Because I don't like being told what to do."

"Who said anything about me asking nicely?" he purred.

Before Emilie could catch her breath, Ezra picked her up and tossed her onto the bed. She landed softly, bouncing slightly before she managed to sit up halfway and stare at him where he stood at the end of the bed. The look in his eyes suggested that he was gauging her reaction and waiting for any indication to slow down, but Emilie wasn't going to give him that.

She smirked. "Well played."

Ezra unbuttoned his shirt without taking his eyes off of her, then yanked it off and carelessly dropped it onto the carpet. The metallic clicking of his belt buckle filled the room as he quickly did away with his trousers.

"Red suits you," he said to her, eyes raking up and down her body. Emilie bit her lip to hide a smile. She was glad someone was appreciating the overpriced lingerie, even if it wasn't Ben.

In fact, Ben was the furthest thing from her mind in that moment.

When Ezra was in nothing but his briefs, showcasing a toned chest and stomach that made Emilie's mouth water, she wanted nothing more than for him to put his body on top of hers and make her forget her own name. However, he caught her off guard by kneeling at the foot of the bed with a teasing smirk.

"What are you—"

Emilie's question was cut short when Ezra reached up and grabbed behind her knees to yank her down toward him. She squealed with delighted surprise at his strength, too dizzy with desire to play hard to get as he draped her legs over his shoulders and pressed a kiss to the inside of her thigh.

They hadn't even kissed yet and he was already going down on her?

Emilie appreciated a man who cut right to the chase.

He pushed aside the flimsy fabric of her underwear and ducked his head, bracing one elbow on the mattress next to Emilie's hip. Her pulse was racing, her need for him so intense that she was seconds away from tangling her fingers in his luscious hair and pulling his head down between her legs without ceremony.

"Is this okay? I don't want to make you feel uncomforta—"

"If this wasn't okay, your balls would already be on the other side of the room," Emilie assured him, winking to soften her threat.

Ezra chuckled. "Noted."

He carried on, covering her thighs with feverish kisses before finally, *finally* flicking his tongue against her center. Emilie moaned and dug her hands into the bedsheets. As he lapped at her delicate womanhood with ravenous insistence, Emilie unraveled beneath him, but he didn't stop until she was panting for breath and begging for more.

When he decided to give in to her pleading, he slid off the red thong and chucked it behind him. Emilie scooted back on the bed and drank in the sight of his gorgeous body as he stripped down fully and climbed on top of her. Their mouths collided in a desperate, open-mouthed kiss.

"I'm on the pill," she breathed, wrapping her legs around his hips and tugging him closer. She wanted to feel him inside her. "And I'm clean."

"Mhm," he moaned into the curve of her neck. "Me, too."

When their bodies finally came together, it felt like heaven. Emilie always thought it was foolish that romance novels described two people as fitting together like puzzle pieces, but she understood all at once that it wasn't just a metaphor. She truly felt like her body was meant to blossom for his. It was euphoric, unlike anything she'd felt before.

While they made love on top of the satin duvet, Emilie forgot everything else in the universe. She forgot where she was, how she got there, and all the nagging emotions that led her to that fateful bar in the first place.

There was only him.

***

In the morning, it appeared as though London was fed up with the sunshine. When Emilie's heavy eyelids dragged open, she saw nothing but pearlescent gray skies outside the windows.

That, and an empty bed.

He was gone.

With a groan, Emilie sat up and took stock of her sore limbs. They'd been at it most of the night, thanks to his unrivaled stamina. She didn't want it to end, but exhaustion had eventually claimed them.

She listened for the sound of footsteps in the bathroom around the corner or the rush of running water, but there was nothing to indicate Ezra was still there. Frowning to herself, she glanced at the empty sheets beside her and noticed a piece of hotel stationery placed neatly on the pillow he had been using. Emilie snatched it up, scanning the tidy scrawl with tired eyes.

I am so sorry to leave you, but something came up with work and I had to catch the first flight back to the US. It was great to meet you.

The note was signed with a simple *E* for Ezra.

Emilie huffed, disappointment pooling in the pit of her stomach.

"It was nice to meet me?" she hissed mockingly out loud, as if the room could answer her back and provide an explanation for the flippant phrase.

However, as quickly as the frustration appeared, it just as easily melted away. Even though Ezra was clearly as obsessed with his job as Ben was, that didn't mean Emilie had a right to be annoyed at him for it. He was just a beautiful stranger she was lucky enough to cross paths with. It wasn't like they were going home to the same city after this wedding. Emilie didn't even know what he did for work.

And she didn't need to know, she reasoned. She'd had a blissful night of mind-blowing sex with a gorgeous guy and, thanks to that, she was already over Ben Wang and his lame flightiness. That was nothing to be disappointed about.

Chapter One: Present Day (Six Months Later)

"Today's a big day," Annie told Emilie as they walked down the busy Manhattan streets together. "Are you sure you don't want to eat something more substantial for breakfast?"

Emilie rolled her eyes at the pointed glance Annie aimed toward her iced latte. She swore Annie regularly forgot that Emilie was the older sister, not her. Perhaps it had something to do with the fact that, despite being a few years younger than Emilie, Annie had several inches on her.

"I'm too nervous to eat anything," she replied to her sister. "Stop worrying about me. I'm the one who's supposed to be worrying about you. Did *you* eat anything for breakfast?"

Annie laughed and tucked her arm into the crook of Emilie's arm.

"I'll grab a bagel on campus," Annie explained, glancing over her shoulder as they approached the younger sister's usual bus stop on the corner of their block. "And I've got to catch this bus. Good luck, Em!"

"Thanks," Emilie replied, waving goodbye as she dashed off to the stairs leading down to the subway platform. It was barely eight in the morning, but it was a Monday in New York. The city was bustling with commuters, jostling the crowd as they rushed to their destinations and commitments.

Finally, Emilie was one of them. Six years after graduating, she had finally landed a real job in her career field. Well, sort of. Working as a graphic designer in the marketing department of an international transportation company wasn't exactly what she'd had in mind when she started her art degree all those years ago, but it was better than waitressing and making coffee. Plus, having a salaried job at Hudson Enterprises meant she could finally earn enough money to start a savings account and work toward her real future goals.

Not to mention, it would be nice to not have to work almost every day of the week. The idea of working nine-to-five on weekdays and having the weekends off was so foreign to Emilie at that point in her life, she felt as if she had accidentally stumbled upon a rare luxury not intended for her.

But it was intended for her. She had earned this. The offer letter still sitting proudly in her email inbox was proof that she deserved the role at Hudson Enterprises. It didn't matter that she barely knew anything about highspeed trains or avian engineering. All she had to do was draw up a few logos, design a couple of ads, and fly under the radar until she had enough money in her bank account to quit and devote every second of her days and nights to painting real art.

That's what she wanted. Ever since Emilie had been little, she had wanted to be a painter. People warned her left and right that she would struggle to find employment in a field like that, but she never listened to them. One day, when her paintings were hanging in the most famous galleries in the world, Emilie would prove that her hard work had been worth it.

Until then, she was trading steaming plates and bustling tables for clicking keyboards and gray cubicles. It was a small upgrade, but an upgrade nonetheless.

Emilie rode the F train uptown. There was a man sitting across the aisle from her in a perfectly pressed black suit and white shirt. He was handsome, but after a few minutes of observation, she realized that the suit was not as expensive as she had originally thought, and there was a gold nametag affixed to his tie. That, alongside the fact that very few upper-level executives rode the subway, led Emilie to believe that the man was merely a doorman or a chauffeur on the Upper East Side.

Still, for a second, he almost reminded her of—

Nope.

Emilie sighed quietly and refocused her gaze on her hands resting in her lap. Thoughts of the sexy stranger she had shared a rapturous night with six months ago in a posh London hotel usually sat in the furthest reaches of her memory. She revisited them occasionally when she was wrapped in the peace and quiet of her bedroom's shadows, but otherwise kept them under lock and key. When Emilie had returned home from Lena's wedding, she hadn't told a soul about the man.

Not even her sister.

It was strange for Emilie to keep things from Annie, especially since they lived together in a cramped apartment that hovered on the border of Little Italy and Chinatown. Emilie wanted to keep Ezra to herself. He was a delicious secret and she worried that telling someone about him would ruin the glimmering aura of mystery.

She didn't think it was wrong to not tell anyone. Ben was long gone. The fact that they never defined their relationship—and the fact that he had decided to blow her off and leave her alone at a romantic event taking place on a totally different continent—meant that Emilie hadn't cheated on him. And, in terms of the sex itself, it was meaningless. She had gone into it knowing there was a high chance she would never see Ezra again, and she was okay with that.

She was more than okay with that. She had goals now. She was going to do well at her new job, save every spare penny, and spend her newfound leisure time rebuilding her portfolio. Emilie didn't have time for dating. Handsome men were nothing but a distraction. If Ezra had ended up staying in that luxurious hotel bed in London until the morning, or God forbid, any longer than that, Emilie knew she would have fallen for him. How could she not? From what she could recall, he was witty and well-spoken and irresistible—a recipe for disaster.

It was better if he was nothing more than a distant memory.

When the subway screeched to a halt at the Fifty-Seventh Street station, Emilie dragged herself out of her thought spiral and exited onto the platform. She didn't spend much time in this part of Manhattan, though it was the area that tourists were more familiar with. Skyscrapers crafted from glass and steel burst from the concrete, stretching up so high into the sky that Emilie had to tilt her head all the way back to see the top of them.

It was louder, too. There were more taxis, more buses, more people. Businessmen, construction workers, and tourists alike mingled on the pavement, weaving across the congested lanes like ants marching in neat rows. Although she had grown up in New York, Emilie was dazzled by it. Queens was a small, suburban town in comparison to the jungle of midtown Manhattan.

Things happen here, Emilie thought to herself as she directed her steps down the avenue to her new place of employment. *Big things.*

Hudson Enterprises was located on the top ten floors of a modern high-rise that overlooked Central Park to the north. Emilie signed in with security at the front desk on the ground floor and smiled in thanks when the guard ushered her toward the bank of gleaming gold elevators. Her stomach squirmed with excited yet nervous energy as she rose to the twentieth floor and the doors slipped open with a pleasant *ding*.

On her left was a glamorous lobby with plush armchairs for waiting visitors. On her right was a large welcome desk made of black marble. Emilie's patent leather brogues clicked on the glossy floor as she made her way toward the young, impeccably dressed secretary.

"Hi," Emilie said, wondering if she should have worn a suit. Her new supervisor had stated in the welcome email that the dress code was business casual and Emilie decided to overdress to impress on her first day by wearing a skirt and a collared blouse, but the fashionable secretary was making her feel a bit frumpy.

That was part of the younger girl's job, though. She was the first person people saw when they stepped into Hudson Enterprises. Of course she had to look good.

Emilie straightened her spine and smiled at the secretary.

"I'm Emilie DeGaulle," she said. "I'm the new—"

"Right!" chirped the secretary, standing up and reaching across the desk to shake Emilie's hand. "Yasmina told me to look out for a twenty-something blond woman. I'm Koni. I'm basically glued to this desk, but if you need anything or have any questions, you can feel free to ask me."

"It's nice to meet you, Koni," Emilie replied, relieved that the first person she met on her first day was friendly. "I—"

"Shoot!" came the sound of a feminine voice to Emilie's left, causing her to pause in the middle of her sentence. "I knew you'd be five minutes early, so I was trying to beat you here!"

Yasmina Nagim, the woman who interviewed Emilie down in the building's first-floor café last month, hurried to the front desk. She was Emilie's new boss, though she didn't look a day over thirty-five. Emilie was relieved to see that Yasmina was dressed casually in black jeans and a loose sweater, her long braids piled in a bun on top of her head and secured with a pretty silk scarf.

"Hello," Emilie said to her. "Sorry about that! I'll try to be more punctual next time."

"No worries at all! Being early is never a crime," Yasmina grinned, ushering Emilie toward the elevators. "Let's head up to the twenty-third floor where the majority of the marketing department lives."

Emilie waved goodbye to Koni and disappeared into the elevator with her new boss. Everything in the building was pristine and state-of-the-art, down to the stylishly embossed elevator buttons. Despite the warmth she had experienced so far, Emilie was intimidated. This office was a far cry from the dusty cafes and local eateries where she had spent the past several years slaving away.

"Now, as you know, I'm head of the marketing's design unit," Yasmina babbled as they disembarked from the elevator and began weaving through rows of cubicles teeming with life. "You'll report to me, but I report to the president of marketing, which is Paul. He's in a meeting right now, but I'm sure you'll meet him by the end of the day. We've got a big team of graphic designers and we love to bounce our ideas off each other, so—"

As Yasmina talked Emilie through the basics of her new job, Emilie followed behind her and offered polite nods at the appropriate moments. It was a lot to take in, but Emilie was determined to show that she belonged there. The maze of cubicles wasn't nearly as desolate as she expected them to be. Most of the barriers between desks were made from plexiglass, making the separation less obvious. Several curious faces turned in her direction as she trailed after Yasmina. Her new boss didn't give her time to stop and introduce herself to everyone, so she merely smiled and waved hello, knowing she would get the chance to meet the others in time. Hudson Enterprises was a huge company after all, and New York City was only one of many locations where they had an office. There were hundreds of employees all over the globe.

But Emilie would probably be gone before she could meet every single one of them.

"This is your desk," Yasmina told her, stopping abruptly and pointing to an empty cubicle nestled amongst a pod of others that clearly belonged to fellow designers. Sketchpads, pencils, tablets, and industrial erasers were scattered all over the place, as well as dozens of prints in various stages of drafting. "Everything you need should already be here for you, but if not, there's a supply closet down the hall to the right."

"Great," Emilie nodded. "Thanks."

"I would introduce you to the rest of the crew, but most of them don't arrive until nine or nine-thirty. I'm pretty lenient about hours as long as you work a full forty by week's end and get all of your assignments done," Yasmina explained, gesturing for Emilie to take a seat at her new desk.

She obeyed, admiring the expensive technology at her disposal. Emilie's medium of choice was acrylic paint and a blank canvas, but her fingers were already itching to get her hands on the kind of digital drawing equipment she could never afford for herself.

"Let's turn this monitor on and make sure the IT department has your email up and running," Yasmina said, leaning over to flick on the sleek computer. For the next twenty minutes, she gently lectured to Emilie about passwords, software, and basic protocol. It was all very straightforward and simple enough, just as Emilie had hoped it would be.

As Yasmina provided a brief demonstration on how to use the company's private messaging system, Emilie found herself wishing that she had done more thorough research on

Hudson Enterprises before she arrived. She knew enough to get by in her interviews and what to expect day-to-day, but she was suddenly much more curious about the leadership behind the empire. The atmosphere was so welcoming and the amenities so luxurious that she couldn't help but wonder what kind of person ran such a pleasant workplace.

Suddenly, a wave of murmurs and greetings came from around the corner. Neither Yasmina nor Emilie could see who was approaching, thanks to the way Emilie's cubicle was situated, but from the cacophony that erupted at this person's presence, it was clearly someone who everyone knew well.

"Oh, goodness," chuckled Yasmina, stepping away from Emilie's desk to catch a glimpse of the marketing department's visitor. "It looks like you're going to meet the president much sooner than I thought. His meeting must've ended early."

Nervously, Emilie stood and prepared herself to shake a very important person's hand. The only thing she knew about him was that his name was Paul, and she hoped he would be as nice as everyone else she'd met so far.

"Is his desk down here, too?" Emilie asked.

Yasmina opened her mouth to respond, her eyes still trained on a faraway point that Emilie couldn't see, past a large cabinet of tablet charging docks.

"That's unexpected," Yasmina gasped. She quickly stepped close to Emilie and lowered her voice. "This is very rare, but it seems that my boss's boss has decided to take a stroll with him on one of the lower floors."

Emilie cocked her head to the side in confusion. "What does that mean?"

Yasmina shrugged and let out a baffled chuckle. "It means that you're about to have the honor of meeting the CEO of Hudson Enterprises on your very first day!"

Emilie tried not to look as nervous as she felt. The CEO? As in, the owner? The universe must have heard her thoughts, answering her questions about the leader of the company a little too literally.

Before she knew it, a middle-aged man came into view, his bald head bobbing over the tops of the cubicles. He spotted Yasmina and grinned, bustling over to Emilie's cubicle. There was a taller man behind him. He was younger and had thick, dark hair.

"Paul, this is our newest designer, Emilie DeGaulle," Yasmina said. "Emilie, this is Paul, president of the marketing department."

Her hands were shaking as she accepted his handshake and smiled.

"It's very nice to meet you, sir," she choked out, forcing herself to look directly at Paul instead of ogling the man next to him.

"Likewise, Emilie," Paul replied with a smile. "Now, allow me the honor of introducing you to the CEO of Hudson Enterprises, Mr. Hudson himself."

Emilie didn't know CEOs could be that young. Or that handsome.

But Emilie didn't need an introduction. Though it seemed like the most impossible thing in the world, she already knew the CEO of Hudson Enterprises. She had met him six months previously and didn't even realize it.

Mr. Hudson was... Ezra.

Chapter Two

It was her.

The woman that Ezra couldn't get out of his mind from the moment he first saw her six months ago. She was so beautiful that Ezra had worried he was hallucinating when he spotted her perched on a barstool by herself, her slim figure adorned in red silk.

Her name was Emilie.

"With an *ie* at the end, not a *y*," she had informed him when she introduced herself last September. "My mother thought the spelling was unique, but it's really just a pain in the ass."

She was funny, he remembered. Bold. Sexy.

And the way she had moaned in his ear—

Ezra blinked, thrust back into the present day by the sheer unlikeliness of the situation in front of him. Sure, she had mentioned she was from Queens, but she didn't say she still lived in New York. Ezra had meant to clarify, meant to bring up the fact that he also lived in the city, but he was so distracted by her emerald eyes and golden hair—not to mention the mental fog from the vodka—that he could hardly think straight that night.

What were the chances that, six months after he forced himself to leave her bed at a luxury hotel in London to deal with an emergency contract issue in Chicago, Emilie would land a job at his company? What was her role? Where were they?

The marketing department. Paul was his marketing president and Yasmina was head of the design team.

She's a designer, Ezra thought. *An artist. I had no idea.*

All those thoughts raced through his head in a matter of seconds, quickly enough for Ezra to maintain his composure and offer Emilie a smile.

"Emilie," Ezra said aloud, nodding his head in welcome. The barrier of her cubicle wall made it too awkward for them to attempt a handshake. "Welcome to Hudson Enterprises. Is this your first day?"

Ezra's first fear was that Emilie wouldn't recognize him, but the expression on her face told him that she did. She wore a combination of barely concealed shock and embarrassment. Clearly, she was horrified to discover the interesting new way that fate had decided to weave their paths together. Ezra was just as surprised, but was neither ashamed nor disturbed. Ever since he'd left London, he had wanted to look for the mysterious woman who had set his entire world on fire in the best way possible, but he didn't know where to start.

"Yes, it is," Emilie answered him. "It's nice to meet you, Mr. Hudson."

Mr. Hudson. It was an awkward formality considering Ezra was younger than many of the employees, but when he tried to encourage everyone, even the janitors, to call him by his first name, it never caught on. Everyone was apparently determined to maintain that boundary, so Ezra let it go.

There was a beat of awkward silence in which Paul and Yasmina glanced between Ezra and Emilie with confusion. They could sense the tension, but Ezra wasn't about to embarrass Emilie even further on her first day. He hoped she wasn't thinking of quitting now that she knew who she worked for. Hudson Enterprises was a competitive corporation, and although Ezra didn't meet every single new person who was welcomed on board, he was very specific about his hiring standards. If Emilie had made it this far, she was not only incredibly smart and talented, but she also deserved to be there.

"You as well, Miss—I'm sorry, but I don't think I caught your last name," Ezra replied, yearning for a crumb of information about the woman who had plagued his thoughts for the past six months.

"DeGaulle," she answered. "Like the airport in Paris."

Ezra chuckled. "Are you of any relation to the late officer Charles de Gaulle?"

He remembered that she had mentioned her trip to London was only her second time leaving the United States, but that didn't mean she couldn't have French ancestry.

Emilie laughed as if he had told a joke. "No. I'm of no importance whatsoever."

"That's not true," Ezra responded automatically before pausing and glancing at Paul and Yasmina. "Everyone at Hudson Enterprises is important."

Of course, what Ezra meant to say was that Emilie was important because she was beautiful, bold, and impossible to forget. That was not something a CEO could say to an entry-level employee without raising a few eyebrows, so he kept it to himself.

"That is absolutely true, Mr. Hudson," added Paul cheerfully.

Ezra smiled politely at him and then nodded at Emilie and Yasmina.

"If you don't mind, I should be getting back up to my office," he explained, already stepping away from the scene. "I have a few calls to make."

Everyone said their goodbyes to him, but the only thing Ezra paid attention to was Emilie's nervous wave as he retreated to the elevators. His heart was pounding in his chest, and he wanted nothing more than to take her hand and pull her out of the building to ask her a thousand different questions.

That would be impossible, though. There were too many prying eyes. Plus, Ezra didn't need to ask to know that Emilie wasn't keen to have her new coworkers find out what had happened between them. Ezra was going to have to handle the situation tactfully and gracefully.

Deep down, however, he wanted to relive their night together in London. He wanted to experience it over and over again. As the elevator took him to the thirtieth floor—the top level of the building where the executive suites were located—Ezra's imagination ran away with him. Even though he barely knew Emilie, he already knew that it was going to be difficult to keep his fantasies in check now that she was so close to him.

But Ezra was used to getting his way. Not because he was spoiled or entitled, but because he was highly intelligent and worked hard for every ounce of success he enjoyed. There was a reason that he owned a billion-dollar corporation. He could formulate a plan and follow through.

Now Ezra had to strategize how best to approach Emilie and make her his.

Unfortunately, Matt was waiting for Ezra inside his office. Matthew Sanchez was the CFO of Hudson Enterprises and Ezra's righthand man. They had gone to college together, engaging in friendly competition throughout the duration of their undergraduate years all the way up to the day they earned their MBAs. A year later, when Ezra started Hudson Enterprises and reached out to ask Matt to join him, it took barely any convincing at all.

"Where have you been?" Matt asked, lounging casually in one of the tufted leather seats facing Ezra's desk. "Your assistant said your morning was clear."

Ezra quirked an eyebrow at Matt and settled down in his desk chair, which was an impressive feat of ergonomic engineering that cost him thousands of dollars but was totally worth it.

"Why are you bothering my assistant?" Ezra snorted. "Just text me."

"I did," Matt smirked. "Turns out Jess is ten times much more adept at communication than you are. You should give her a raise."

"Yes, I probably should," mused Ezra, leaning back and crossing his arms against his chest. All he wanted was to be alone and think about Emilie, but he didn't want to be rude to his business partner. "What do you need from me?"

Matt's expression melted into a frown as he rested forward with his elbows on his knees and sighed loudly in frustration.

"Blackwell got the land in Vermont," he announced.

Instantly, Ezra's mood darkened. He placed his palms on top of his desk and sat up straight.

"Since when?" he asked Matt.

"Since last night, apparently. The punk had already sent out a press release by eight this morning."

The punk Matt was referring to was Anderson Blackwell, the CEO of Blackwell Capital. His company was Hudson Enterprises' biggest competition in this sector of the transportation industry and had been nothing but a thorn in Ezra's side for years. Blackwell was constantly blocking Ezra's contracts, snatching up his clients, and causing endless inconveniences.

Despite that, Ezra usually managed to come out on top. He didn't believe in playing dirty. Rather, he was convinced that making smart, well-calculated decisions was the key to staying ahead in the competitive market. It was undeniable that Hudson Enterprises was a better company than Blackwell Capital, not only because their stock was more valuable and their business was more publicly reputable, but also because Ezra didn't spend his time seeking out ways to get in Blackwell's way. He didn't have to. He just had to stay true to his principles and carry on with his vision.

"He didn't even put a bid on the Vermont land," Ezra said.

"He must have done it at the last minute."

"Classic Blackwell."

Matt sighed. "I don't really know what to do. This isn't the first time he's tried to snatch up land before us, but usually we've been able to block the sale. I'm assuming he presented the property managers with an offer they couldn't refuse."

Ezra nodded and tapped the trackpad to wake up his computer. The company in Vermont that Hudson Enterprises was planning to purchase land from was family-owned and financially struggling. Ezra had offered them a fair deal, promising only ethical construction and minimally invasive structures on the land, and was under the impression that the contract was practically in his hands.

"What's his plan, anyway?" Ezra scoffed. "He's barely got a foothold in the railroad industry and that land can't be used for much else."

"The press release stated that Blackwell Capital intended to use it to build a factory," Matt groaned.

"You're joking."

"I wish I was."

Ezra fought the urge to chuck the crystal paperweight resting on his desk through the window. Not only was Anderson Blackwell determined to be a continuous nuisance, he was also hellbent on being a generally awful human being.

Hudson Enterprises constructed, owned, and operated an extensive series of railroads throughout the United States under the brand of Samson Railways—named after Ezra's grandfather. One of his biggest missions was to expand mass transit in the country and make it more affordable for everyone. So far, it was going phenomenally well. So well that Ezra was planning to buy the land in Vermont to start expanding the railways into Canada. He had already jumped through the legal hoops to make it possible, but those months of headaches were going to go down the drain if Blackwell got his way. Instead of helping people become more mobile without the need for vehicles, Blackwell intended to pump ridiculous amounts of carbon emissions into the air to construct more of his foolish, gaudy jets.

Ezra's nose wrinkled with disgust. Some people's morals were truly in the wrong place. Matt waited to hear what Ezra's plan was, but Ezra wordlessly picked up his phone and pressed the button that connected him directly to his assistant down the hall.

"What's up, Mr. Hudson?" chirped Jess. She was a spunky Yale graduate with a no-nonsense attitude and unparalleled work ethic.

"Hey, Jess," Ezra sighed. "Can you please schedule a meeting for Matt, Cassie, and me in the legal department as soon as possible? This afternoon would be ideal."

"No problem," she replied on the other end of the line. "I'm pulling up her calendar right now. What should I tell her the meeting is for?"

"I need to see what I can do about blocking a sale," he explained. "It's Blackwell again."

"Say no more, Boss. I'll confirm in the next five minutes."

"Thanks, Jess."

His assistant hung up before him, the sound of her furiously typing on her keyboard in the background cutting off abruptly.

Ezra glanced at Matt. "Cassie's a bulldog. She'll figure something out."

Matt shrugged and stood. "Sounds good to me. I can't stand that bastard."

"You and me both," Ezra agreed as Matt made his way out of the office. "Hey, would you mind closing the door on your way out?"

"No more open-door policy?" joked Matt.

Ezra rolled his eyes.

"I promised my mother I would call her," he lied smoothly.

Matt laughed as if he understood exactly what Ezra meant by that statement alone.

"Give Nadia my regards," he said before ducking through the doorway and closing the door behind him.

The truth was that Ezra's mother was not expecting a call from him any time soon. She was on a meditation retreat in Nepal, but Ezra knew she wasn't exactly roughing it. He pictured his mother surrounded by a dozen other wealthy, middle-aged women with nothing better to do than pretend to be devout Buddhists for the month.

Nadia Hudson, born Nadia Nachkeva, was the only daughter of a wealthy couple who'd struck gold in the oil industry in the seventies. She was an heiress to hundreds of millions of dollars, never had to work a day in her life, and had the privilege of marrying for love rather than status.

But that didn't mean Ezra's father was a nobody. Major Jonathan Hudson was a respected army engineer with a degree from MIT and handsome looks that caused many to ask why he didn't become a model or actor. Nadia fell in love with him instantly, embarking on a romance that would take her all over the world.

When Ezra's father died eleven years prior, Ezra was only twenty years old and was in the middle of his sophomore year of college, but he was more worried about his mother than himself. Nadia had always been unpredictable and ruled by her emotions; Ezra feared that she would go completely off the rails at the loss of her husband. She surprised him, though. Rather than losing her mind, Ezra's mother devoted herself to wellness and serenity. Ezra understood that the overpriced yoga retreats and exclusive foreign spas were just a distraction for his mother, but if they kept her reasonably stable, he wasn't going to intervene.

He cared about her, but he wasn't the parent.

Ezra cleared his throat and opened his email inbox. There was already a note from Jess confirming his meeting with the legal department that afternoon right after lunch, but that wasn't what he was looking for.

A man less ruled by his heart might have spent his morning fulfilling his CEO responsibilities, but Ezra was a romantic person on a mission. He bypassed his assistant's email and opened the company directory. There were hundreds of employees in New York alone, dozens of whom went by the name Emily, but only one who spelled it with an *ie* at the end. Ezra's sharp memory was both a blessing and curse; he could replay every single detail of the night he first met Emilie, even if it felt like torture to know that he might truly never see her again.

He was glad that he'd held out hope for this long. The IT department was quick at setting up new employees in the system. He found her name in the directory within seconds.

Emilie DeGaulle.

"Like the airport in Paris," Ezra whispered aloud, a wistful smile on his face. He felt like a teenage boy experiencing a crush for the first time. Emilie was a complete mystery to him, but she fascinated him. He had to know more about her.

He clicked on her name. It revealed the extension that would connect him to the landline at her desk, as well as her title and her location in the building.

Junior Graphic Designer, Marketing, 23rd Floor, Suite 8

It was a roadmap to her, but he couldn't follow it, literally. He couldn't go back down there just to see her emerald eyes and charming smile again. She would have to explain why the CEO kept speaking to her and he didn't want to cause anyone to feel suspicious toward her. He wanted to make her life easier, not more difficult.

Scratch that. He didn't just want to make her life easy. He wanted to make it magical. Blissful. A dream come true.

But he was getting ahead of himself.

Ezra opened a blank template and copied Emilie's email into the address bar. His fingertips drummed on the keys for several minutes. He had to be professional. All of the company's emails were archived and stored in a massive hard drive. Not only was it safer and more convenient to make it impossible for employees to fully delete any communications, but it was also a necessary legal measure. Hudson Enterprises dealt with many serious clients, including governments. Everything had to be pristine.

Miss DeGaulle, Ezra wrote. *I wanted to formally welcome you to the company and wish you the best of luck in your new role. I'd like to discuss how I can personally make your goals as a designer at Hudson Enterprises more attainable. Please meet me in my office on the 30th floor at 11 this morning if you are available.*

He hesitated, reading over the words of the email to ensure that it sounded reasonable and respectful. Ezra often met with personnel to discuss their future trajectory within the company, but he rarely took the time to sit down with lower-level employees. Still, maybe it was something he should consider putting into practice moving forward. As he had told Emilie, everyone at his company was important. They all deserved a chance to speak with the man in charge.

That's what Ezra told himself to calm his nerves.

Yours, he almost signed the email, but quickly hit the backspace button and went for *Warmest regards* instead. Hopefully, Emilie would be able to read between the lines and understand, that while Ezra was more than happy to actually discuss her career goals with her, there were other, more immediate things they needed to talk about.

For example, he was desperate to know if Emilie was as deliciously haunted by that night in London as he was. There was a chance she thought of it as nothing more than a random hookup, which happened often in the wake of boozy wedding receptions. Either way, Ezra had to know.

He sent the email and sat back in his chair, staring at the computer screen and trying to imagine what her face would look like when she saw a message from him pop up in her inbox. More than anything, he hoped she would see his name and smile.

Chapter Three

Emilie was overwhelmed, but not unpleasantly so. She could already tell the days at Hudson Enterprises would be fast paced, but she preferred chaos over boredom anyway. Since she had set foot in the building two hours ago, she'd met her cubicle neighbors and given her opinion on at least ten different designs currently being drafted for a variety of projects. She could hardly believe that anyone cared what she thought about a design, given that it was only her first day, but the creative team didn't seem to care about any of that. Rather, they appeared excited to pick her brain.

Half the morning rushed by before Emilie noticed. By the time she was able to sit down and open her new email account, her mind was spinning with all the information she'd absorbed in such a short span of time.

But that was nothing compared to how she felt when she saw an unread message waiting in her inbox. The sender's name was printed boldly in the subject line, impossible to ignore.

Ezra Hudson. That was it. Not *Ezra Hudson, MBA, CEO of Hudson Enterprises.* Just Ezra. He was confident and dominant, but he was also humble. There was a small part of Emilie that wished he was a pompous douche bag, that she would discover the man she'd had a passionate one-night stand with was nothing to waste time daydreaming about.

That would make it easier for her to finally move on from what had happened in London. She could brush away the tendrils of memories like cobwebs from the corners of her mind and throw every ounce of her mental energy into following her dream of becoming a painter.

Unfortunately, Ezra wasn't complying with her secret wishes. He was polite and modest. Everyone seemed to like him or at least respect him. If only she'd done the responsible thing and looked up information on who managed the company where she was working ahead of time. If she'd known that the CEO was Ezra—

Emilie frowned, her mouse hovering over his email.

If she'd known, would she have taken back her acceptance of the job offer? Would she have gone back to working for minimum wage seven days a week just to scrape by? Would she have willingly taken a step away from an opportunity that would bring her closer to her ultimate goal?

No. Emilie knew herself. Not only would she have been too curious about Ezra once she found out he was the CEO of a massive company, she was also not easily deterred from her goals. Sure, it was incredibly awkward that the boss of her boss's boss was the same guy she'd had a drunken hook-up with at her friend's wedding last summer. But it wasn't embarrassing enough to cause Emilie to give up a rare and precious opportunity.

People hooked-up all the time. Young and old, rich and poor. It didn't have to mean anything more than two people enjoying pure human pleasure for an evening and moving on. Emilie was sure Ezra felt the same way. He probably dated heiresses and models, not starving artists who wouldn't land their first salaried position until several years after graduation.

She opened Ezra's email and frowned at the screen.

I wanted to formally welcome you to the company.

Did he do that for all new employees? Probably. She shouldn't get ahead of herself and think that she was receiving special treatment from him just because—

"Hey, Emilie! Do you want to come look at—oh, good! Your email account is working!" Yasmina chirped, popping around the corner of Emilie's cubicle with a smile on her face and catching a glimpse of the message open on Emilie's screen.

"Yes," Emilie nodded. "I have an email from Ez—Mr. Hudson."

Yasmina's grin crumpled into a confused frown.

"Mr. Hudson? Ezra Hudson? The CEO?"

"Yes," Emilie repeated, gesturing to the email to indicate that her supervisor was welcome to read it herself. Maybe Yasmina could clarify what to expect from the meeting.

Yasmina's visible confusion grew more pronounced. When she was done reading, she stood up straight and furrowed her brow at Emilie.

"That's odd," she said. "Must be a new thing he's trying out. It's nice of him actually."

So, it wasn't normal for the CEO to request meetings with minor employees on their first day. At least, not historically.

Emilie glanced at Yasmina, hoping that the nervousness she felt at the idea of being alone in a room with Ezra again translated into anxiety about speaking with someone who in Yasmina's eyes was such an important man.

"I wasn't expecting this," Emilie admitted. "Should I have prepared something?"

Yasmina waved off her questions. "No, Mr. Hudson is a very easygoing, casual man. I mean, you met him earlier, so you know how nice he is. He really goes out of his way to make people comfortable."

"Right."

"You should get going, though," Yasmina continued, glancing down at her watch. "You've got about five minutes to get up to the thirtieth floor. Good luck! I'll catch up with you when you get back."

Emilie had no choice but to stand and find her way back to the elevators. She pressed the button marked with a *30* and smoothed down the front of her wool skirt. Did she look okay? Her outfit was a far cry from the lowcut jumpsuit she'd worn at Lena's wedding, and it was also nothing like what she wore when she wasn't working. She felt as if she were playing dress up with her mother's clothes, but at least she appeared professional.

There was another welcome desk on the top floor of the building, but it was manned by a girl who was too absorbed by a pile of paperwork in front of her to be as bright and cheerful as Koni. Emilie paused, glancing around awkwardly and internally kicking herself for not asking Yasmina how to get to Ezra's office. Then again, maybe she didn't know. Clearly, this floor was reserved for very important executives. It was much quieter and there wasn't a cubicle in sight. Rather, intimidating doors leading to large, luxurious suites with expensive desks and plush chairs.

"Hi," Emilie said to the busy girl. "Sorry. I have a meeting with Mr. Hudson at eleven. Which one is his office?"

The girl looked up instantly when Emilie mentioned Ezra's surname. Her expression wasn't unkind, but it was obvious that she was trying to figure out why someone like Emilie would have a meeting with someone like Mr. Hudson.

"I didn't know he had another meeting," said the girl. "Who are you with?"

She understood that the girl was doing her due diligence, not wanting to let a potential sociopath wander freely up to Ezra's office, but Emilie blushed with embarrassment nonetheless.

"I work in the marketing department," Emilie explained. "It's actually my first day. Mr. Hudson asked to see me."

"He did?"

"Yes."

The girl, who didn't bother introducing herself, confirmed what Yasmina had implied—Ezra was acting out of the ordinary.

"Okay," she shrugged. "It's down that hallway over there, keep walking until you hit the end, then take a left. His office is at the end of that hall. You can't miss it. There's a gold plaque on the door."

"Thanks," Emilie breathed, quickly turning down the marble-floored hall the girl had indicated. She didn't wear a watch, but an avant-garde clock on the wall told her that she was about to be late.

Just as the girl had said, Ezra's office was hard to miss. It was slightly separated from the others, taking up more space on that floor than the others. The other doors had plaques on them, but Ezra's was the only one that had *CEO of Hudson Enterprises* printed on it, so Emilie was able to locate it easily.

His door was closed. She took a deep breath, composed herself, and knocked on the smooth mahogany.

"Come in," called a masculine voice from within.

Willing her hand not to shake, Emilie turned the knob and timidly poked her head inside the office.

"Hi," she said, offering a small smile to the tall, broad-shouldered man seated behind the desk. Ezra stood up the second he saw her, waving her inside.

"Hi, Emilie," he replied with a polite grin. "Please come sit down. Also, please close the door behind you if you don't mind."

For some reason, Emilie felt like a schoolkid who had been sent to the principal's office for bad behavior. Ezra's formality grated her the wrong way, but she understood why he was acting this way. This was his company. He couldn't go around suggesting that there was anything other than pristine professionalism going on between them.

Emilie approached one of the leather chairs and lowered herself onto the surprisingly comfortable material. Ezra sat down in his seat and rested his elbows on the armrests. Silence spanned the distance between them, but it wasn't uncomfortable—rather, it was tense in a way that made her stomach flip and her heartrate increase.

She couldn't stop thinking about how unreasonably attractive he was. It wasn't fair for someone like Ezra Hudson to walk around the planet looking like that. How was anyone supposed to sleep at night knowing beauty like that existed? Her thoughts were verging on blatantly overdramatic, but Emilie couldn't help herself.

The last time she had seen Ezra, he was lying beside her in the tangled sheets of a king-size bed in a posh hotel suite. Back then, she was fascinated by him because he was handsome, charismatic, and unbearably sexy. Over the past few months, she'd wondered if her memories were making Ezra seem better than he really was, enhanced by the alcohol and the ambience of a romantic wedding.

Now, however, Emilie still believed that he was all those things and so much more. In fact, her memory barely did Ezra justice. Not to mention, he was friendly and polite, as well as outrageously wealthy and successful. Ezra was the total package.

Emilie was doomed.

"So," Ezra said, puffing out an exhale from between pouted lips.

"So," Emilie echoed, crossing her legs and boldly meeting his gaze.

"Where have you been?" he asked.

She cocked her head to the side. "What?"

"Since the wedding," he clarified. "Have you been in New York the whole time? How have I not seen you before today?"

Emilie's lips curved into an amused smirk. "I don't think we run in the same circles, Mr. Hudson."

"Please call me Ezra," he responded quickly. "And what makes you say that?"

She couldn't believe he was forcing her to explain. Ezra knew he was a billionaire. He had become a CEO before turning thirty. Emilie was… just Emilie. She was twenty-eight, worked an entry-level position, and barely had a penny to her name. On top of that, New York was a huge city. It made perfect sense that they had gone six months without stumbling into each other again.

Instead of saying all those things aloud, Emilie cleared her throat and sat back in the chair.

"I don't know why you're asking me those questions," she quipped. "You're the one who was gone in the morning. You left a note, but you didn't leave your number."

Ezra groaned and raked a hand through his hair. The motion left it so seductively tousled that Emilie had to avert her eyes for a few seconds and focus on the Manhattan skyline outside the windows.

"I know," he sighed. "I didn't even realize I forgot the most important part until I was on my jet and halfway across the Atlantic. Part of me was tempted to ask the pilot to turn around and bring me back, but I was telling the truth when I mentioned I had to leave for a work-related emergency. Believe me, though. I definitely did not mean to leave you high and dry."

Emilie was surprised by his confession. Everything that happened after the night they'd shared suggested Ezra was content to treat it as a meaningless fling. Urged on by her desire to stay focused on her art career, Emilie had followed suit.

She shrugged, remembering the reason Ezra was at the wedding in the first place was because Lena's new husband was an old friend of his.

"You didn't ask Pierre to get it for you?" she inquired.

Emilie wasn't close with Pierre, but it would have been simple enough for Ezra to ask his friend to inquire for her contact information from Lena.

Ezra shrugged sheepishly. "Pierre and I are good friends, but we don't really know each other like that. It would've been a bit awkward to explain that I needed him to ask his wife to get me one of her friend's numbers because I left the reception early to hook up with said friend."

Emilie blushed. "Fair point."

It wasn't as if Emilie expected Ezra to exhaust all his available resources to find her again. She wasn't self-absorbed like that.

"What about you?" Ezra asked.

"What do you mean?"

"Why didn't you ask Lena to pester her husband for my number?"

She sighed quietly. She was glad the office door was shut. It was nice that Ezra cared enough to keep up appearances with his professional email and closed doors. Although it was more for his reputation than hers, it showed that he was a respectful man.

"I actually didn't tell Lena about what happened," she admitted. "I haven't told anyone."

"Really? That embarrassed?" Ezra was smirking, indicating that he was joking. Emilie fixed him with a stern stare, but her heart wasn't in it.

"No," she replied. "I had a good time. I am very shocked to learn that you own the company I work for, though."

"Well, congratulations. Without intending to sound egotistic, I know it's quite difficult to receive an offer from Hudson Enterprises. You must be very talented," he told her, hazel eyes twinkling with a mixture of emotions that Emilie couldn't decode. "I didn't even know you were a graphic designer."

"It's not like we did much talking before," she replied before quickly pressing her fingertips to her mouth; she didn't mean to make the suggestive comment out loud. "But maybe we shouldn't discuss that while we're here at our respective jobs."

"Would that make you more comfortable?" Ezra asked. "I didn't mean to upset you, by the way. You know, with the weird email? I just knew I couldn't sit around for the rest of the day knowing that the girl who eluded me for six months was just a few floors below me."

Emilie blinked. Had Ezra really been that fixated on her? Given how attractive he was, she figured she was just one of the many women he had charmed into bed. She didn't mind. She wasn't needy like that. Ezra was just some hot guy she had known for less than twenty-four hours; she wasn't expecting a dozen roses and a marriage proposal the morning after.

"It's okay," Emilie assured him. "But I would like to keep this whole situation behind closed doors. As in, it would probably be best if no one else knew that we've met before in general."

Perhaps she was mistaken, but Ezra appeared vaguely disappointed by her statement. He nodded and straightened in his chair.

"I understand. In that case, how about we have dinner tonight?"

Emilie's lips parted in surprise. "Dinner?"

"I'm not going to lie to you, Emilie," Ezra began. "I've thought of you pretty much constantly since leaving London. Now that you've miraculously stumbled across my path, I'll do whatever it takes to convince you to give me a proper chance."

"A… chance?"

He leaned forward, gazing deep into her eyes. "One date. Just dinner. Tonight. You can even walk out on me in the middle of it if you're not completely charmed."

"I don't think that's a good idea," Emilie protested. Even as she spoke the words out loud, her stomach sank with dread. She didn't want to reject him, but it was the right thing to do.

"Why not?" he replied.

"I'm busy tonight," she lied.

It wasn't that much of a lie. Emilie had plans that night to lock herself in her bedroom and paint. She wanted to refresh her current portfolio before she started sending inquiries to galleries. The works that were displayed on her basic website were outdated, paintings from years prior when she wasn't utterly exhausted from her endless string of dead-end jobs.

"Busy doing what?" Ezra pressed. He wasn't being rude, his tone merely curious as if he only wanted to know more about her life.

Emilie fought the urge to sigh again. "I just don't think it's a good idea for me to see you outside of work hours. I don't want to draw any negative attention toward myself before the end of my first week."

"Nobody has to know," he said. "It's not like either one of us would be lying by keeping it to ourselves. Everyone has private lives that they don't discuss at work."

She should say no. She should put her foot down and tell him to find another woman to pursue. The dinner invitation was obviously not of a professional nature and Emilie wasn't interested in getting involved with the company's CEO in that way. On top of that, her priority needed to be her art. She wasn't going to get anywhere as a serious artist if she was gallivanting around the city with a dashing billionaire.

And yet... this was the man who had danced on the borders of her mind for months, who crooned in her ear when he moved inside her, who caused goosebumps to erupt on her skin with a singular glance. He was alluring and he was obviously interested in pursuing her.

How could Emilie possibly find the strength to say no to Ezra Hudson? Her heart and her mind agreed it was the last thing she wanted to do.

Sensing her hesitation easily, Ezra softened his gaze.

"Just one dinner," he pleaded. "Let me make up for my disappearing act in London. If you decide afterward that you're not interested, I'll leave you alone. I promise."

She turned her face away, observing the bookcases stuffed with hundreds of tomes, most of them nonfiction works about transportation and engineering. Beside the bookcase were two college degrees framed on the wall, but Emilie was too far away to catch a glimpse of the words on them.

Finally, she took a deep breath and nodded.

"Fine," she said. "We can have dinner."

Ezra's face glowed when he smiled at her.

"Great. We can leave right from here together. Six o'clock? Or my chauffeur Henry can pick you up around the corner if you don't want anyone to see you getting into my car," he offered.

"Sure," Emilie agreed. "Sounds good to me."

Even as she accepted Ezra's dinner invitation, she was simultaneously overcome with trepidation and excitement. The warring emotions jostled for dominance, but neither was able to gain the upper hand.

A few minutes later, as Emilie made her way out of his office and wove through the executive floor of Hudson Enterprises, she couldn't help wondering what on earth she'd gotten herself into.

Chapter Four

Ezra wasn't a fool. He could tell that Emilie was reluctant to accept his dinner invitation, but he was relieved when she'd eventually agreed. However, he desperately hoped that she hadn't done it just to appease him.

He hoped she genuinely wanted to come.

But he understood her hesitation. It was her first day of work and she was likely already overwhelmed by that adjustment alone. Adding onto the fact that a random hook-up of hers was the CEO and was not shy about his attraction to her was probably not helping with the nerves.

Despite that, Ezra would show her that she wouldn't regret taking a chance on him. He hadn't imagined the connection between them in London. It was undeniable, even in the quiet formality of his office. The air was full of electricity whenever Emilie was around him, as if a thunderstorm was brewing on the horizon.

Ezra glanced at the time and then whipped out his phone, dialing the number for one of the most exclusive restaurants in the East Village. He wanted to impress her.

"Thank you for calling the Orange Rose," answered a French-accented voice after several droning rings. "How may I help you?"

"Good morning. Would it be possible to make a reservation for dinner tonight?" Ezra inquired.

There was a brief pause. Ezra already knew what was coming, but it wasn't going to be a problem.

"Sir, we are fully booked for the next three weeks," answered the man firmly. "Unfortunately, we would not be able to accommodate you this evening, but if you'd like to reserve a table for next month, I'd be happy to assist you."

Ezra smiled to himself. "My apologies, sir. I should have introduced myself beforehand. This is Ezra Hudson of—"

"Mr. Hudson!" exclaimed the man, needing no more prompting than those few words alone. "Ah, *monsieur*, why did you not say anything sooner? *Oui*, it will be no problem at all to get you a table for tonight."

"Are you sure? I don't want to be a bother," Ezra replied, hoping to allow the man to regain at least some of his dignity.

"Of course, of course! How many seats will you be needing at your table, sir?"

"Just two," he responded. "We should arrive around seven."

"No problem, Mr. Hudson. See you tonight."

"Thank you very much."

Ezra let out a quiet chuckle when he hung up. He wasn't a big fan of flaunting his money and influence, but sometimes it came in handy for him to be who he was. Not even in the sense that he owned Hudson Enterprises, but for a different reason entirely. The Orange Rose was a celebrated restaurant in New York, but they didn't bend over backward for every wealthy person who called and asked for a table. It helped Ezra's case that his mother was best friends with the wife of the Orange Rose's owner and had financed their expansion to Chicago, Los Angeles, and Houston. Because of that, the Lees were welcome there any day, any time.

The rest of the day dragged by. Ezra's only distraction from thoughts of Emilie was his meeting with Matt and the legal department, during which they explored options to thwart Anderson Blackwell's purchase of the land in Vermont. He walked out of the meeting feeling optimistic that he would regain the upper hand and floated through the rest of the afternoon, buoyant with hope and confidence.

It took every ounce of willpower within him not to email Emilie again or to send her a note on the company's private messaging system. He didn't want to distract her, but by midafternoon, he was attempting to formulate a reasonable excuse to go down to the marketing department and catch a glimpse of her golden hair and bright green eyes for just a second.

He managed to hold himself back. If he came on too strong, he would scare Emilie away. She was already timid, either because she wasn't nearly as into him as he was into her or because she felt uncertain about indulging the interest of an executive at her place of employment.

At six o'clock sharp, Ezra told his assistant to go home for the evening, then said his goodbyes to the rest of his colleagues on the thirtieth floor. He took the elevator to the parking garage in the basement where his chauffeur was already waiting for him. He slid into the backseat of the sleek black Bentley and grinned through the rearview mirror at the old man in the driver's seat.

"Henry," Ezra said to his chauffeur. "Can we swing around the block to pick up a friend of mine? She should be waiting on the corner of Fifty-sixth and Seventh."

"Of course, Mr. Hudson. And then we're off to the Orange Rose, yes?"

"Yes, please."

Ezra's stomach twisted nervously as Henry navigated the evening traffic around the block. Part of him was worried that Emilie would flake on him, that she would change her mind and quit her job and leave New York behind just to ensure she would never cross paths with him again. It was a ridiculous fear, but his mind was often a melodramatic place.

He let out a relieved chuckle when he saw her standing on the street corner in her puffy green parka. It wasn't that cold outside, but she was bundled up as if it was still the dead of winter. When Henry pulled up to the curb and Ezra rolled down the window to signal for her to climb in the backseat beside him, her legs looked adorably skinny poking out from under her coat while she hopped over a puddle of melted snow and scurried over to the door. Normally, Henry would have parked and opened it for her, but the traffic was too dense and their current position wasn't an ideal place to stop for longer than a few seconds.

When Emilie was inside the car, she flung back the hood of her coat, let out a breath, and glanced at Ezra.

"Seriously?" she laughed. "A Bentley?"

Ezra smirked. "What's wrong with Bentleys?"

"Nothing, just—"

"I've also got a Tesla," Ezra continued. "And an Audi. Would you prefer it if we took one of those?"

"I would *prefer* to use the subway," Emilie pouted. "Why do you have more than one car if you use a chauffeur? Do you even have a driver's license of your own?"

Her tone was playful, but there was a flicker of judgment in her case. Ezra realized he had made a misstep by lightheartedly joking about his expensive cars. He was beginning to understand that Emilie wasn't like most people in New York. She wasn't impressed by ostentatious displays of wealth.

"Of course I have a license," Ezra replied. "It's just that it's more convenient for me to have a driver in case I need to do work on the way to my next destination, but I can drive myself if necessary. Do you have a license?"

Emilie snorted. "Of course not. I was born and raised in Queens and now I live in Manhattan. Why on earth would I need a car? I'm not too good for the subway."

She was certainly not going to let Ezra live down the fact that he was willingly driven around town in a luxury car, which he admired, but before he could pretend to defend himself further, Emilie leaned forward and smiled at Henry in the rearview mirror.

"Hello, by the way," she said to him. "I'm Emilie. Emilie DeGaulle."

Ezra didn't think anyone had bothered to introduce themselves to his chauffeur before.

"Hello, Miss DeGaulle," he replied, winking at her in the mirror and then glancing at Ezra with a twinkle of amusement. "I'm Henry. Allow me to assure you, despite the Bentley and the chauffeur, Mr. Hudson is an admirably humble man."

Satisfied with his testimonial, Emilie smiled and sat back in the seat. She ran her palms over the burgundy leather upholstery and sighed.

"I guess it is a nice car," she murmured.

Ezra chuckled. "So how was your first day?"

"Good! You have a lot of very nice people working for you. They've all been very helpful and welcoming."

"I'm glad to hear it," he replied. "How long have you been working in graphic design?"

She bit her lip, gazing out the front window as they slowly cruised the avenue toward the lower east side. It was as if she was reluctant to answer his question, but she eventually sighed and turned to meet his eyes.

"Approximately one day," she admitted.

Ezra raised his eyebrows in surprise. That wasn't the answer he was expecting.

"Wait, really?" he laughed. "How did you—"

"How did I get the job with absolutely no experience on my resume?" Emilie finished his question for him. "Beats me. I mean, I have a portfolio of digital designs, a few logos and random marketing materials I've done for some cafes and restaurants I was working at over the years, but I really never expected to even be invited back for a second interview."

He nodded slowly. "I don't place much importance on properly formulated resumes. I think it's more important to hire people who have obvious talent and who can work well in a team atmosphere. That's it."

"What do you know about my teamwork abilities?" she smirked.

"Well, didn't you say you worked in food service prior to this? That requires a lot of patience and collaboration. I'm sure Paul and Yasmina picked up on that right away," Ezra told her. "Plus, you're quite charming. I'm sure everyone already considers you a positive addition to the company."

Emilie's smirk grew more pronounced. "I'm charming? I spent the first five minutes of this drive berating you for your transportation preferences."

"And I was charmed by it."

She pressed her lips together, falling quiet. They stared into each other's eyes in the backseat for several long seconds. Ezra wanted to reach out and touch her. He wanted to kiss her. He wanted to tell Henry to redirect the car to Soho where Ezra could take Emilie to his penthouse loft and make love to her again. The one night they'd spent in London wasn't long enough. He needed a million more nights with her.

Henry cleared his throat, breaking the spell that hovered between them. Ezra hadn't noticed, but they had arrived at the restaurant. Emilie blinked and peered out the tinted window.

"The Orange Rose? This is where we're having dinner?" Emilie asked. He couldn't tell if she was happy about it or not.

"Have you been here before?"

Emilie shot him a look over her shoulder. "Me? Definitely not. I didn't know we were going to such a nice place. I don't think I'm dressed properly."

"Nonsense," Ezra said gently. "You look beautiful. Anyway, just because this place is Michelin-star doesn't mean you have to wear a ball gown to be let inside. Come on."

At that moment, Henry opened Emilie's door. Thankfully, it didn't take any more prodding for her to climb out of the car. Ezra slid out after her, nodding at Henry as he drove away, and guided Emilie toward the restaurant with a hand on the small of her back.

Inside, the hostess recognized Ezra immediately.

"Mr. Hudson! It's been a while!" she grinned from behind the podium. "We have your table ready for you this way."

He could feel Emilie's eyes on him, undoubtedly with a questioning gaze at the familiar welcome he received. He began to feel uneasy, wondering if he should have thought twice about bringing Emilie to a place like this. It wasn't that he wanted to show off, but rather that he was accustomed to showing affection for others by providing them with the best things his money could afford.

They sat down, Emilie smiling gratefully at the hostess when she offered to take their coats and hang them up instead of leaving them draped on the backs of their chairs.

"The chef would like to offer you a complimentary bottle of Bordeaux, Mr. Hudson," said the hostess. "Shall I bring it out?"

"Ah, how kind of him! Yes, please," he replied.

When the hostess disappeared, Ezra looked at Emilie across the table. The restaurant was busy—fully booked, of course—but it was designed so that conversations wouldn't carry from table to table and disrupt the individual patrons' privacy.

"So, what gives?" Emilie smirked. "Do you own this restaurant or something?"

"What? No. The owner is just a family friend."

"Of course. Where do rich people find all of these wonderful family friends?" she joked. "The only family friends of mine that I can think of are my mom's sorority sisters from college and the only perks I get from them are backhanded suggestions to get highlights and a spray tan."

"Your mom was in a sorority?" Ezra laughed.

"Yep. It didn't rub off on me and my sister, though," Emilie said. "Annie and I aren't really the type."

"Annie is your sister? Is she older or younger?" He felt like he was drinking from the sweetest fountain with each detail he gained about her life. Everything she said fascinated him. He wanted to know everything.

"Younger," Emilie said. "She's artsy too, but more in terms of curation than appreciation. She's living with me while she finishes her master's degree in museum curation."

"Oh, wow. This is the perfect city to live in for that kind of career path."

"I know, right? She's smart, too. She'll probably end up working at the Guggenheim or the MoMA," she replied. "Maybe if I had gone to graduate school, I wouldn't have spent the past six years making lattes for impatient Wall Street guys and Upper West Side mommies."

Ezra snorted. "Grad school isn't the right choice for everyone. Honestly, most people really shouldn't bother—"

"Your wine, as promised," announced the waiter, placing a dark bottle and two glasses on the table. They fell silent as he uncorked it with a flourish and poured an appropriate amount in each glass. "Now, would you like to hear what the chef is cooking up this evening or would you like to be surprised?"

Ezra grinned. The Orange Rose didn't have a set menu. The chef served something different every evening and there was no way to find out what it was ahead of time until you were seated at a table. It was one of the quirks that helped the restaurant stand out among the saturated world of New York cuisine.

He glanced at Emilie, raising his eyebrows to indicate that it was her decision. She shrugged at the waiter.

"Surprise us," she told him, though it was phrased more like a question.

"Very well, madam," he nodded. "I will return shortly with your first course."

When he disappeared, Emilie lifted her glass of wine to her nose and sniffed it gently.

"It smells expensive," she said, then glanced at the label on the bottle. "It's from 1997, imported directly from France. So, each sip must cost about twenty dollars?"

Ezra chuckled. He didn't mind her fixation on cost and displays of wealth. It was her way of showing him that she was very much out of her element without explicitly saying so.

"I don't think it's *that* premium," he replied. "Anyway, let's toast to your first day of work. Welcome to the Hudson Enterprises team, Emilie."

Even in the dim candlelight, he could see the faint blush rise to her cheeks.

"Thank you," she murmured as their glasses gently touched. They sipped the wine, which was rich and smoky but simultaneously fruity and sweet. Ezra wasn't much of a wine person, but his parents were, so he had grown up learning about it through them.

"So, what about you?" Emilie asked him. "Do you have any siblings?"

"Nope. Only child."

"Really? I guess that makes sense."

"What's that supposed to mean?" he laughed.

"You seem like you're used to having things your way," she replied. "Not in a bad way. It's just... the way you carry yourself. You're very confident."

"Well, I—"

Once again, Ezra's response was interrupted by another person's voice. This time, however, it wasn't their waiter. The second Ezra heard the familiar masculine tone, his stomach dropped and his mood instantly soured.

"Ezra Hudson? Is that you? In the flesh?" boomed a voice dripping with faux joviality.

Ezra took two full seconds to compose himself and plastered a wide smile on his face, turning in his chair to greet his greatest business rival—who was conveniently at the exact same exclusive restaurant that evening. God, did this guy have Ezra bugged or something?

"Anderson," Ezra said, holding out his hand to shake Anderson Blackwell's and fighting the urge to squeeze hard enough to break one of his fingers. "Long time, no see. What brings you here?"

Anderson gestured to the two men who flanked him, both very large and very fair—resembling traditional Scandinavians—and dressed in sleek black suits. Ezra wondered what he was plotting with the two men and if it would mean another headache for Hudson Enterprises.

"Just boring old business, I'm afraid," Anderson grinned cheekily, though his eyes gleamed maliciously. "Looks like you have much lovelier company than me tonight."

He smiled at Emilie and shook her hand.

"Yes, this is my… friend," Ezra said, not wanting to tell Anderson that she was his employee or a woman he was reconnecting with after a one-night stand that had occurred six months previously. "Emilie."

"It's a pleasure to meet you, Emilie," replied the tall, dark-skinned man. "I'm Anderson Blackwell of Blackwell Capital. If it weren't for me, this handsome fellow wouldn't have an ounce of competition in the transportation industry!"

Emilie smiled thinly, visibly picking up on the tension between Ezra and Anderson, but not wanting to appear rude.

"Nice to meet you," she murmured to him.

Anderson nodded and turned back to Ezra, ignoring his so-called business partners for the moment. "Sorry about the Vermont fiasco, by the way, chum. Should've sunk your teeth into it a little more firmly!" He threw back his head and laughed as if he'd told the funniest joke in the world.

Despite the fact that Ezra wanted to shove his butter knife into the man's throat, he forced a few humorless chuckles and nodded.

"Yes, it seems I need to learn to be several more steps ahead of you than I already am!" Ezra exclaimed, affecting his tone so it sounded like he was merely teasing, even though he meant it as a threat.

He could tell Anderson understood the hidden message from the flash of annoyance in his eyes, but Anderson simply laughed again and clapped Ezra firmly on the shoulder.

"Fair enough," he crooned. "I'll let you and this beautiful lady get back to your dinner. See you later, Ezra."

Ezra nodded in goodbye, relieved when Anderson and the mysterious businessmen continued following the hostess and disappeared around a corner. When he looked back at Emilie, he could sense that she was deeply uncomfortable by the tense, shallow exchange. It appeared as though she wanted to ask him what all of that was about, but she didn't know how to phrase her question.

He gazed at her, straight-backed and nervous in the posh restaurant, glancing around self-consciously and probably wishing she was literally anywhere else in the world. Ezra had definitely screwed up. If he had taken her somewhere else, somewhere less ostentatious, he might have avoided a run-in with Anderson and been able to show Emilie that he wasn't a total snob.

But the night was still young. He wasn't going to give up on her yet.

"Hey," he whispered, leaning forward conspiratorially. "Do you want to get out of here?"

Chapter Five

Did she want to... what?

Get out of there? Was he asking her back to his place already? Before the first course even arrived at their table?

Emilie felt a flutter of shame. She should have known better. Ezra had asked her the same question once before and she barely thought twice before agreeing. Maybe he thought she was easy, that all he needed to do was impress her with complimentary wine and a public pissing contest with another handsome and successful business partner. In his eyes, that was all she needed in order to open her legs for him again.

God, she was an idiot.

She eyed Ezra across the table. "Excuse me?"

"I'm serious," he murmured. "It's not too cold out. I know a place in the West Village where we can get a much more satisfying dinner than this fancy nonsense, no offense to this restaurant's outstanding chef."

Oh. *Oh.* He wasn't asking her to go back to his place with him. Somehow, Emilie's discomfort had been obvious enough to signal that she was totally unaccustomed to eating in restaurants where one plate cost over a hundred dollars, and the waitstaff wore uniforms that cost twice what she had paid for her entire outfit.

"Are you sure?" Emilie asked him. "I don't want to be rude."

Ezra shook his head. "It's okay. They can give our table to somebody on the waitlist. Shall we make a run for it?"

His eyes were sparkling with a dare. Emilie figured that any place he suggested would be better than the Orange Rose. She was sure the food was lovely, but felt like Ezra had the wrong idea of her in his head. It wasn't his fault. They'd met at an incredibly luxurious wedding that was being held in one of the most exclusive neighborhoods in London. Both Lena and Pierre were blessed with generational wealth. Ezra probably assumed that, because she was there and because she said she was close with Lena, she lived under similar circumstances. She should have found a way to make it clear that wasn't the case before he went to all the trouble of securing them a table at one of the most notoriously elite restaurants in the city.

It was her mistake for thinking Ezra would understand her background based off the singular fact that she was an entry-level employee with a pathetic resume.

"Um, sure," she replied.

Ezra offered her a lopsided grin and reached in his back pocket for his wallet. He pulled out two crisp one-hundred-dollar bills as if they were nothing more than coupons clipped from the Sunday newspaper and slipped them under his wine glass. Then he stood and held out his hand. Timidly, she stood and placed her hand in his, gasping when he tugged her through the tables, grabbed their coats from the antique hooks by the door, and pulled her outside.

"Mr. Hudson, is everything okay—" the hostess called out to their retreating forms in a panic, but they were long gone. Giggling like schoolchildren ditching class, they jogged down the block and turned the corner before slowing down to a walk.

"I'll send the chef an apology bouquet tomorrow," Ezra told her, clearly determined to ensure that Emilie didn't think he was rude for instigating their escape.

"You can blame it on me," she suggested, pulling on her coat and bundling up against the early March chill. "Just say you weren't aware you were slumming it with the lower class."

Ezra snorted and nudged her in the side with his elbow. "Don't be ridiculous. I'll blame it on myself. I'll say that I'm such an abominable snob that I forgot not every woman on earth is impressed by hefty price tags."

Emilie rolled her eyes, immediately forgiving him for the chauffeur, the Bentley, and all the pomp in between. How could he know that it wouldn't dazzle her? He barely knew her. It was only through moments like this that they could gain even ground.

But was that a wise thing for Emilie to desire? Perhaps she should have insisted they stay at the Orange Rose and had a somewhat miserable evening eating pretentious courses and drinking overpriced wine. At least then she could have told herself that Ezra was definitely not the man for her and swiftly moved on from her little crush.

Oh, well. It was too late.

"Aren't you cold?" Emilie asked him as they walked west down Eighth Street, noticing that he'd left his lightweight trench hanging open.

Ezra shrugged. "No, it's nice outside."

"It's freezing," she argued.

"It's, like, fifty degrees at most."

"No, it's definitely only forty."

He chuckled and pulled out his phone, tapping the weather app on his screen to indicate that it was precisely forty-five degrees Fahrenheit in Manhattan that evening.

"I guess we were both wrong," Ezra laughed. "You like being right, don't you?"

"Of course I do," she said. "Don't you?"

"Of course I do."

They exchanged a smile, then looked down at their feet in unison. They walked in silence. Although the days were starting to get longer, it was already dark at that hour. It was barely half past eight o'clock in the evening, and Emilie realized with an irregular thump of her heart that it was the same time she had decided to duck out of Lena's wedding reception six months ago. She'd spent about an hour at the bar by herself before Ezra showed up, and then they were both locked away in her hotel room by the time the clock struck eleven.

She had no intention of the current evening taking the same turn, but it was funny to think of the parallels. Back in early September, the sky was still light at this time of night in southeast England. The air was warm. She didn't need a coat or boots. She missed summer weather, but at least for London, winter was mostly over at that point.

After a few minutes, Ezra paused outside a grimy dive bar on the corner of a street lit with old-fashioned lanterns. Emilie loved the West Village, loved its antique charm and quaint hamlet vibes, but never in her wildest dreams could she afford to live there.

"This is it," Ezra announced, gesturing proudly at the pub. It was tucked away, barely noticeable with its lack of signage, but she could tell that it was a neighborhood staple.

She grinned and followed him inside, sighing happily when they were greeted with a wave of warmth from a crackling fireplace. The woman behind the bar barely glanced up as the bell above the door tinkled to signal their entrance but shouted for them to sit anywhere they wanted. Emilie took the lead, choosing a booth in the back corner. The bar wasn't very busy, but it was a weekday night. It was dimly lit and almost everything was constructed from darkly stained wood. A soft folk song hummed from the sound system and the pleasant clink of glasses behind the bar provided a sweet harmony.

It was cozy. Emilie was instantly at ease, tossing her coat beside her on the seat and resting her elbows on the tabletop. Ezra seemed more relaxed too, rolling up his sleeves and loosening his tie.

The woman who welcomed them in bustled over with two laminated menus.

"Welcome," she said. "Will you be drinking or dining?"

"Both," Ezra replied. "Can I start with a Brooklyn lager?"

"Sure thing, sweet pea," said the waitress, her voice warm and patient despite the fact that she was barely smiling. From that alone, Emilie could tell that she was a born-and-bred New Yorker as well. "And what about you, gorgeous?"

"What do you recommend?"

"Well, we've got a seasonal draft that the boss chuffed about. Some kind of berry-flavored beer they brew locally in Bushwick."

"I'll have that," replied Emilie.

The woman wandered away. It looked as if it was just her and a college-aged guy working, who was so similar to her in appearance that Emilie deduced he was either her son or her nephew. Even though it was just the two of them, the atmosphere wasn't stressful. The current scattering of customers was calm, chattering amongst themselves and displaying no signs of neediness. Emilie loved it when bars and cafes were like that. When she was a barista, it made her life easier to serve people who weren't fussy about pristine politeness and formalities.

"Is this better?" Ezra murmured, eyeing her nervously.

She nodded. "Much better. I do appreciate the fanciness, though. I hope you don't think I'm ungrateful."

"No, not at all," he replied, shaking his head. "Actually, I'm kind of embarrassed that I pulled a stunt like that. I'm so used to impressing colleagues and clients and—"

"—and women?" Emilie interrupted, waggling her eyebrows at him.

Ezra rolled his eyes playfully. "Believe it or not, I don't woo as many women as you might think. In fact, meeting you in London was the last time it happened."

"Are you saying you wooed me back then?"

"Considering the way you were sighing my name—"

Emilie gasped and swatted at his forearm. Ezra snickered, not even flinching at the light smack. He was bold, but she didn't find it annoying the way she did with most men who dared to make similar commentary. In spite of his alpha-male presence, there was a somewhat nerdy innocence underneath Ezra's intimidating exterior shell. Emilie wondered how much harder she would have to try to shatter it and uncover what else he might be hiding.

The waitress arrived with their drinks. They ordered burgers and fries, both pointing to the first thing they saw on the menu because neither one of them had been paying attention to anything in the past five minutes except each other. It was a far cry from the wine and caviar they might have enjoyed at the Orange Rose, but the fact that Ezra appeared to have no issue with their change of pace told Emilie he wasn't as snobby as his job title or his net worth suggested.

"So you never got to finish telling me about how you're an only child," Emilie said when they were alone again, thinking about the odd interruption made by Ezra's colleague. Or rather, rival. The man who had introduced himself as Anderson Blackwell was handsome and suave, only a few years older than Ezra by the looks of it, but there was a sliminess to his mannerisms that made Emilie feel uneasy.

Ezra nodded. "Well, there's not much to it. My parents fell in love, had me, decided that was enough, and that was that."

"Did you ever wish you had a brother or sister?"

"Yeah, when I was little," he replied, pausing briefly to take a sip of his drink. "We moved around a lot, so even though I got to meet a lot of new friends, none of them got to come with me when it was time to go again. It would've been nice to have had a sibling around during all of that, but I got used to it easily enough."

"Oh, that's right," Emilie murmured. "Your parents were in the military, right?"

"Just my dad," Ezra corrected her, raising his eyebrows as if he were surprised she remembered the information he'd shared with her months ago. "He was a Major in the army."

"Is he retired now?"

Emilie watched as something changed in Ezra's expression. It was subtle, but she didn't miss it.

"He passed away about ten years ago," he revealed. "Of all things, he died in a random civilian plane crash."

"Oh, my God," Emilie whispered. "I'm so sorry."

"Thank you, but it's okay," Ezra shrugged. "I didn't mean to darken the mood, but I didn't know how else to answer your question, honestly. He was a tough father, but a good man."

"What about your mom? If you don't mind me asking—"

Ezra smiled softly. "Yeah, she's fine. She's… unique. Unlike my dad, she was blessed with a trust fund and ample inheritance. She spends most of her time doing yoga in faraway places, but she's got a good heart."

"That sounds nice," she replied, moving her arms off the table as the waitress came bustling back with two heaping baskets, each loaded with a massive burger and way too many fries for one person to eat on their own. She dropped them off with a silent wink and hurried away to help the patrons at the booth behind theirs.

"And you?" Ezra asked, popping a fry into his mouth. "Are you close with your parents?"

"My mom is great," she answered as she cut her burger in half. "I mean, she barely leaves Queens, but she's always done her best for us. She raised us by herself. Our dad left when Annie was a baby."

"I'm sorry to hear that." From the look in his eyes, Emilie could tell he meant it.

She shrugged. "It's okay. I barely remember him, so I don't really know any different from having had a single mom. She dated every once in a while over the years, but she always told us that we were the priority."

"She sounds amazing," Ezra replied.

"Yeah, she's cool."

They had more in common than Emilie thought. No father. Well-meaning mothers trying to navigate their own broken hearts. Of course, the circumstances that landed either of them in that situation were very different, but the outcome gave them something to bond over. Emilie realized that she liked learning about Ezra. He was full of surprises. Hours ago, he was toiling away in an executive suite on the top floor of a modern high-rise in midtown, dressed in a custom suit and silk tie. Now, however, he looked like a regular guy. An outrageously handsome regular guy, but regular nonetheless. He was like a chameleon, changing effortlessly to fit his surroundings, but nothing about him seemed fake or shallow.

Deep down, Emilie wished she could be like that. She wished she could be whisked away to an expensive dinner in a luxury car and not bat an eye at the cosmopolitan ambience. It must be wonderful to feel natural no matter where you were, she thought. But at the end of the day, she was who she was and there was little she could do to pretend otherwise.

"I really want to ask you something, but I don't want to seem like I'm prying into your personal life," Ezra said after they had eaten in silence for a few minutes.

"What is it?"

"When we met in London, you said that you were alone because your date never boarded his plane," he began. "Did he ever reach out to you again?"

Emilie sighed. Ben Wang. She blamed him for her bias against wealthy, successful men. He was a workaholic, so caught up in his career that Emilie often wondered why he bothered to date in the first place.

"He texted me with an apology when I got back to the city," she told Ezra. "But I never replied, and he never pushed it. It wasn't like we broke up or anything. We were hardly dating in the first place."

"Regardless, he's a fool," Ezra told her. "I'd sign away the entirety of Hudson Enterprises right now if it meant I could have a second date with you."

Emilie laughed, caught off guard by the grand declaration. "I wouldn't let you do that, but I appreciate the sentiment."

They spent the rest of the evening chatting about lighter topics, skirting away from the subject of flaky dates and their shared workplace. Emilie felt comfortable around him, opening up little by little. She knew there was a reason he kept popping up in her mind over the past few months. He was engaging and funny and flirtatious, all without being over the top. Ezra was a true conversationalist, turning poetic phrases but then listening carefully to every word she said.

She was falling for him, but she wasn't sure she was ready to admit it.

When they finished eating, Ezra paid the bill, then insisted that she let his chauffeur drive her home. The temperature had dropped several more degrees during the time they were in the bar, and it wasn't convenient for Emilie to get to the subway from their current location, so she obliged.

The Bentley was idling on the curb outside when they left the pub, Henry leaning against it casually while he waited for them. He opened the door and Ezra gestured for her to climb inside before him, but instead of sliding all the way to the opposite window, she stayed in the middle seat and bit her lip to hide a smirk when Ezra got in and noticed her purposeful proximity.

The ride to the ancient brick building on the lower east side that Emilie called home was quiet. Henry had the radio station tuned to classical music, but Emilie couldn't hear it over the hammering of her heart.

She and Ezra had their faces turned out the window, but their focus was on each other. Their thighs were pressed together and, seconds after Emilie fastened her seatbelt, Ezra had grabbed her hand and entwined their fingers in his lap. As they rode through the streets, his thumb rubbed delicate circles over her knuckles.

Her free hand rested on his knee, her body turned inward toward him instead of facing front. The tension was unbearable. She could feel the warmth of his skin through the fabric of his trousers and wanted nothing more than to allow her fingertips to trail further upwards, but she didn't want to embarrass Henry.

All she could think about was the way he had touched her in that hotel room last September. She was so desperate to taste him again that she could hardly think straight. Ezra cleared his throat quietly and shifted slightly in his seat, subtly adjusting his pants. Emilie fought to keep the satisfied smile off her face at the tangible evidence of his attraction to her.

"This is my street corner," Emilie announced suddenly. "It's probably easiest to park here."

Quick to obey instructions, Henry pulled over on the corner of the block where he would be able to idle for a few minutes without getting a ticket.

"I'll walk you to your door," Ezra whispered, already halfway out of the car.

Emilie nodded, his grip tightening on her hand as he helped her onto the sidewalk. Shutting the door without a backward glance, Emilie took the lead and pulled Ezra toward her stoop, which was located about midway down the street. He followed behind, matching her brisk pace, but before they made it to the front door of her building, Emilie turned into a hidden alleyway and tugged Ezra along with her out of sight.

Ezra was quick to respond, understanding her intentions immediately. He pressed her up against the brick exterior of the building and, before Emilie could take her next breath, captured her lips in a kiss. A rush of heat raced down her spine. She grabbed fistfuls of his jacket and pulled him closer so that his body was flush to hers. He moaned as she molded her body to his and deepened the kiss.

There it was. The undeniable truth. The chemistry they'd experienced in London wasn't a one-time thing. It persisted without the vodka, without the aura of romance that a wedding brings, and without the thrill of a foreign city. There was something real between them that Emilie couldn't deny.

They spent several minutes like that, wrapped around each other in the alley, making out like teenagers. The only thing stopping Emilie from inviting him inside and tearing off his clothes was the fact that her sister was definitely home.

That, and a gentle reminder in the back of her mind that she wasn't supposed to be welcoming distractions like Ezra into her life.

She pulled away from the kiss, breathless. Ezra followed her lips with his for a second, unwilling to break apart, but eventually lifted his face and let out a quiet exhale of laughter in the quiet alley.

"So, I guess this means tonight went well and you don't completely regret giving me a chance?" he whispered.

Emilie smiled, straightening out the wrinkles she'd created in his shirt and jacket during the heat of the moment.

"I had a nice time," she answered. "But I should go now."

Ezra nodded and stepped away. She led him out of the alley and allowed him to follow her to the stoop. Undoubtedly, Henry knew exactly what was taking Ezra so long to return, but he didn't seem in a rush to get back to his waiting car. She dug her keys out of her purse and hovered by the door.

Ezra reached out and lifted her chin with the tip of his index finger, kissing her softly one last time before making his way down the steps. He waited until she turned the key and was safely inside before walking away. Emilie could feel his eyes on her the whole time. As she walked up the stairs to her apartment, her body felt heavy and slow as if it was begging her to stop putting distance between her and Ezra.

What a day.

Chapter Six

Ezra woke up with the taste of Emilie on his lips.

Like a lovesick fool, he opened his eyes and smiled as he greeted the day ahead. He couldn't wait to see her again. He didn't care what he had to do; he would find a way to subtly cross her path at the office that day.

He went through the usual motions of his morning, but she was on his mind the entire time. While he jogged on the treadmill in his personal gym, showered under the high-tech rain spout in his en-suite bathroom, dressed in a sleek gray suit, and brewed a cappuccino with his elaborate espresso machine... all he could think about was Emilie. He thought about doing all those things with her, about waking up with her and having a daily routine with her.

Her, her, her... he was a goner.

By the time he arrived on the thirtieth floor of Hudson Enterprises, his head was so far in the clouds that he knew he was doomed to experience a rude awakening the second the smallest dose of reality came his way.

Sure enough, Cassie from the legal department was waiting for him outside his office door. He glanced at his watch. It wasn't even nine in the morning yet, but she looked as if she had a lot of news to deliver. Assuming that the attorney was about to tell him that their meeting yesterday afternoon had reaped no positive results and Blackwell had firmly secured the land in Vermont, Ezra braced himself.

"Morning, Cass," he said. "You look like you mean business today."

"Morning, Ezra," she replied curtly, one of the few people at the company who actually called him by his first name. "I do. I know you're a busy man, so I wanted to track you down before anyone else could snatch you away. I have an update regarding the Vermont contracts."

He unlocked his office door and gestured for Cassie to follow him inside. While he busied himself with turning on the computer and getting settled for the day, Cassie perched on the arm of the leather chair opposite his desk.

"Just rip off the bandaid, please," Ezra sighed. "Did my arch nemesis win this round or not?"

Cassie smirked. "You'll be pleased to know that he didn't."

Ezra raised his eyebrows at the stern woman in front of him. She was ferocious and meticulous—they'd been lucky enough to poach her from one of the most prolific corporate law offices in New York.

"Seriously? It worked?" he gasped.

"Turns out that sometimes getting your way is as simple as appealing to their human sensibilities," she replied.

In their meeting yesterday, after brainstorming for half an hour about ways they could reverse the sale of the land to Blackwell, they had decided to go for an unorthodox solution. They composed an email to the owner of the land in Vermont, asking him to rethink approving the transfer of property to Blackwell Capital in favor of the more humanitarian and progressive project that Hudson Enterprises had planned. They also offered to match Blackwell's offer if the landowner agreed to go back on the sale. It was a long shot. If the landowner didn't give a damn how his land was used once it was out of his hands, Ezra and his company would lose.

However, as luck would have it, the landowner cared about the property being used for a good cause. An affordable railroad was a lot more favorable than a massive factory, so it was no question that Hudson Enterprises had better intentions.

"So, it's done? They sold it to us?" Ezra asked.

Cassie nodded, smiling with satisfaction. "Their attorney called first thing this morning and said the landowner didn't sign the paperwork yet, so they shredded the contract with Blackwell Capital. I'm drafting up a fresh one to send over to them by noon today, but it's pretty much set in stone. They're going to inform Mr. Blackwell of the change themselves."

Ezra grinned. He recalled the particularly pompous attitude Blackwell had shown last night at the Orange Rose, likely due from the fact that he thought he had bested Hudson Enterprises. He was too arrogant for his own good. Hopefully this would be a lesson to him. The Vermont landowner clearly wanted to work with someone who had good intentions and a strong moral compass, and had only been led astray because of the ridiculously high offer Blackwell had made. Luckily, money wasn't an issue for Ezra and his company. If it came down to it, they could have doubled Blackwell's offer.

Satisfied to have won yet another round with that menace, Ezra dismissed Cassie and spent the rest of the morning humming to himself, answering emails, and signing off on all the little things that came across his desk. While he toiled away, he thought mainly of Emilie. It was difficult to resist sending her another email or instant message, but he didn't want to plague her inbox with notes from the CEO and arouse any suspicions that might embarrass her.

After all, Ezra wasn't a fool. He was a firm believer in gender equality. He understood how difficult it could be for young women to be taken seriously in the workplace. More often than not, they had to work ten times harder than men for half the respect. If any of Emilie's coworkers found out that she was involved with him, they might be led to believe that was how she had gotten the job in the first place. It didn't matter if neither one of them had any idea they would run into each other yesterday; rumors would fly, and the bulk of the negativity would land on Emilie's shoulders. It was unfair and ridiculous, but society couldn't be changed overnight.

That wasn't the only reason Ezra left Emilie alone that morning. Truthfully, he didn't want to distract her from her new role as a graphic designer. He meant to ask more about her artwork last night, but the conversation naturally moved in other directions. But that was okay. They had plenty of time to get to know each other. They lived in the same city. Miraculously, they were also in the same borough. The lower east side wasn't that far from Ezra's place in Soho; they could easily see each other outside of work.

He placated himself with such thoughts until lunch time when Matt appeared in his doorway and demanded he join his colleague for sandwiches at the deli on the corner. Ezra obliged and they made their way down to the street, joining the varied crowd of people lined up outside the deli, construction workers and top-level executives rubbing shoulders without batting an eye, in true New York style.

"Shelby wants to have you over for dinner at some point in the next week or so," Matt informed him. Shelby was his wife. She was an adorably petite woman with bright red hair who was currently about seven months pregnant with their first child.

"Your wife is very fixated on feeding me," Ezra joked. At Shelby's insistence, Ezra regularly came to the Sanchez household in Greenwich Village for dinner.

"I think she's worried that you're going to accidentally starve yourself with your bachelor lifestyle," Matt replied as they slowly made their way to the front counter of the deli. "She keeps asking me when you're going to meet a nice girl, as if I go to work every morning to gossip with you about your nonexistent love life."

"Hey! It's not completely nonexistent."

"Oh?"

Matt raised his eyebrows at Ezra. He instantly regretted defending himself. There was no way he could tell Matt about Emilie, not even vaguely. He knew his friend. Matt would poke and prod and pry until he got every single detail out of Ezra, and he didn't feel comfortable putting Emilie in that position without talking to her first about how she wanted to handle whatever was going on between them. If Ezra was going out of his way to keep their situation from the marketing department, he certainly couldn't go blabbing about it to the company's CFO.

"Well—" Ezra trailed off and shrugged, an expression meant to indicate that Matt had a point. It was better for him to give in to his friend's teasing than to defend his pride. At least for now. Maybe there would come a point when Emilie would be okay with him telling the whole world how much he liked her.

Matt couldn't interrogate him further at that point because the men behind the deli counter demanded their attention. They ordered their sandwiches and went back to the top floor of the company, chatting about the weather and solidifying Ezra's agreement to come to dinner the following weekend.

They were busy men though, so they didn't have the chance to sit down and enjoy their lunch together. They parted ways and went to their respective offices to eat and work at the same time, much like they'd been doing since they had started Hudson Enterprises.

Ezra only had the opportunity to enjoy about two bites of the sandwich when his assistant poked her head through the doorway and tapped her knuckles lightly on the threshold. She noticed he was eating and instantly got an apologetic look in her eyes, but Ezra waved her in.

"What's up, Jess?"

"I've got some news, boss," she sighed. "But I don't want to ruin your lunch."

"So it's bad news?"

"It's not ideal."

Ezra frowned and pushed aside his food, gesturing for Jess to sit down.

"What's wrong? You're not quitting are you?" Ezra asked.

Jess smirked. "God, no. Like I said in my interview, my long-term goal at this company is to eventually take your job. I'm not going anywhere."

Ezra chuckled. He remembered her bold statement during her interview; it was one of the main reasons he had decided to hire her on the spot. He appreciated people who took risks and who weren't afraid to show others how ambitious they were.

"Good to hear," he nodded. "But what else could possibly ruin my lunch?"

She flinched. "It's Blackwell Capital."

"Again?"

"I'm afraid so."

Ezra sat back in his chair and let out a long, low exhale. Usually Blackwell's attacks were spaced out over several weeks. He didn't expect to get the news that he was up to something again mere hours after that morning's victory. Did this have anything to do with the physically imposing men Anderson brought to dinner the night before?

"Go ahead," he groaned. "What is he doing now?"

"It's Monaco," she deadpanned, gritting her teeth as if waiting for a blow.

"No," breathed Ezra, his stomach plummeting. "How could he possibly insert himself into that?"

Hudson Enterprises wasn't an international billion-dollar company based on rural railroads alone. They formed transportation contracts with some of the most powerful entities in the world. For example, they recently won a bid with the government of Monaco to upgrade their entire private fleet of royal jets. It was a massive deal with huge financial rewards which would trickle down to even the lowest level of employees at the company.

Though it wasn't signed yet, he had assumed the contract was in the bag. The press release was ready to go out before the ink had a chance to dry. He was already having the design team working on mock-ups of modern royal branding.

"According to their representative's assistant, the royal family decided to go for Blackwell's bid instead," Jess explained. "They didn't say why."

"I didn't even known Blackwell had a bid. It's not exactly an accessible playing field."

Jess merely shrugged. "I have no idea. He usually sticks to the private sector. I don't think he's ever worked with a government before."

"No, he hasn't," Ezra confirmed, reaching for his phone. "Hold on a minute. I'll call my contact."

Landing a job as high-profile as updating an entire fleet of jets for literal royalty was no small task. For a company based in the United States, it was practically unheard of. Ezra went to great lengths to even make it possible, spending countless evenings at networking events to schmooze with anyone who might offer him an international connection. He researched all the security measures and regal protocol that his engineers would need to adhere to and was practically an expert in French diplomacy at that point.

There was no way he was losing this contract to Anderson Blackwell, of all people.

Ezra scrolled through his contacts and pressed *dial* on the man who worked in public relations for the Monaco royal family, a man named Maurice whom he was lucky enough to meet at a fundraising gala a few months ago. He checked his watch, realizing that it was almost seven in the evening in Monaco at that point, but he knew that Maurice worked long hours and rarely turned off his phone.

Sure enough, he answered on the third ring.

"This is Maurice," the man said in lieu of hello.

"Maurice, it's Ezra Hudson at Hudson Enterprises," he responded, switching the call to speaker so Jess could overhear the conversation. "We received a rather confusing message from your assistant a moment ago, so I wanted to connect with you regarding the status of the—"

"Mr. Hudson, I apologize, but there is no use in pleading with me," Maurice cut him off, his usually jovial tone inexplicably cold and curt. "I am low on the totem pole and the royals are very rarely swayed from their decisions once they have been made. The fact of the matter is that they are not interested in doing business with immoral men, as they fear it may have political repercussions."

"Immoral men? What do you mean?" Ezra asked, furrowing his brow at Jess across the desk. She whipped her phone out of her pocket and started typing furiously.

"Mr. Hudson, I do not have time for this. I must bid you goodbye."

Without another word, Maurice hung up on him.

"Immoral men?" he whispered when he placed the receiver back in its cradle. "And yet they're doing business with Blackwell?"

"Oh, God," muttered Jess all of a sudden. "I see what the problem is."

"What? What is it?"

Wordlessly, Jess placed her phone on the desk and slid it toward Ezra so he could see the article she'd pulled up. It was from a trashy tabloid, the kind that survived off baseless rumors and clout. There was a grainy photograph which depicted Ezra inside the Orange Rose, his features totally visible from the unknown photographer's vantage point. It was obvious that there was a woman sitting across from him, but it could have been any woman with blond hair and slender shoulders.

Ezra was rarely the victim of paparazzi, but his billionaire bachelor status had been known to gain him some unwanted attention over the past couple of years.

When he read the article's headline, he cursed aloud.

CEO of Hudson Enterprises Caught Wining and Dining an Elite Escort at Manhattan's Exclusive Orange Rose

An escort? They thought Emilie was an escort? What would give them that idea? She'd been dressed in a long-sleeve blouse and a perfectly appropriate skirt yesterday evening. She was unreasonably gorgeous, but she looked like any other professional woman in New York.

Of course, the truth didn't matter. Ezra knew exactly who was responsible for this blow to his reputation. Blackwell must have taken the photo before he approached the table, then sent it to the tabloid, pretending to know that Emilie was a well-known escort despite the fact that he'd only just met her. Then, when the tabloid happily published the news that golden boy Ezra Hudson had to pay women to go on dates with him, he'd sent it over to Monaco right away.

Blackwell was playing dirtier and dirtier every time. It was getting out of hand.

Poor Emilie, Ezra thought. At least there was no way to identify her from the photo. At least her reputation was intact.

Ezra handed Jess back her phone.

"Well, obviously, that's not an escort," he muttered.

"I assumed so."

"I appreciate that."

"Not that there's anything wrong with being a sex worker," Jess continued. "I mean, they work just as hard as the rest of us. Anyway, it's not like those Europeans have much ground to stand on in that respect."

"Right," Ezra sighed. "I'm assuming you already know what I'm going to need you to do, but please get in touch with the PR department and let them know we need to have that article removed. That wasn't an escort. That was—"

That was my lower-level employee who is younger and more naïve than me.

Ezra cringed internally. The truth sounded worse than his taking a prostitute out to dinner.

"That was just a friend of mine," he finished.

"Of course," Jess nodded, standing up. There wasn't an ounce of doubt in her expression. Though Ezra didn't mention his run-in with Blackwell last night, Jess was smart enough to understand that the two stunts were connected. If Anderson couldn't earn large contracts with work ethic and skill, he would find another way. Ezra didn't understand why the guy was so determined to ruin his company. If the transportation industry wasn't working out for him, he should have pivoted to something else. It wasn't Ezra's fault Blackwell didn't have the resources to outpace him the honest way.

When Jess left, Ezra knew it was time to give in to his nagging thoughts and text Emilie. He doubted she read the tabloids and hoped that she wouldn't accidentally stumble across it. She would probably be so horrified to have her privacy violated that she would never want to see him again.

For that alone, Ezra was going to find a way to put a stop to Anderson Blackwell's mischief once and for all.

Chapter Seven

"Hey, Jack! You and Emilie can press pause on the new royal jet insignias," Yasmina called out from her cubicle. "I just got a memo that the entire Monaco project is on standby."

Emilie's coworker Jack, a skinny guy with long dreadlocks and thick-rimmed glasses, poked his head over the barrier that separated their two cubicles.

"I wonder what happened," he whispered to her. "That was supposed to be one of the company's biggest projects to date."

"Really?" she frowned. Ezra hadn't mentioned it, not that she expected him to bring up pending contracts over dinner.

"Yep," Jack chirped. "But at least this will give us more time to work on the marketing for the Vermont railroad project. We're going to need, like, a thousand different things for that. Signage, brochures, timetables, maps… I'll give you access to the folder where we're keeping the drafts so you can look through them."

"Cool, thanks," Emilie replied with a polite smile.

Discussing which font to use for signs in a train station wasn't exactly her idea of a thrilling afternoon, but at least she got to be somewhat creative. The closest she'd gotten to using her artistic creativity as a waitress were the sculpture-esque piles of plates and cutlery she balanced in her arms on the way to the kitchen.

Emilie's cell phone buzzed with a message on top of her desk. It wasn't the kind of company where employees were expected to keep their phones off until leaving work at the end of the day, which was nice.

Her stomach flipped when she realized it was a text from Ezra. She glanced around, but Jack had dipped out of sight and no one else was around to read over her shoulder. She was being paranoid, but she really didn't want any of her new coworkers to find out that she was familiar with the CEO. Very familiar.

Can I see you again tonight? read his message.

Emilie felt the corners of her lips turn upward ever so slightly in an involuntary smile. God, she wanted to kiss him again. Or rather, she wanted to do so much more than kiss him, but she would settle for another make out session in the alley if that was her only option.

I would love to, Emilie typed back. *Unfortunately, I already have plans.*

It wasn't a lie. When Emilie woke up that morning, there was a message in the email inbox connected with her art website from a gallery. A real art gallery. She recognized the name immediately. She had sent an inquiry to them months ago and never heard back, so she assumed that was a rejection. But apparently the gallery owner had a client cancel on him last minute and she was being given the rare opportunity to meet with him that evening to discuss the possibility of selling a few of her pieces there.

There was no way she could reschedule. She wouldn't dream of it.

What are your plans? Whatever they are, I promise I can be more fun, came Ezra's swift reply.

I can't cancel, she replied. *You'll have to show me how much fun you are another night. Challenge accepted*, Ezra texted back.

Emilie sighed quietly and set her phone aside. She was unbelievably attracted to Ezra, but she was timid about the distraction he presented, especially now that she had a real career and a meeting with a gallery on the books. Her dreams were so close she could taste them. Not even a man as perfect as Ezra could convince her to give them up.

***

When work was over, Emilie practically ran out of Hudson Enterprises. Luck was on her side as she raced home, so that she wasn't late for her meeting with the gallery owner. The subway was on time and running smoothly, rolling up the second she stepped onto the platform and coughing her out into her neighborhood twenty minutes later.

She took the stairs up to her third floor apartment two at a time, tearing off her work clothes the second she was through the door. Her sister was still on campus, so she saved time not having to explain herself as she exchanged her blouse and trousers for a loose-fitting romper and black tights that would fit her artsy persona better. She shoved her feet into thick-soled, lace-up boots and piled her long hair into a bun at the top of her head. It was important that she looked professional, but not boring.

After touching up her makeup, Emilie grabbed her portfolio case and made sure her best paintings and sketches were neatly stored in the plastic dividers, threw on her coat and ran right back out the door.

As if fate was smiling on her, the gallery was only a few blocks from her apartment. She walked briskly, too full of optimism to move at a normal pace through the rush-hour pedestrian crowds.

She arrived at the gallery with five minutes to spare and fought the urge to do a victorious dance on the curb before walking inside just in case the owner noticed and thought she was too unhinged to do business with.

The gallery itself was small, but clean and well-situated. The lower east side was quickly becoming one of the most fashionable neighborhoods in downtown Manhattan. What had once been home exclusively to ne'er-do-wells and punk kids was transforming into a trendy, artistic district where people from higher income brackets were interested in gobbling up the reasonably affordable property. It meant that Emilie's rent was probably going to skyrocket in the next couple of years, but it also meant that there were more residents interested in buying art.

"You must be Emilie," said a wiry old man with thick spectacles and hunched shoulders from behind a desk in the corner of the room. Other than him, the gallery was empty, but she knew from the online reviews that pieces were snatched up quickly by ambling foot traffic and professional art buyers on the prowl more during normal business hours.

"Yes," she replied, shaking his frail, wrinkled hand. "It's very nice to meet you. I really appreciate you reaching out to me and giving me this opportunity."

"Of course, dear," he said, hobbling around the side of the desk to stand beside her. "Now let me see what you've brought with you. I saw a few pieces from your website, but I'm an old man and I'm not very good with all of that technology nonsense."

Emilie smiled and nodded, placing the large case on the desk and unzipping the cover. She stepped aside and clasped her hands in front of her, waiting quietly. This was the first time she'd ever had the chance to meet with a gallery owner and, although they were informed about the general process in art school, Emilie realized that it was very different when it was actually happening. She didn't want to hover or to speak too much for fear of over-explaining her art and taking away the experience, but she also didn't want to seem too passive or apathetic.

The old man was paying no attention to her mannerisms as he looked through her work, bending over and squinting at various paintings and drawings. Emilie glanced around at the other artwork on display while he scrutinized her work. There were a lot of incredible pieces on the wall in a variety of styles and themes. It was clear that the gallery owner preferred obvious talent and beauty over sticking to a specific concept.

After about ten or fifteen excruciating minutes during which Emilie was trying her hardest not to appear as antsy as she felt, the old man straightened, readjusted his glasses, and fixed her with an unreadable stare.

"I like many of these pieces, especially the woodblock prints," he told her. "Do you use acrylic paint?"

"Thank you. Yes, I do. I prefer acrylic over oil."

"As do I."

Emilie nodded. If he liked them, did that mean he wanted to sell them? She didn't want to be too forward.

He flipped to a painting in the back of the portfolio. It was a photographic scan of a painting she had done years ago when she was fresh out of school. Full of bright colors and youthful energy, Emilie hadn't painted anything like it in a long time. She'd never sold it, and instead it hung in the hallway of her tiny apartment between her bedroom and her sister's room.

"This one in particular is very lovely," he murmured. "Do you have more like it?"

"My style has changed slightly since I finished that piece, but I'd be more than happy to revisit it if that's what you'd like to see more of."

He grinned at her response. "A diplomat, I see. I have dealt with many artists who have responded to the same question by telling me to kiss their ass."

"Oh, goodness."

He chuckled. "My dear, it's very clear that you have talent. I have been in this business for decades and have seen thousands of artists rise and fall or go absolutely nowhere at all, and so do not take this lightly when I say that you show great promise."

"That's very kind of you—"

"That being said," he continued, holding up his hand to stop her bashful interruption. "At this moment in time, I run a very small gallery. In my old age, I keep a tight list of artists on these walls. I have to be very competitive about what goes on display and I have to be certain that it can sell."

Emilie tried to keep the disappointment off her face. She knew the beginnings of a rejection when she heard it.

"I understand," she replied.

"I fear your lack of name recognition will make it difficult for either one of us to profit," he told her. His voice was kind, but he didn't mince words. Even though Emilie was basically being told to go try again elsewhere, she appreciated that he was at least taking the time to let her down easily and honestly.

It was frustrating. How was she supposed to gain name recognition if no galleries would put her art on display? She could play the social media game and spend hours each day attempting to market herself online, and perhaps even create an online shop for generic prints, but that wasn't really the kind of artist career she wanted. As foolish as it seemed, she wanted to be successful via the traditional route.

Before Emilie could formulate a response, the door to the gallery opened and a tall man in a dark suit came inside.

Emilie blinked in surprise. She recognized him.

"Hello," said the visitor. "I'm so sorry—are you closed for the evening? I saw the light was on and you two were in here, but—"

"No, no! It's quite alright! Feel free to browse, sir," said the older man. "We're just finishing up here."

Emilie was still staring at the tall stranger. It was the same man from last night, the one who had come up to their table in the Orange Rose and joked around with Ezra for a few minutes. He was one of Ezra's business partners, though their exchange was ripe with fake smiles and shallow laughter, hinting at a deep sense of competition between the two men.

What did he say his name was? Andrew? Alexander?

Though she was dressed in a completely different style than the night before and had her hair up, he seemed to recognize her, too. His expression brightened and he let out a light chuckle, walking right over to Emilie and the old man.

"I always say that New York is just like a small town!" he exclaimed. "We just met last night. Anderson Blackwell of Blackwell Capital. And you're Emilie, correct? Ezra's friend?"

She felt a flicker of guilt for not remembering his name when he clearly remembered hers but accepted his handshake and smiled warmly. He didn't seem nearly as sleezy as he had last night; perhaps it was all an act to impress the two men he had with him at the restaurant.

"Yes, that's right," she replied. "I'm Ezra's... friend."

"Well, I didn't know Ezra was friends with an artist," said Anderson, glancing past her at the portfolio that lay open on the desk. "These are amazing. Do you mind if I look?"

"No, go ahead," Emilie murmured, shocked about the strange coincidence of it all. From the way Ezra reacted to Anderson, she had assumed that he wasn't a good guy, but he was acting perfectly polite and respectful.

The gallery owner stepped aside to make room for Anderson's broad form, quiet during their entire exchange. He threw glances at Emilie, perhaps rethinking the conclusion he had drawn about her being a nobody.

Anderson flipped through the paintings, pausing on a charcoal sketch. It was a study of the Washington Square arch, though Emilie had taken some liberty with the famous landmark's surroundings. Instead of drawing the monument amongst the concrete and crowds, she'd translated it into a peaceful forest. Lush trees and overflowing hydrangea bushes flanked the arch. Her sister said it was an interesting commentary on one of the grimiest, most crime-ridden parks in Manhattan, but that wasn't quite how Emilie meant for it to be interpreted. Rather, she thought it would be interesting to take something that was directly associated with a place—in this case, New York City—and put it somewhere completely different.

Emilie had made other sketches like that. She drew the Eiffel Tower on a tropical beach. She put Big Ben underwater. There was an unfinished piece in one of her sketchbooks at home in which she attempted to put the Taj Mahal on the moon, but that was proving to be much more difficult than she expected.

"I love this," whispered Anderson, touching his fingertips to the protective layer of plastic. "How much?"

He looked at Emilie expectantly when he asked the question, rather than at the gallery owner. She froze, shocked that he liked her silly charcoal drawing so much that he wanted to buy it… just like that.

"Oh, I don't—" Emilie began, but the old man came to rescue.

"Two," he replied smoothly.

Anderson smiled. "Sold. Do you accept AmEx?"

"We do, sir."

Anderson pulled out his wallet and winked at Emilie.

Two… two what? Two single dollars? Two hundred?

"We will have it framed and delivered to your home in five to seven business days, sir," said the gallery owner while Emilie tried to make sense of what was happening. "Unless you'd like to come pick it up when it's ready?"

"Delivery is fine," Anderson replied. "Thank you."

In a matter of minutes, Anderson paid for the drawing, signed the receipt, provided the owner with his delivery address, and shook Emilie's hand a second time.

"It's a beautiful piece," he told her. "I'll definitely be coming back to see what else you create."

"Really?" she replied before she could stop herself. "That's very nice of you to say. Let me give you my card."

Emilie fished around in her bag for her wallet, her fingers fumbling nervously. Last year for her birthday, her sister's gift had been a set of business cards for Emilie's budding art career. They were simple but pretty, embossed with gold lettering on textured white cardstock with her name, website, and email.

She handed one to Anderson and he tucked it away in the inside pocket of his suit jacket, then reached back into his wallet and handed her one of his cards. True to his surname, the business card was black. Silver lettering spelled out *Blackwell Capital, Inc.* in curling script.

"Thank you," she told him, carefully tucking it away in her bag.

"Good luck, Emilie," Anderson told her as he made his way out of the gallery. "Give my regards to Ezra when you see him again."

She nodded. Obviously, Anderson didn't know that she actually worked for Ezra, but she didn't think it was necessary to mention it, because then she would have to explain why she was having a romantic, candlelit dinner with her boss the other night.

When he was gone, Emilie turned back to the gallery owner. The old man burst out laughing.

"I love to be proved wrong!" he chirped, placing his palms over his stomach while he giggled. "I hope you don't mind that I intervened, but you looked a bit like a deer caught in headlights. Obviously, because we haven't agreed on a contract, I will happily transfer the full two thousand to you for this sale, as I can hardly take my usual percentage after speaking to you the way that I did."

"Two thousand?" Emilie gasped. "Dollars?"

"Yes, madam," he chuckled. "Congratulations. Is this the first piece you've sold?"

"Yes," she breathed, so shocked that she hardly knew what to say.

The man tapped her portfolio. "Do you mind if I keep this for a few days to fully soak in the work? In the meantime, I'll have my assistant draw up a contract and email it to you tomorrow. Typically, we do an even fifty-fifty cut. Is that acceptable?"

He wanted to take fifty percent of Emilie's sales. It was a steep request, but not unheard-of in the art world. Plus, if Emilie sold another simple charcoal drawing for two thousand dollars, that meant she would still make a thousand. She didn't mind that at all.

"Yes, that sounds good," she nodded. "I have more at home, too. And I can make more. Obviously."

"Of course, dear. I'll be in touch. I look forward to doing business with you."

Fighting the urge to pinch herself to make sure she wasn't dreaming, Emilie practically skipped out of the gallery and back down the street toward her apartment.

She'd done it. She'd sold a piece of art. She had a pending contract with a gallery. There were no promises that she was on the road to success, but it was more than she'd ever experienced before.

Finally, for the first time, Emilie could call herself a professional artist.

Chapter Eight

Anderson Blackwell was often impressed by how easy it was to make people fall under his spell. He always had a knack for charming others. It was like a sixth sense. Somehow, he knew what people wanted to hear and he was more than happy to tell it to them if it meant he gained more power over them.

Emilie DeGaulle was an easy target, just like her choice of companion, Ezra Hudson. Finding out more about her was like taking candy from a baby. All Anderson had to do was call one of his assistants, a young guy named Dan who was eager to please, to come to the Orange Rose under the guise of joining him and his colleagues for dinner. The original plan was for Dan to bug Ezra's table using his natural gift for sleight-of-hand by slipping a mic underneath one of the plates being delivered to their table.

It sounded like something straight out of a spy movie, but Anderson wasn't above espionage. The thing was, it was a happy accident that he and Ezra had ended up at the Orange Rose on the same evening, but he took it as a sign from the universe that he had a golden opportunity right in front of him. The second he saw Emilie, with her big green eyes and Rapunzel hair, he knew he had stumbled upon treasure.

The thing was, Ezra was notoriously single. He didn't date. Love and romance were such easy tools for manipulation and destruction, but Ezra had yet to give him the chance to delve into it… until last night.

Sending the photograph and the escort rumor to the tabloid and Ezra's connection with the Monaco government was just the beginning of a long string of victories he knew were on the horizon.

When Ezra and Emilie left the restaurant before their first course was served, Dan admitted that he was taken off guard. Thankfully, he thought fast and smart. He tailed them all the way to a pub on the west side and slipped into a booth next to them without being noticed. Their conversations were boring, but flirtatious and basic enough that it was easy to deduce their romance was new.

Anderson smiled to himself as he walked away from the art gallery and hailed a taxi on the bustling avenue. A yellow cab pulled over immediately and he ducked inside.

"Tribeca, please," he said to the driver.

Pulling out Emilie's business card, he wanted to laugh at how easy it was to have her in the palm of his hand. Dan, dutiful and determined, kept notes on everything the young couple spoke about. Then, when Ezra's ridiculous chauffeur picked them up, Dan quickly rented a city bike and pedaled after them without being detected.

Apparently, Ezra and Emilie shared a heated moment in the shadows by her apartment. Then, watching from the opposite side of the street, Dan tracked Emilie through the old windows of her building as she stepped inside alone and made her way up to the street-facing apartment on the right side of the hall.

When Ezra and his chauffeur were long gone, Dan approached the stoop and found the little button marked with Emilie's apartment number. *3FR*. Third floor, front of the building, right side. Her last name was printed on a label next to the doorbell.

DeGaulle. Her name was Emilie DeGaulle.

That was all Anderson needed and Dan was proud to deliver it to him.

Anderson's day had been busy. When he wasn't unraveling Ezra's plans for the contract with the royal family's jets in Monaco—and dealing with the annoyance of the loss of the land in Vermont—he'd been busy researching Emilie DeGaulle.

Compared to other women her age, Emilie had a small online footprint. However, Anderson had a lot of resources at his disposal. He learned that she had graduated from the Pratt Institute six years ago. He even found pictures of the series of paintings she did for her senior thesis.

He found her art blog, her phone number, and a handful of email addresses she'd cycled through in the past decade, but he couldn't find her employer.

Thankfully, Dan was already on the case. He followed Emilie from her apartment on the lower east side that morning all the way to midtown where she got off the subway and marched right into Hudson Enterprises. That was where Dan's trail ended, but he figured she'd be back down soon enough. Both he and Anderson assumed she was merely paying Ezra a visit.

Lo and behold, Emilie didn't leave Hudson Enterprises until five o'clock sharp, but at that point Anderson had already had one of his other assistants hack into their employee database and discover that Emilie DeGaulle was not just a friend of Ezra's, but also an employee. She was a graphic designer for the marketing department.

Anderson had a good laugh about that one. Ezra Hudson, who was always so polite and well-behaved, was secretly dating one of his junior employees. It was scandalous and ripe with potential for ruination, but Anderson decided to play a long con. There had to be something more he could do than suggest that the CEO of Hudson Enterprises was taking advantage of a young woman who worked below him.

That was too simple. Too easy. People would lose interest too quickly. It wasn't enough to destroy Hudson Enterprises.

Because that's what Anderson wanted to do, and he wasn't going to stop until he accomplished it. He wanted to take everything from Ezra. It wasn't personal. It wasn't as if Ezra had wronged him in the past and he was plotting an elaborate revenge.

The truth was, Anderson was tired of getting beat time and time again for land and contracts in an industry where Ezra had too much control. Transportation engineering was a billion-dollar enterprise, but it wasn't easy. Anderson would do anything to win a monopoly. It was the only way he could expand the drug empire he had inherited from his father into international markets. There was no such thing as dirty money, but there was such a thing as those too weak to acknowledge it. Ezra was too moral, too pure. He wasn't going to last long. Anderson would simply speed up that process and make his life a little bit easier.

In the meantime, while he waited for the right time to swallow Hudson Enterprises whole, Anderson would continue to take the smaller things. Contracts and connections and land. He'd even take Ezra's girl.

Sure, Emilie wasn't his usual type. She was pretty, but in a petite and awkward way that made her seem somewhat girlish. Anderson liked women. Women with curves and attitudes and little regard for morality.

Still, Emilie was a talented girl. Dropping a couple thousand dollars for a nice drawing was like handing pocket change to a busker in the subway, but he could tell that it meant the world to Emilie. If she was poor and desperate, how hard could it really be to woo her?

Sooner or later, Anderson was going to make sure Ezra lost everything. That's the way the world worked. The powerful beat the weak. It was the natural order of things. Criminal enterprise aside, Anderson figured he was just doing what he needed to keep the universe in balance.

***

The second Emilie walked through her front door and saw her younger sister in the kitchen, she squealed happily and launched herself into her arms. Annie caught her at the last minute, hugging her back with a confused grunt. Emilie rarely displayed that much enthusiasm, but she couldn't contain herself.

When she finally let her sister go, she stepped back and beamed at the taller girl. Annie's green eyes were slightly darker and her blond hair was cropped to her shoulders, but the two sisters looked undeniably similar. When they were younger, they had often been mistaken for twins.

"Care to explain why you just attacked me?" giggled Annie. "Did you have a really good second day at work or something?"

"I sold a painting," Emilie blurted out.

"You—what?"

"Actually, it was a drawing, but I sold it! For two thousand dollars, if you can believe it! It was crazy. I mean, one minute, I swear the gallery owner was about to tell me to get lost, but the next minute this rich guy comes in and walks right over to my portfolio and insists on buying one of the sketches!" Emilie babbled.

Annie furrowed her brow. "I need you to slow down and backtrack. Which gallery, which rich guy, and which drawing? Also… two thousand dollars? Are you serious?"

Emilie let out another excited squeal and bounced on the balls of her feet. Before she'd left the gallery, she gave the owner—whose name was Steven—her banking information. She would be two thousand dollars richer by morning. She explained everything to her sister with more detail but left out the part about how she'd already met the buyer before.

Annie didn't know Emilie had gone on a date last night, let alone with someone she'd randomly slept with at Lena's wedding last September. Throw in the fact that Ezra also turned out to be the CEO of the company where she worked, and Emilie would have to spend the next week performing a monologue to her sister just to explain everything. It wasn't that she was purposefully keeping Annie in the dark. She'd tell her eventually. She trusted Annie more than anyone in the world.

But, for now, Emilie didn't think it was necessary to get into the mess of it all when she still wasn't certain if it was a good idea for Ezra and her to proceed any further.

"That's so amazing," Annie murmured, hugging Emilie close when she was finished with her explanation of the evening's events. "Congratulations! We should get champagne or something."

"I don't think we can afford champagne."

"We can definitely afford, like, a six-dollar bottle of sparkling wine from the bodega, though."

"True. I'm in."

"Wait, before we go," Annie called out, tapping Emilie's shoulder when she turned to head toward the door. Emilie felt too full of joy to stay inside the apartment, twirling away from Annie.

"What?"

"Something arrived for you about an hour ago. I ran into the courier at the door when I got home," she replied.

"Huh? I wasn't expecting anything."

Wordlessly, Annie gestured to the coffee table in their tiny living room, which served as a dining table, a study desk, and a storage center all at once. On top of the cheap, glossy white painted wood pulp surface sat an unfamiliar object.

Resting in a gorgeous clay pot was the long stem of a stunning purple orchid. It was beautiful, so richly colored that Emilie could hardly believe it was real. Who the hell would send her such an expensive gift?

It only took her two seconds to answer that question on her own.

Emilie let out a chuckle as she walked over the orchid and lifted the little notecard that was tied to the flowerpot with a white ribbon. It was folded to conceal the message within, but Emilie knew Annie would have already peeked at it.

Em, it addressed her. *Roses are red, violets are blue, orchids are purple, and I can't stop thinking about you. Sorry for the terrible poem. Ez*

Em and Ez. She had to admit, the nicknames sounded cute together. Plus, the awful poetry made her laugh. He was ridiculous. Although they'd already slept together, they barely knew each other at all, and yet he was sending her flowers on an otherwise inconsequential Tuesday evening just to say he was thinking of her.

Emilie wished she had a tougher heart. It was impossible to resist falling for Ezra.

She sighed and glanced up at Annie, who was grinning and waggling her eyebrows expectantly, waiting for the juicy details.

"Hold on," Emilie told her. "Let me make a call."

When Emilie pressed call on Ezra's name in her phone, he picked up right away.

"Hi, Emilie," he murmured, an obvious smile in his tone.

"Hi, Ezra," she replied, rolling her eyes despite the grin on her face. She plopped onto the couch, ignoring her sister who didn't care one bit about being impolite and listening in on Emilie's end of the conversation.

"Are your evening plans already over?"

"Yes, they are."

"Can I see you?"

Emilie laughed. "It's late."

"Come over. I can bring you to work tomorrow."

Her stomach flipped at his suggestion. "I can't. Thank you for the flower, though. It's very pretty."

"You're welcome. Did you like the poem?"

"It was very entertaining, yes."

"Can I see you tomorrow night?" Ezra implored.

Emilie pressed her fingers over her lips and ducked her head to hide the smile on her face and the blush on her cheeks from her sister, but Annie's snort of laughter told her that she caught it anyway.

Maybe it was just the triumph she felt from what had happened at the gallery, but Emilie was in too good of a mood to say no to anyone.

"Fine," she replied. "Tomorrow night."

"We can have dinner at my place in Soho. I'm actually a fairly decent cook," Ezra told her. "Does that sound good?"

Soho. Trendy, expensive Soho, where celebrities and millionaires ambled about on the narrow cobblestone lanes, purchased overpriced lattes from artisanal cafes, and browsed through cashmere sweaters at luxury boutiques. Emilie didn't have to see it for herself to know that Ezra's home was opulent. But that wasn't why she hesitated. She didn't expect a man like Ezra to live in a humble neighborhood and she was bothered by the prospect of visiting a place that was so expensive she was sure she could never afford it even in her wildest dreams.

Rather, Emilie was hesitant because she knew exactly what would happen if she went over to Ezra's place for dinner. They would drink wine and nibble on whatever meal he whipped up. They'd stare longingly into each other's eyes and reveal more of their hearts to each other. Like magnets, they would be drawn together, incurably attracted.

Emilie would end up in bed with him again. She didn't bother trying to fool herself into thinking she would be able to exercise restraint and go home before things went too far. Then, because it was his place, he would still be there in the morning when she woke up. It wouldn't be the way it was in London. She would see him in the morning light. She would see the way his lashes fell on his cheek when his eyes were closed, and taste his skin in the sunshine. He probably had sheets with an astronomically high thread count and a silk duvet spun from the rarest silkworms in the world.

It would be heaven. It would be the final straw.

Emilie couldn't give in to him. Not yet. She had sold one piece of art and was about to sign one gallery contract, but that didn't mean she could let herself be distracted. If anything, she needed to be more focused than ever on her art.

Because she knew she couldn't walk away from Ezra completely—and not just because they worked in the same building—she rationalized that she was going to have to find a way to slow things down between them.

Emilie's mind raced through those thoughts in the span of just a few seconds. When she reached her conclusion, she cleared her throat.

"Can you hold on a second?" she asked Ezra.

"Sure—"

Emilie pressed the phone to her chest to muffle the microphone and met Annie's pleading, desperately curious gaze.

"Are you going to be home tomorrow night?" Emilie whispered to her.

Annie quirked an eyebrow at her sister but followed her lead and kept her voice low when she replied. "Duh. It's not like I have a life outside of studying."

Emilie gave her a thumbs-up and pressed the phone to her ear again.

"What if you came over to my place instead?" Emilie asked Ezra. Annie made a face, attempting to communicate how utterly lost she was, but Emilie held up a finger to indicate that she needed to be patient for a little bit longer.

"Your place?"

"Yeah. Why not? We can have dinner here, right?"

Emilie's reasoning was simple. If Ezra was desperate to see her, she didn't have the willpower to fend him off. However, if she flipped the script and invited him to her miniscule, humble abode while her little sister was home, the opportunity for romance would be limited. The likelihood of them passionately making love in Emilie's closet-sized bedroom with Annie on the other side of the paper-thin wall was nonexistent.

They could spend the evening together, and Emilie's heart would remain safe. At least, for the most part.

She hoped.

"Sure," Ezra replied, audibly amused by the turn of events. "Your place sounds great. What time should I come over?"

"How about eight o'clock?"

"Eight o'clock, it is."

"Goodnight, Ezra."

"Goodnight, Emilie. Sleep well."

The second Emilie hung up the call, Annie leaped across the room and snatched the phone out of her sister's hands. Emilie pouted while Annie cackled victoriously.

"You can get this back when you tell me what on God's green earth is going on," Annie said, settling on the couch beside Emilie.

Emilie groaned and flopped back against the cushions. "I thought we were going to buy gross fake champagne."

"Screw the bubbly. I'm much more interested to hear about this person you invited over for tomorrow night," Annie giggled.

"It's a long story."

"I've got time."

"Okay," sighed Emilie, realizing that there was no way Annie was going to let her keep Ezra to herself another minute. It was a six-month-long secret, but it was time to spill. "Remember when I went to London for Lena's wedding last summer?"

Chapter Nine

Ezra stood on Emilie's doorstep with a bottle of wine, a bouquet of yellow roses from the bodega on the corner, and his heart in his hands. After work, he'd hurried home to abandon his suit for a pair of dark jeans and a simple black tee. He wanted to prove that he could be casual and look like any other guy on the lower east side.

Emilie opened the door, her cheeks flushed and her eyes bright. She was so beautiful, all he could think about was kissing her. Instead, he hugged her and stepped inside the little apartment, offering her the roses.

"More flowers?" she asked.

"They reminded me of you," he shrugged, offering no further explanation when Emilie led him further inside toward the small kitchen where she dug a mason jar from the cupboard for the flowers.

"Thanks," she murmured.

The truth was that he saw the roses and thought that their yellow hue reminded him of sunshine, which in turn reminded him of Emilie's warm, enchanting aura, but he figured that was a bit too much to admit out loud.

"Um, and I brought wine, too," he said. "I didn't know what we were eating, but I had a bottle of chardonnay I kept meaning to open, so—"

"Chardonnay is great," she replied, quickly snipping the stems and plopping them into the jar. "The truth is that I'm terrible at cooking, so I ordered Mediterranean food from a restaurant a few blocks away. It should be here in a few minutes."

Ezra laughed. He had offered to cook for her in his home, but she insisted on dinner at her place even though she had to have the meal delivered. Was she nervous about going over to his house? Was she trying to prove something by inviting him to her humble home?

He glanced around. Honestly, it was a nice apartment. It was old, but in a cool and classic Manhattan kind of way. Exposed brick, old-fashioned steam radiators, and thick windows that overlooked the brown brick buildings on the other side of the street. It was small, of course, but who needed thousands of square feet when the most incredible city in the world was outside? Even Ezra's loft wasn't unreasonably spacious.

"I like your apartment," he told her, watching as she brought the yellow roses over to the coffee table and settled them beside the orchid he'd sent her yesterday. Everything in the home was a different color or different pattern, but the chaos worked. It suited Emilie.

"Really? It's small."

"Nothing wrong with small."

"Let me give you a tour while we wait for the food," she offered. "It'll take about twenty seconds."

He approached her, watching as she bit her lip when he came to stand so close there was barely an inch of space left between them.

"Okay," he whispered, brushing a strand of hair out of her face. The thick waves were pulled back in a ponytail, but a few rebellious pieces had escaped to frame her face. She looked like a wild, untamable angel.

Emilie cleared her throat and took a deep breath before stepping away from Ezra. It brought him great satisfaction when her voice trembled slightly as she spoke.

"Well, you've already seen the grand foyer, the chef's kitchen, and the formal sitting room," she joked. "The luxury marble bathroom is down the hall that way, and this door right here leads to my sister's room. She's definitely listening very closely on the other side of it right now."

Ezra was surprised when, sure enough, the door to his left opened and a taller version of Emilie with short hair poked her head out.

"Hi," grinned the girl. "I'm Annie. You must be Ezra. It's nice to meet you."

They had the same mannerisms. The same playful sparkle in their eyes and the ever-present humor in their tone. Ezra smiled and shook her hand. He didn't realize that anyone else would be home when he came over, but it explained why Emilie asked him to come over to her place instead. In spite of the time they had shared together so far, Emilie clearly wasn't ready to be alone with him in his house.

That was fine. He understood. If she was still too timid to trust him, he could change her mind.

"Nice to meet you, too," he replied.

Annie winked. "Don't worry about me. I'll be quiet as a mouse, just minding my business in here studying Dadaism. However, if there are any falafels leftover from dinner, I'd love a bite."

Emilie rolled her eyes. "Okay, Annie. Goodbye now."

"Bye-bye," crooned the younger woman, shutting the door slowly.

"What's Dadaism?" Ezra asked Emilie as he followed her to the open door at the end of the hall.

"It's an art movement," she explained. "Super weird, but kind of cool."

Ezra remembered Emilie mentioning that her sister was studying to be a museum curator. Two artsy sisters living together, joking around like best friends. Ezra thought it was sweet. He didn't mind if there was a quiet third person hanging out on their date. He was grateful for every glimpse he got into Emilie's life.

There were paintings and drawings hung up all over the walls, covering nearly every inch of available space. He wanted to ask if they were Emilie's creations, but the second she flicked on the light inside the next room and glanced over her shoulder at him, his mouth went dry.

"This is my room," Emilie said, nodding her head for him to follow her inside.

He tried to remind himself that he was a grown man and there was no reason for him to feel butterflies in the pit of his stomach as he followed a beautiful woman into her bedroom. It was no use. As far as Emilie was concerned, Ezra was a pathetic pile of mush.

Emilie watched him observe his surroundings.

"It's very... green," he murmured.

She laughed. "Green is my favorite color."

The sheets, the comforter, the rug, and every tiny bit of furniture crammed inside the room were a different shade of green, but it wasn't tacky in the slightest. Obviously, Emilie had a very good eye for design. The monochrome décor was feminine and mature, but it also revealed her youthful, energetic spirit.

"I like it," Ezra told her. His eyes were drawn to a bookshelf by the window, which was stuffed full of sketchbooks, brushes, tubes of paint, and various other supplies that he couldn't identify. Dozens of canvasses in a variety of sizes and in various stages of completion were scattered about the room, leaning up against the wall in stacks or resting precariously on every available surface.

"It's kind of weird, but I actually don't use green in any of my paintings," Emilie told him, clasping her hands behind her back. She looked anxious as he took in the dizzying sight of an artist's den. He knew with absolute certainty that the artwork he'd noticed throughout the rest of the apartment was her doing.

"Why not?" Ezra asked, leaning forward to get a better look at a canvas covered in abstract strokes of purple and red.

"I don't know," she said. "Art is meant for display, so, I think I like green so much that I want to keep it for myself. Does that make sense?"

He nodded. Her mind was a fascinating whirl of thoughts. If he could, he would give up everything to spend the rest of his life decoding her.

"I don't know if I have a favorite color," Ezra admitted.

Emilie tutted her tongue at him. "Impossible."

"I'm serious," he laughed. "I'm not very good at picking favorites."

But she shook her head and moved over to the shelf. She grabbed a handful of tiny paint tubes and held them out to him.

"Pick one," she instructed.

"What?"

"Pick a color."

Ezra frowned at the selection. There were dozens of colors in her hands. He didn't know that paint came in such small containers. He felt like she was testing him, so he chose the first color that drew his eye. It was blue, dark and sultry like the night sky.

"Interesting," she murmured.

"What's interesting?"

"I had a feeling you would choose that one," Emilie smirked, returning the paint back to the shelf and crossing her arms against her chest as they continued to stand together in the cramped space.

The bed was so close. The bottom corner of her duvet brushed against his calf. He couldn't stop thinking about it, but remembered that her little sister was only a few feet away.

He had more class than that.

"I didn't even know you were a painter," Ezra told her, saying the first thing that came to mind. "I mean, I knew you were creative because of your job position, but I had no idea you were this amazing. What are you doing working for my boring company? Paul and Yasmina are forcing you to make stupid advertisements, but you're capable of *this*?"

Emilie waved off his compliments. "Believe me, I'm grateful for the graphic design job. It's stable, unlike most careers in art. And now that I'm not working in the service industry seven days a week, I actually have time to work on my art. Half of these paintings have been works in progress for months—some of them for more than a year."

"Oh, wow," Ezra breathed. He didn't realize she had been working so hard before she'd landed the job at his company. Even though it didn't have anything to do with him, he was glad that getting the role gave her a chance to work on her art. "So, this must be your true goal in life. You want to be a painter?"

Emilie shrugged. She looked like she didn't want to respond to Ezra's question, as if she was embarrassed to admit that working in a corporation's marketing department wasn't her life's purpose.

Ezra chuckled and reached out to lightly pinch her forearm. "It's okay. Pretend I'm not the CEO. I can promise you won't offend me. Even I know corporate jobs are a unique form of torture."

She relaxed and let out a quiet exhale. "Okay, yeah. Ideally, I could become a full-time painter. Yesterday, when I couldn't—"

The doorbell buzzed, cutting Emilie off. She pouted and led Ezra back to the living room, instructing him to sit on the couch while she pressed the button to allow the delivery person into the building, then waited by the door while he made his way up the stairs. Once she collected the bag of food, Ezra watched as she hummed under her breath while gathering bowls and cutlery from the kitchen.

She sat on the floor and started dishing out the food into bowls arranged on the coffee table. Ezra realized there was no other table in the apartment and that this is what they were going to be using as a dinner table. Endeared by the simplicity of it, he joined her on the hardwood floor.

"I forgot to ask if you had any food allergies," she chattered. "I figured you weren't a vegetarian, since we ate burgers together, but—"

"It's okay," he told her, shaking his head. "I'm not allergic to anything. This is great. You're very good at ordering food."

Emilie laughed and handed him a container of yellow rice. "I guess I also should have asked if you even like Mediterranean food—"

"I'm not picky," he insisted. "What were you saying about yesterday?"

"Right. Well, when I told you that I couldn't see you because I had plans, the truth was, I was meeting with a gallery owner," Emilie told him, sitting cross-legged with her back against the front of the couch. She looked adorably comfortable. Ezra was relieved that she could relax around him. "It's really a totally insane story, the more I think about it."

"Really? What happened? Did he like your stuff?"

"He liked it, yeah," she shrugged. "But he was going to reject me anyway. He was in the middle of telling me the fact that I have no name recognition value meant neither one of us would profit from a partnership when that business friend of yours from the Orange Rose walked in!"

"My—who?" Ezra frowned in confusion. He didn't remember seeing any colleagues during their brief time at the Orange Rose.

"Anderson Blackwell," Emilie clarified. "Isn't that crazy? Like, he just happened to run into you at the restaurant and then also happened to be at the gallery? I swear the universe works in the most mysterious ways sometimes—"

While Emilie trailed off and ate a few bites of food, Ezra tried not to look like he was about to punch a hole through the floor. What the hell was Blackwell doing at the same gallery where Emilie was having a meeting? There was no way it was a coincidence. After the stunt he pulled with the tabloid—which thankfully was now taken down and cleared up—there was no way Blackwell had innocently crossed paths with Emilie a second time.

He was up to something.

But Ezra didn't want to waste the evening explaining to Emilie that Blackwell was a bad guy. What evidence did he have other than the fact that he was constantly attempting to thwart the growth of Hudson Enterprises? Of course he was. Ezra was his competition and Blackwell didn't care about appropriate business ethics. Not many people did nowadays. If Ezra tried to illustrate those things to Emilie, she might think that he was trying to turn her against a man that she personally had no reason to dislike.

For now, Ezra would have to keep a close eye on the situation.

"So, what happened? Did Blackwell know the gallery owner or something?" Ezra pressed.

"No, not at all. It looked like he was there to browse, but then he noticed my portfolio was open and asked if he could look at it. I figured there wasn't any harm in saying yes, so I let him," Emilie explained. Ezra couldn't tell if she was picking up on the tension in his body, but hoped he was putting up a good front. "And then he really liked one of my drawings, so he asked if he could buy it."

"He did? Seriously?" Ezra exclaimed, then quickly backtracked. "I didn't know he was such an art aficionado."

"He doesn't seem the type, but he seemed to really like the sketch," she replied, moving her food around in her bowl thoughtfully. "Anyway, when he asked how much it was, I totally blanked. The gallery owner stepped in to save me and named a price. After Anderson left, he apologized and offered me a contract. My mom is looking it over for me right now since she's worked as a paralegal for most of her life, but if it looks good, I'll officially have a gallery in the city selling my art!"

"Wow, that's incredible, Emilie. Congratulations!"

"Thanks. I mean, I'm just lucky that Anderson showed up. I thought he had a weird vibe when I met him at dinner, but I guess he's actually really nice."

"Hmm," Ezra replied, nodding while avoiding her eyes. If she noticed that he was acting strange, she didn't pry.

Thankfully, after that they spoke about other things. Emilie explained Dadaism to him in further detail, and then, when prompted by Ezra, who just wanted to hear her talk for hours and hours, explained surrealism and modernism, too. When she spoke about art, she became more animated. He could tell she was passionate about the subject.

There was a part of him that was ashamed he didn't know she was such a talented painter. On top of that, he was annoyed that Anderson Blackwell would always be the first person to have purchased her art. Emilie would always remember him that way, and Ezra would never be able to change that. Even though she likely wouldn't allow it, Ezra wanted to buy every single piece of art she'd ever created. He'd do anything if it meant she could follow her dreams. Maybe it was ridiculous to think that way about a woman he was still getting to know, but Emilie was more than just some girl he was dating. She was more than a one-night stand or a missed connection.

She was… everything.

After dinner and the bottle of chardonnay were both nearly finished, they continued sitting on the living room floor. They sat facing each other, propped up with their arms resting on the cushions. Annie never emerged from her room, either asleep or too absorbed in her studying that she forgot to bother them for falafel.

"Did you always want to be the CEO of a major international corporation?" Emilie asked him. A smirk danced on her lips, mesmerizing Ezra's wine-dizzy mind.

He chuckled. "Not exactly. When I was little, I wanted to be a pilot."

"What changed?"

Ezra shrugged. "The thought of having so many lives in my hands scared the shit out of me."

"Fair enough."

"So, after that, I decided I wanted to be just like my dad. I wanted to be an engineer. I even started out majoring in it when I went to college."

Emilie nodded along, paying attention to every single word he spoke.

"Did you not like it?" she prodded.

"It wasn't really my thing," he admitted. "I wasn't very good at science or mechanics. Working with my hands didn't come naturally to me. I was really good at math, though. Statistics and calculus and all of that, so I switched to finance. I was still interested in planes and trains, but more so on the business side."

She smiled as if he had said the most interesting thing in the world, but her face quickly dissolved into a frown. "It must be hard for you to work in that field, right?"

"Because of what happened to my dad? Not really. Honestly, part of the reason why I'm so passionate about transportation technology is because I want to be at the forefront of making it as safe as possible," Ezra replied. "No one should have to lose somebody that way."

"You're amazing."

"I'm nothing compared to you," Ezra whispered.

"I disagree."

"Is this our first fight?"

Emilie giggled, but Ezra couldn't take it anymore. The sweet sound of her laughter was quickly muffled by his kiss. Instantly, she melted into him and draped her arms around his shoulders. He wanted her closer, set on fire by the way she whimpered ever so slightly into his mouth when he squeezed her waist.

Without breaking the kiss, Emilie pushed the coffee table away and swung her leg across Ezra's lap so that she was straddling him. His hands roamed her body, torturously barred from her skin by the fabric of her jeans and sweater.

After a few minutes, Emilie broke away. She was breathing fast, her cheeks flushed and eyes dark.

"I want you so bad," he murmured.

She looked like she might say yes. As if she were just a few seconds of begging away from hopping in a cab with him to his place in Soho. She would look so good naked in his bedsheets.

"I… I think we should… sorry. I didn't mean to—I shouldn't have—" she stuttered, climbing off his lap. His body pleaded for her not to go, but he didn't want to force her to go further than what she was comfortable with.

Ezra inhaled deeply and tried to will the stiffness in his jeans to calm down.

"It's okay," he told her. "I understand. I hope you don't think that I expect you to—I mean, just because of what happened in London—"

Emilie bit her lip. "I don't know what came over me that night. I normally don't do stuff like that."

"Me either," Ezra grinned. "But we don't have to pick up where we left off."

"Good to know."

"Actually, I was wondering about something," he began. "I know you're not into the snobby wealth scene, but there's a fundraiser gala this weekend that I was invited to. The charity helps fund youth art programs in underprivileged school districts throughout the city. Would you be interested in accompanying me?"

Emilie raised her eyebrows high. "To a gala? I've never been to one. Aren't they really fancy?"

"They can be, but they're also a good opportunity to meet some really impressive people. If anything, we can get dressed up, stop by long enough for me to write a check, and then go get drunk at a dive bar," he offered.

"I don't really have anything to wear to something like that," she protested, though he could tell she was considering it.

"Don't worry about that. I'll take care of it."

Emilie frowned at him. "Ezra—"

"Please? Pretty please?" he pleaded, leaning forward to kiss her slowly. So slowly that he swore time slowed down between the breaths they took.

He pulled away, but just barely. Their noses brushed against each other.

"That's not fair," Emilie whispered. "You're coercing me with your lips."

"I can use my tongue, too," he purred.

She clutched a fistful of his shirt. For a second, he wasn't sure if she was going to pull him closer or shove him away. However, after a few seconds, she simply loosened her grip and let out a slow exhale.

"Okay," she finally said. "I'll go with you to the rich people event."

"That was easier than I thought," he chuckled.

She rolled her eyes. "Shut up."

He smirked. "Make me."

And she did.

Chapter Ten

When Emilie arrived at work the next morning, her body was tired but her mind was buzzing with electricity. Ezra didn't leave her place until shortly before midnight the night before and Emilie had spent the next handful of hours tossing and turning in bed, kicking herself for pumping the brakes on their make out session in the floor of her living room.

I want you so bad.

Those words Ezra had spoken to her played over and over in the back of her mind. He had sounded so raw when he told her that, like nothing else in the world was truer than how much he wanted her.

Ezra Hudson was going to drive her crazy.

To make matters worse, there was a note waiting on her desk when she stepped into her cubicle. She didn't need to question who would leave a folded letter underneath her keyboard, barely visible to anyone who might walk by. Did Ezra sneak down to the lower floors before anyone else arrived just to leave it for her? How early had he arrived that morning? Did he manage to get more sleep than she did?

Emilie glanced over her shoulder to make sure no one was paying attention to her, then opened the note.

Em, I think 23 is my favorite number now because it's the elevator button I can press to get to you, read the message. *I hope you make fun of me for how lame that is of me to say. Yours, Ez*

Smiling to herself, she slipped the note into her purse and sat down to boot up her computer for the day. While the rest of the design team slowly trickled in, she pulled out her phone and texted Ezra.

You're the cheesiest man I've ever met, she sent to him.

A few minutes later, her phone buzzed with a response.

I can do worse than that, he replied. Then, a few seconds later, a longer message appeared: *I wish this didn't have to be a secret. If I could, I would run yelling through the halls of Hudson Enterprises about how beautiful you are.*

Emilie drummed her fingertips on top of her desk. This was one of the topics they had discussed last night during dinner. They had agreed it was better for them to keep it under wraps that they were seeing each other, though the conversation skirted around clearly defining the relationship. Were they merely dating? Though it made Emilie nervous to admit it, it certainly felt like it was much more than that.

Well, in that case, I think your employees are indebted to me for keeping you contained, she typed back.

I want you to be my girlfriend, he responded an instant later.

Emilie froze. There it was. Plain as day. Ezra didn't just want her physically. He wanted to be in a relationship with her. She didn't know how to reply. The idea wasn't repulsive—the opposite, in fact—but Emilie knew that a committed relationship would take away even more of her precious painting time. She'd already lost every evening so far that week.

When Emilie didn't reply, Ezra sent another text.

I mean it, he wrote. *I'll buy every single page of your sketchbooks for one million dollars each if it means you can quit this dumb company of mine and be my girlfriend publicly without all the current complications. I know you want to do it by yourself and I respect that, but I also think you should consider the benefits of taking advantage of a guy with ample disposable income and zero self-respect.*

Emilie almost laughed out loud. She knew he was mostly joking about the million-dollar offer, but there was also a part of her that felt certain he would truly do it if she let him.

But, no. He was right. She did want to do it by herself. She didn't want to make it as an artist because a rich guy who knew of her, through her connection to Ezra, liked a couple of her drawings. She also didn't want to make it because a different rich guy had such a big crush on her that he offered outlandishly high prices for her work just for the chance to date her without having to sidestep company policy.

There were so many people who were given unfair advantages in life. People who had endless opportunities handed to them on a silver platter just because they were lucky enough to be born into the right family. People who were rich or famous or important, people who knew people that could give them a leg-up. The creative industry was saturated with artists who— regardless of talent or skill—were successful because they had money on their side.

Emilie had never had money. She and her sister had never been dirt poor, but they'd had to learn to make do with the few things they had. She'd always told herself that she was going to prove she could become a successful artist without selling her soul to the upper class. As easy as it would be, Emilie didn't want to let Ezra buy up all her art. She didn't want him to hang her paintings in his loft and his yacht and his glamorous office so that he could tell all the other wealthy people in New York about her.

As kind as he was, she didn't want to be indebted to him. If she was going to be someone noteworthy, she was going to do it on her own. Maybe it was unrealistic or downright impossible, but Emilie was determined either way.

And yet... she could picture the life Ezra was painting for her. She could help her sister pay off her student loans and give her enough cash to afford rent for the next year while she slaved away in the bowels of a museum internship program. She could quit Hudson Enterprises and become Ezra's girlfriend and move in with him and spend her days sprawled out in his luxurious Soho apartment, painting to her heart's content.

She could be happy like that, but not for long. She would know it wasn't genuine, that her happiness existed only because she had allowed her attraction to a man distract her and reshape her entire future.

Emilie decided to keep her reply to Ezra relatively lighthearted.

As tempting as the offer is, I'm going to climb this ladder on my own. Now stop texting me and get to work, Mr. Hudson!

She hoped Ezra wasn't too disappointed by her rejection. It wasn't that she hated the idea of being his girlfriend. If circumstances were different and Emilie had a little more luck and privilege on her side, she wouldn't hesitate. Ezra was a great guy. Most girls would kill for the chance to date someone like him.

The problem was she didn't know how to tell him she liked him a lot, just not enough to give up her dignity.

Luckily, Ezra's reply was brief and mocking.

Yes, ma'am! his message read.

Emilie placed her phone face down on the desk, took a few moments to clear her mind as much as possible, and opened the design team's to-do list for the day.

One of the good things about working at Hudson Enterprises was that there was always a lot to accomplish. Everyone was busy, bouncing ideas and drafts off each other for suggestions. If Emilie's true passion was graphic design, she could see herself loving her position at the company and staying there for a long time.

Part of her felt bad that she was using the job as somewhat of a stepping stone, especially because it was obvious that the rest of the team were living out their dreams in the marketing department. She knew she had rightfully earned her place there, but she also couldn't help thinking that there was someone else out there who would be ten times happier than she was to doodle on a tablet in a cubicle all day.

Oh, well. That person could take over her role once she sold enough paintings to quit Hudson Enterprises.

During her lunch break, Emilie walked to Central Park and claimed a spot in the sunshine atop a boulder. It was finally getting warmer in the city and Emilie felt like a lizard sunning on a rock in the forest, soaking in the fresh springtime air.

It was almost seven in the evening in England, but Emilie had a handful of texts from Lena begging her to call and catch up as soon as she was available.

After the wedding, Lena and Pierre had taken a month-long honeymoon to backpack through East Asia. The pictures they posted were incredible, their smiles bright from the beauty of being in love. When they returned home, Lena and Pierre had to leap right back into their demanding jobs. With the time difference between New York and London added on top of that, Emilie hadn't had many chances to talk to her old friend.

When Lena picked up the call, she sighed happily.

"Ah, the soothing sounds of Manhattan," she crooned in lieu of hello. "I missed hearing all those noises."

Emilie laughed. She was so used to her hometown that she barely registered the noise, but Lena was right. At that very moment, there were engines revving, horns honking, children squealing, and a jet passing overhead.

"London isn't noisy enough for you?" Emilie asked.

Lena giggled. "It's plenty loud, but we've got this little house in Kensington where it's so quiet and peaceful that I sometimes forget we live in one of the biggest cities in Europe. You could never accomplish something like that in New York."

"You talk like never getting a moment of silence is a good thing."

"Oh, but isn't it?" Lena giggled. "Silence is so boring. Anyway, how are you? What are you up to? What time is it there? How's your new job?"

Emilie was used to the way Lena talked. She was extremely energetic and, thanks to a touch of attention deficit disorder, was prone to peppering people with a handful of questions at once because she would otherwise forget to ask.

"I'm good," Emilie replied. "I'm just in the park on my lunch break. It's about half past noon. My new job is… interesting."

"Interesting? In a good way?"

At that moment, Annie was the only one who knew the truth about who Ezra was. Emilie had told her sister everything, not daring to mince words as she explained their hook-up in London and the realization that, six months later, he was the man who signed her paychecks. Annie was unfailingly nonjudgmental, which made it easy to open up to her.

Lena, while easygoing and sweet, was someone who Emilie thought twice about before telling her secrets to. She wasn't gossipy, but she did have a loose filter. If Emilie told Lena about hooking up with Ezra at her wedding and then running into him again six months later, Lena wouldn't be able to stop herself from blurting it all to Pierre, who was friends with Ezra. Knowing them, the pair of social butterflies would stop at nothing to ensure that their friends ended up together.

And, as Emilie reasoned earlier, she wanted to do things on her own, at her own pace.

"Yes, in a good way," Emilie finally answered her. "I'm learning a lot and my coworkers are nice."

"I never thought you'd go into graphic design. What's the name of the company again?"

Emilie froze. She was glad that Lena was on the other side of the ocean and couldn't see her expression. Emilie was a terrible liar.

"It's just a really small, independent marketing firm," Emilie lied. "You wouldn't know it."

"Oh, I swore you mentioned that it was something to do with planes," Lena murmured. "I think Pierre has a friend who works in that industry."

Her stomach flipped. She did her best to sound casual.

"Really? That's cool," she replied. "How are you, though? How's the British Museum?"

"You know… British," Lena laughed. "I thought I'd get used to how formal and slow they are about things, but I'm an incurable American at heart. I mean, I've been working there for five years and I'm only just now getting the chance to spearhead the creation of a new exhibit."

"Seriously? That's incredible! Congratulations, Lena."

"Thanks, but it's really not as big of a deal as it sounds. I don't get much creative liberty," she lamented. "Really all I'm doing is rearranging a few artifacts."

"Well, that still sounds like a great opportunity."

"Hey, Em… can I tell you something?" Lena asked suddenly.

"Of course."

"I'm actually thinking about quitting."

"Quitting? Quitting the bloody British Museum?" Emilie couldn't believe her ears. It was one of the most famous museums in the world. It was home to some of the most notable relics of humanity throughout history—many of them stolen during Britain's colonial era, but still. Emilie remembered how amicably jealous she was of Lena when she was hired to work there almost immediately after graduating college.

"I'm actually thinking of going back to school," Lena admitted. "Curation doesn't get my blood pumping anymore. I'm not obsessed with it like your sister is, but there's a program in Paris for artifact restoration. I'd have to take a bunch of chemistry courses and whatnot, but it sounds so cool."

"Wait… Paris?"

"Oh, yeah. I forgot to mention that, too. Pierre got a job offer to teach at the Sorbonne," Lena giggled. "He hasn't accepted it yet, but we're thinking about it. It's still a big city, but it would be a nice change of pace to be in mainland Europe."

Emilie closed her eyes for a brief moment, reminding herself that it was better to focus on being happy for her friend than to kick herself for being far less impressive.

"You're living my dream life," Emilie told her.

"Nonsense. The grass is always greener on the other side," Lena lectured her. "I'm just a boring married woman now. By the way, are you *still* single? Have you gone on any dates in the past, like year?"

"I'm too busy to date," Emilie replied. It was technically the truth.

"One is never too busy for love," her friend sang back.

"I'll keep that in mind. I should get back to work soon, though."

"Okay! Please come visit London soon! Or you can come see us in Paris. You'd love France. Plus, you have a French name—"

"Yes, I'll try to figure out a good time to come."

"Yay! Bye, Em! Love you!"

"Love you too, Lena."

When the line went dead, Emilie dropped her phone into her lap and hugged her knees to her chest. Catching up with Lena always left her with a mixture of emotions. On one hand, she was thrilled to hear about the endless string of successes that she and her husband accomplished. Not only were they beautifully matched and sickeningly in love, but now Pierre was going to be teaching at one of the best universities in the world and Lena was going to grad school for a program that was probably almost impossible to be accepted into.

It was hard for Emilie not to compare herself. She was pathetically single, practically broke, and living in a cramped two-bedroom apartment on the lower east side with her sister. She worked in a cubicle. It had taken her six years to sell a single piece of art and the fact that it happened at all was the result of a random twist of fate.

Emilie's mom would tell her to stop beating herself up. She would say that everyone did life at their own speed and that there was no rule book. Emilie always nodded along when her mother had gone on those rants, but she had never truly believed her. In Emilie's eyes, there was a rule book. Graduate college, get a good job, fall in love, get married, maybe have a kid or two, and live happily ever after. Everyone knew that's what you were supposed to do. No matter how often people insisted that you didn't have to color inside those lines, there was always a sense of disapproval reserved for those who failed to abide by the unwritten guidelines.

There were other rules that Emilie had failed to follow, too. Don't hook up with random strangers at your friend's wedding. Don't date the CEO of the company where you work. Don't slack on your dreams.

Emilie had a few more minutes before she had to be back at the office, so she reached for her phone and checked her personal email. Steven, the gallery owner, was supposed to be getting back to her shortly about more of the kind of pieces he wanted to see from her. However, instead of a message from him, she had an email from someone else entirely.

Anderson Blackwell.

For a second, she forgot she had given him her card, never expecting him to actually reach out to her.

Emilie thought about the way Ezra had tensed up when she had mentioned Anderson's name over dinner last night. It was obvious that Ezra didn't like him, but she couldn't tell if it was because of the natural competition between them or if there was something darker going on beneath the surface. She figured that, if it was important, Ezra would tell her.

She opened the email, curious to know what Anderson could possibly be contacting her about. Was the drawing he had purchased less satisfactory than he originally thought? Did he want a refund? No, that couldn't be it. Only two days had passed since that night at the gallery— the piece hadn't even been delivered to him yet.

Emilie, I hope this finds you well, the email began. *I am looking forward to hanging up your drawing in my home, but I must admit that I am a curious and impatient man. I became so eager to see more of your work that I spent more time than I'm willing to admit scrolling through your website and admiring your talent. It is truly remarkable.*

Emilie was flattered by the kind words, but she was also confused. Had Anderson emailed her just to compliment her? Was he interested in her?

She continued reading. *I'm reaching out to you because I fear Blackwell Capital is experiencing a dire lack of color in our entrance lobby. Do you accept commissions? If so, would you be willing to do a custom mural for our headquarters? Please let me know—I'll be happy to triple your regular rate if that helps to convince you. Sincerely, A. Blackwell*

Emilie read the email several more times. She couldn't believe it. Anderson wanted her to paint an entire mural in the lobby of his company headquarters? Knowing his empire had to be big to be considered Ezra's competition, Emilie understood how huge the opportunity was. Her painting would be seen by everyone who walked into Blackwell Capital, from fellow businessowners to potential clients to government officials. People like Anderson and Ezra dealt with very important individuals.

Not to mention how much money he was offering her. Emilie had no idea how much to charge for a mural project, but she knew they didn't come cheap. And he was apparently offering triple the typical price.

Standing up slowly, Emilie made her way back to the office. She didn't know how to respond to Anderson. Was it wrong for her to accept a commission from Ezra's main competitor? Would she be betraying him by going to Blackwell Capital and creating something unique and special for them?

She figured it wasn't necessary to answer Anderson's email right away. She could take some time to think about it and decide in the next day or so. In the meantime, she wouldn't mention it to Ezra. Whatever was going on between Anderson and him was none of her business.

Chapter Eleven

It was a miracle that Emilie agreed to go with Ezra to the gala. It was even more of a miracle that she accepted the gown he gifted her, a floor-length velvet dress that hugged her delicate curves in all the right places. The fabric was bright red, just like the outfit Emilie had worn when they first met in London. He wondered if she realized he'd chosen it on purpose.

When Henry pulled up in the Bentley outside Emilie's apartment, she was already waiting on the front stoop. Ezra couldn't keep the grin off his face when he opened the door for her and kissed her on the cheek. She was a vision, her golden hair twisted up into a slick bun like a ballerina. She had paired the Dior gown with her own shoes and accessories, making it her own.

"You look beautiful," he whispered to her in the backseat as Henry drove them uptown.

"Thanks," she breathed. "You look really nice. I've seen you in suits every day, but it's been a while since you wore a tuxedo."

"Should I wear them more often?" Ezra joked. "I'd get dolled up for a Tuesday morning board meeting if you asked me to."

Emilie snorted and swatted him in the arm. Just like the last time they were in the back of the Bentley, she chose to be in the middle seat so she could be closer to him. While the city streets sailed by outside the windows, Ezra admired her in the glow from the streetlamps. Everything she wore was red. Her lipstick, her shoes, her bag, and even the ruby studs in her earlobes. Like her bedroom décor, the monochrome wasn't unpleasant. On her, it looked impossibly glamorous.

Even though Emilie didn't feel comfortable surrounded by the wealthiest and most sophisticated people in New York, she looked as if she belonged among them. She was perfect. More than perfect.

"You're staring at me," Emilie whispered. "Is there something on my face?"

"No," he murmured. "I was just thinking about how flawless you are."

"Don't be silly. I'm incredibly flawed."

Ezra chuckled. "I'm calling your bluff. Name one flaw you have."

"Easy. You witnessed it the other night. I can't cook."

"That's hardly a flaw. It just means that I get to do all the cooking for both of us, which is actually ideal," he said. "Try again."

"Okay, fine," she huffed. "I'm not very good at saving money."

"That's also not a flaw," Ezra quipped. "Money literally exists to be spent. You're actually handling it exactly how you're supposed to."

She laughed, the tinkling sound filling the car like music. "I have a feeling you're going to have an excuse for every single flaw I mention."

"Now you're catching on."

Emilie playfully rolled her eyes. A few minutes later, they arrived at the building where the gala was being held. It was an intimate arts center on the upper east side with wide stone steps that led up to a double door entrance, reminding Ezra of an ancient church.

Henry pulled up and Ezra motioned that he didn't need to get out and open the door for them. There was too much traffic on the avenue, not to mention there was no need to pretend as if they were celebrities arriving on the red carpet.

Standing on the sidewalk beside him, Emilie appeared almost comically out of place. Everything around her was ordinary and dull. The concrete pavement, the graffiti on the parking meters, the dirty cabs that zoomed by… they were part of a world that didn't shine bright enough for her. Even Ezra, who knew he looked rather dapper that evening, didn't feel as if he deserved to be by her side.

And yet, despite the fact that the brightest diamonds would pale in comparison to her, Emilie looked timid and uncertain as she stared up at the colossal, Greek-columned building.

"We can leave as soon as you tell me you want to go," Ezra assured her. "I just want to show my face and make a donation. I would be careful, though. There's a lot of priceless artworks in this building and someone might mistake you for one. Try not to become the victim of an art heist tonight."

Emilie burst out laughing at his lame compliment, visibly relaxing as she tucked her hand into the crook of his elbow and allowed him to lead her inside.

The interior of the building was stunning. The ballroom featured a domed ceiling painted creamy white and a massive chandelier cast a kaleidoscopic array of shadows across it. Emilie stared around in awe, her lips parted as she took in the sight of the lacquered gold crown molding and pastel blue marble floors.

"I feel like I'm in a palace," she murmured to him.

"That's fitting," he responded with a wink. "You look like a queen."

"I'm going to start pinching you every time you offer me a lame compliment," she giggled.

"Pinching is fine," Ezra whispered in her ear. "I like biting, too."

She elbowed him lightly in the ribs and he pretended to be severely wounded, causing her to laugh again. All around them and dressed to the nines, the old money elite of Manhattan floated around the ballroom. Even though the point of fundraising galas was to give money to the needy and contribute to a good cause, the rich couldn't resist turning it into a black-tie affair. Ezra had a feeling that galas were one of the only ways these charities received donations in the first place. If those with financial privilege didn't get to flaunt it when they wrote their checks, they wouldn't do it. It turned Ezra's stomach, but he was glad he wasn't like that. His parents had raised him to be humble no matter what.

"Ezra Hudson, my boy!" called a familiar voice behind him. Ezra whirled to find a friendly face, an older man named George who owned a conglomerate of the most successful airlines on the planet. They regularly did business together. George's wife—or rather, second wife—Nina was by his side. She was gorgeous, but half the man's age. In fact, he was pretty sure Nina was younger than Emilie.

"Hi, George," Ezra said to the man. "Nice to see you here."

"Oh, you know me... I love a chance to whip out the fancy dress and drink champagne with my darling," he chortled, smiling at Nina. To her credit, Nina didn't seem like a soulless gold digger. Rather, she appeared to genuinely like George. She blushed at his term of endearment.

"He's lying," Nina joked. "Convincing him to put on his cummerbund was like trying to get a toddler dressed for school."

"It's true, I'm quite fussy," chuckled George, brushing off his wife's teasing easily. "Now, who is this? I don't believe we've met before."

George glanced at Emilie, and Ezra stepped in to introduce her.

"This is my date, Emilie DeGaulle," Ezra said smoothly. "She's an artist."

"An artist! Well, my boy! I had no idea you were cool enough to date within the artsy crowd," laughed George, shaking Emilie's hand. "Be honest, sweetie. You're just here because he's sexy, huh?"

Emilie and Nina let out twin peals of laughter while Ezra shook his head in embarrassment.

"It's nice to meet you," Emilie said to George and Nina.

"Are you wearing Dior?" Nina asked her.

"Yes, I think so," she replied, glancing down at her dress as if it was her first time seeing it.

"You think so?" laughed Nina. "That's hilarious."

Emilie didn't understand the joke, but George and his wife were pulled away by one of his connections a few seconds later, so she was saved. Ezra thought it was endearing that Emilie, who could identify works by famous artists from a mile away, didn't know the difference between Dior and Chanel. She was always well-dressed, but luxury fashion wasn't her thing.

Even though Ezra had meant it when he said he intended to make their appearance at the gala brief, they were quickly tossed from group to group. He should have realized ahead of time there was no way he could slip in and out unnoticed. His reputation as one of the youngest billionaires in the country—and a bachelor to boot—meant that he was irremediably popular. Emilie was a good sport, smiling each time he introduced her vaguely as his artist date, but he could tell she was uncomfortable around the fake smiles and prying eyes.

He didn't blame her. Ezra often went to events like this by himself. The fact that he had brought a date with him was clearly one of the hottest topics of the evening as everyone milled around with half-finished glasses of champagne in their diamond-dripping hands. Emilie's beauty only exacerbated the inquisitive stares. They asked her everything they could, bypassing Ezra and digging their claws right into the source. They wanted to know what pedigreed family she came from, which Ivy League school she attended, and where in the cosmopolitan world she spent her summers.

Of course, Emilie didn't have any of the answers they were looking for. Ezra wanted to punch himself in the face for not preparing her ahead of time, but he didn't want to scare her away before they even arrived. She managed to do well enough by giving vague, short answers. The rumor mill would paint her as aloof and mysterious, but Ezra figured that was for the best. If they found out she worked in his company's marketing department, their cool stares would turn into haughty glares in an instant. He didn't want to put Emilie through that.

During a blessed moment of respite from the shallow conversation, Ezra took Emilie's hand and pulled her toward the edges of the ballroom.

"Come with me," he murmured in her ear, leading her out onto a balcony into the cool night air. They were alone out there, the other guests too concerned with preening their own feathers to explore the grandeur of the venue.

Emilie leaned against a massive stone column and let out a loud exhale.

"Sorry," she muttered. "I'm really not much of a party person in the first place, but this is a different nightmare entirely."

"Do you want to leave?" Ezra asked her.

She shrugged. "It's okay. We can stay a little longer. I know it's important for influential people like you to network and whatnot."

Ezra smirked at her flippant words and stepped up close to her. She smiled and used his tie to pull him closer until his body was flush against hers.

"Thank you for coming with me tonight," he whispered, lips hovering a centimeter from hers.

"If you kiss me, you're going to ruin my lipstick and end up looking like a clown in the process," Emilie warned him lightly.

Ezra pouted, but it swiftly morphed into a smirk. "That's okay. I can kiss you here instead."

He tilted his head to the side and pressed his lips to her jaw.

"And here," he whispered.

Lowering his mouth, he trailed kisses down her throat.

"And here."

Her collarbone, her shoulder, the skin just below her ear.

Emilie clutched at the sleeves of his suit jacket as if it was the only thing holding her up. When Ezra snuck a glance at her face, he saw that her eyes were closed and her lips parted blissfully.

It took every ounce of willpower within him to stop himself from making love to her right there against the side of the building. How much longer would he have to wait before he could feel her body blossom for his again? He buried his face in the crook of her neck, not bothering to hide how hard he was as he pressed more firmly against her.

Emilie moaned softly.

"I want—" she breathed. "I want you. I want to—can we go back to your place after this?"

Ezra cursed quietly, his voice rough from the strain of trying to stay sane.

"Yes, yes, yes," he replied.

She reached down and palmed him through his trousers, causing him to curse again—this time more insistently. He remembered how bold she was in bed, making her desires known with unflinching brazenness.

"I can take care of this right now if you want, though," she whispered, tightening her grip subtly between his thighs.

Ezra groaned. Was she offering what he thought she was? After resisting him all week, she was giving in. What changed? Was she tired of pumping the brakes? Was she just as unbearably turned on as he was in that moment?

"It's okay," he breathed. "I can wait. Just, um, give me a minute."

Taking a deep breath, Ezra stepped away from Emilie and went over to the balcony railing. He inhaled the crisp air, willing himself to cool down. Emilie laughed quietly but kept her distance. Thankfully, he collected himself quickly and turned to smile at her.

"All good?" she asked, eyes sparkling with amusement.

"For now," he replied. "I just need to say a few goodbyes, then we can head out, okay?"

"No worries," she shrugged, following him as they moved back inside. "You go schmooze. I'm going to hunt down something stronger than that watered-down champagne."

"Are you sure?" Ezra asked. He was surprised that she was willingly going off on her own, especially after facing such a tough inquisition for the past hour, but she was a grown woman who could take care of herself. Furthermore, he didn't blame her for wanting a stronger drink.

"Yes, I'm sure. Don't worry about me. Go do your important business and come find me after, okay?"

Ezra nodded.

When they had first met, she had been nursing a glass of pure vodka after being stood up at her friend's wedding. Ezra knew what Emilie needed to cope with the current situation, and it wasn't to continue hanging off his arm like a pretty jewel, so he kissed her cheek and watched her walk away toward the temporary bar at the far end of the room. She wouldn't be hard to locate in the crowd. She was the only person wearing red.

Still, it wasn't easy for him to turn away from her and return to the throng of tuxedo-clad business partners vying for his attention. But he could get through it now that he knew Emilie wanted him as much as he wanted her. He could endure anything as long as the night ended with her lying beneath him in his sheets, her nails digging into the small of his back, and her voice crooning his name.

"Ezra, you look a bit distracted," said a man to his left. "Are you feeling okay?"

"I'm more than okay, Peter. Just thinking about how good the string quartet sounds," Ezra answered quickly, saying the first thing that came to mind.

"Really? I didn't even notice! You've got an eye for detail, boy. I heard about what happened with the Monaco contract, though. How the hell did that guy worm his way into your deal?"

Ezra sighed. Peter was a good guy, firmly on Ezra's side. He was retired, having just passed on the mining empire he owned to his eldest son, but he was still around to socialize.

He turned to the older man and shook his head.

"Don't even get me started—"

Chapter Twelve

Emilie wasn't surprised that Ezra was a natural when it came to socializing at the gala. It was intriguing to watch Ezra in his element. For all the jokes he cracked about how foolish his rich colleagues were, it was undeniable that he flourished in their environment. Ezra was a natural everywhere, Emilie noticed, but it was difficult for her to stomach.

The thing was, it reminded her that she was wasting her time with him. They had no future together. Emilie could never picture herself becoming the type of person who regularly wore ball gowns and twirled around priceless mansions with powerful people. That was Ezra's life, though, and she didn't expect him to stop going to fancy fundraisers just because she didn't like being there. She didn't want to change for him, so how could she expect him to change for her?

She didn't know why she asked to go to his place after the gala. In the heat of the moment, all she could think about was how desperate she was to feel him inside her again. She immediately regretted asking him to take her home. It was reckless. Sleeping with him a second time was going against every conclusion she had come to over the past few days. She couldn't do it. She was going to have to find a way to politely backtrack on her request, but for the moment, Emilie would let him finish working the room.

On her way to the bar, her eyes were drawn to a series of frames displayed on the walls of the hallway just beyond the ballroom. Temporarily distracted from her hard liquor mission, she redirected her steps to the hall. A few looks were thrown in her direction, but now that she was no longer standing beside Ezra, no one had a reason to be seen speaking with her. Maybe some people would find that offensive, but Emilie was relieved to be ignored for the most part.

The hallway was empty, the loud chorus of chatter from the ballroom fading to a dull hum, leaving her alone with the sound of her breath and the click of her heels on the marble.

Moving toward the frames, Emilie realized they were paintings, clearly created by children. She smiled to herself as she observed the clumsy strokes of bright colors. Many of them were abstract, random splotches left open for interpretation by the viewer. Others were more literal: a dog, a house, a sunny beach.

A sign on the wall explained that the artwork had been made by some of the kids who had benefited from the charity's funding. Kids who grew up in rough communities and went to schools with limited resources. One of the first things to go when a school was short on funding was the art program, but Emilie was happy to know there were charities trying to change that.

She glanced over her shoulder. Why weren't any of the guests out in the hall looking at the adorable art?

The answer was obvious. They didn't care. They were here to perform their generosity for their wealthy friends, and to make themselves feel better about the fact that they had an unfair amount of money in their bank accounts. The physical evidence of what the charity did hardly mattered to them.

Emilie felt a bubble of anger rise in the pit of her stomach. It frustrated her that Ezra played nice with people like that. Maybe he didn't truly see how shallow they all were. Or maybe he did, but it didn't bother him as much as it bothered her.

Frowning to herself, she continued observing the children's artwork. They must have been proud to learn that their paintings would be displayed in a mansion for important adults to view. Emilie remembered being that small. She had always wanted to be an artist, no matter how many times her teachers or friends' parents told her that artists didn't make any money. Her young mind couldn't fathom why everyone was so obsessed with money—did they care about anything else?

All that mattered to Emilie was that her mom and her sister supported her. They had never discouraged her, and for that she was eternally grateful.

"Pretty lame, huh?" came a voice from behind her.

She gasped and whirled around, startled by the realization that she wasn't as alone as she thought she was.

Anderson Blackwell, dressed in a sleek tuxedo, stood a few feet away. His jacket was unbuttoned, hanging loose on his muscular frame. He had his hands shoved casually in his pockets and was smiling at her.

"Hi," she breathed, placing a hand over her heart as if that would help slow its rapid beat.

"Sorry," Anderson chuckled. "I didn't mean to startle you."

"It's all right," Emilie replied, watching him approach her. He maintained a respectful distance, but something about his demeanor told her that his decision to follow her into the hallway wasn't innocent.

She still hadn't answered his email about the commission.

"They're all well aware that these paintings are out here," Anderson told her, nodding his head back toward the ballroom. "It was in the invitation. Obviously, they don't care."

"Well, they aren't Picassos," Emilie replied.

"They could be one day," he replied. "Or they could be even better than that. They could be as good as you."

Emilie waved him off and shook her head.

"Thank you, by the way, for buying my drawing," she told him.

"Thank you for selling it."

She had to hand it to him. Anderson was impressively charming. His flirtations were smooth and natural, as if he barely had to think about what he said beforehand. It was different than the way Ezra spoke to her. He was suave, but it was also obvious that he was trying very hard to say the right thing.

Emilie didn't like that Anderson was a little too poised. It came off as less genuine. On top of that, she was becoming more hesitant about him because of the way Ezra reacted when she mentioned him. She didn't dare ask anybody at work for details, afraid that she would open a can of worms about a taboo subject. However, a quick internet search earlier that day told her that Ezra and Anderson were definitely not friendly colleagues. They were strong rivals. Ezra was inarguably more successful, but Anderson had started to catch up in recent months.

She didn't know what to say, but she felt as if Anderson was waiting for something.

"Sorry, by the way," she said. "I haven't answered your email yet. I don't typically do commissions, so I—"

"It's no problem at all," Anderson cut her off gently. "Take your time. I hope I didn't make you feel awkward, considering your position at my company's largest competitor."

Emilie frowned. "How did you know I worked at Hudson Enterprises?"

"Sorry?"

"I just don't think we talked about it before. At the gallery, I mean."

Anderson faked a laugh. "Right! Ezra must have mentioned it."

He was lying. Emilie didn't need to be a genius to understand that Anderson and Ezra didn't chat outside of the few times they accidentally crossed paths in public. She had a strong intuition.

"Right," she replied lightly, forcing a smile onto her face. "Well, you'll have to excuse me. I should get back in there."

"Don't you want to discuss—"

"I'll get back to you first thing on Monday," she interrupted, already backing away from him.

She didn't wait for Anderson to say anything else, turning and hurrying back into the ballroom. She felt uneasy. Everything was so complicated. Of course, she understood that getting involved with a man with as much wealth and influence as Ezra would be difficult, but there was so much drama she had never imagined would become her problem. Perhaps she was being paranoid, but it almost seemed as if Anderson thought pursuing her was one of the many ways he could engage in competition with Ezra.

But she wasn't an engineering contract or a plot of land. She was a human being. Why didn't Ezra say something before? It was obvious he was uncomfortable when she told him about Anderson buying her artwork, but he had kept his thoughts to himself. Was that part of the competition, too? Did Ezra know that Anderson would be at the gala? Did he beg her to come so that he could parade her around like a shiny toy that Anderson couldn't have?

Deep down, Emilie was aware she was being melodramatic. Regardless, it was impossible for her to acknowledge that when everything about her current situation was out of the norm for her. This wasn't who she was. She didn't wear gowns that cost three times her rent. She didn't attend fancy fundraisers and make small talk with rich people. She didn't skulk around in corners with handsome CEOs and lose her sense of reality in the heat of the moment.

None of this was right. Although she tried to convince herself it wasn't happening, Emilie had allowed her heart to be led astray by a smooth-talking billionaire who wasn't meant for her. If she'd known who Ezra was all those months ago… well, who knows what she would have decided to do? Clearly, Emilie wasn't adept at consistency when it came to making important decisions about her personal life.

Ezra was nowhere in sight when she entered the ballroom again, so she continued in her previous trajectory toward the bar. Thankfully, Anderson didn't follow.

There were waiters floating around the room with trays of champagne and wine, but Emilie was hoping they had something more substantial available.

"Can I get a vodka soda? Easy on the soda, heavy on the vodka?" she asked the man behind the bar who, like the rest of the catering staff, was dressed in a pristine white suit.

"Of course."

While he made her drink, she sank against the side of the bar and rested an elbow on the counter, watching the world she didn't belong to swirl all around her.

"Emilie? Emilie DeGaulle? Is that really you?"

Emilie turned to find an all-too-familiar face staring at her with palpable surprise. She gasped.

"Ben?" she breathed. "What are you—?"

She was so shocked to see him that she couldn't even finish her sentence. It had been over six months since she last saw Ben Wang. The last time being the day before she'd boarded a flight to London. He was supposed to follow her there and be her date to Lena's wedding. When he'd stood her up and offered nothing but a lame excuse about work, Emilie had written him off and crawled into bed with a different man instead—Ezra. It wasn't cheating. Emilie and Ben weren't officially in a relationship at the time, but merely casually dating. Perhaps that should have been Emilie's first cue not to invite him to accompany her to a destination wedding.

How different would her life currently be if she'd realized that back then?

Or would it be completely the same?

"What am I doing here?" chuckled Ben. "What are *you* doing here?"

Ben wasn't a mean person. Emilie honestly believed him when he explained that he missed the wedding because of work, but that didn't mean she was willing to pursue someone who backed out on a promise like that.

It did make more sense for Ben to be at the gala than Emilie. Although he wasn't as prestigious as Ezra, Ben was a successful investment banker on Wall Street. He had plenty of money to give to charity.

"I'm here with someone," she answered, eyes wide with bafflement. "Just some… guy. I didn't know you came to these things. How have you been? Did you get a haircut?"

Ben laughed. "I've been good, but busy. I did get a haircut, yeah. Listen, Emilie, I know we already hashed this out months ago, but I am really sorry for the way we parted ways. It was never my intention to—"

"It's okay," Emilie insisted. Ben was cute. A little nerdy, but definitely handsome. She hadn't thought about him in a long time. "It was so long ago. I'm over it. It's so funny to run into you here!"

"Never in a million years did I expect to see you at a zoo like this," Ben replied. "Who is the guy you're with? How did this even happen?"

"Oh, he's just—" How could she explain that her date was the man she'd slept with after drowning her frustration about Ben with vodka?

"Wait, it's not Anderson Blackwell, is it?"

"Huh?" Emilie replied. She was vaguely aware of the bartender sliding her drink across the counter toward her, but she ignored it.

"The guy who owns Blackwell Capital? I noticed you talking to him in the hallway," he clarified. "Please don't tell me he's the reason you're here."

"No, he's not," she said. It was hard to tell if Ben wasn't a fan of Anderson because he was jealous or for a different reason entirely. "Why? Do you not like him?"

It was a small world. What were the chances the two men she was most recently involved with would both have an issue with Anderson?

"Hmm? No, I don't know him personally, but I know he's bad news," Ben answered. The relief in his expression was evident when Emilie confirmed that she wasn't romantically involved with Anderson.

"Bad news in what way?"

Ben leaned in close and lowered his voice. "Rumor has it that he has ties to a notorious crime family. His father died before the Feds could get him, but the apple doesn't fall far from the tree. I wouldn't be surprised if Blackwell Capital was full of dirty money. You should probably steer clear of him."

"Noted," Emilie said. Her stomach was churning. It wasn't wise to believe gossip and rumors. Sure, Anderson had a strange aura, but Emilie couldn't imagine him being the son of a mafia boss. This wasn't a Hollywood action film.

And yet, Emilie had no problem agreeing to keep her distance from him. She was beginning to think there were quite a few people she needed to keep her distance from.

"Well, I should probably head home," Ben told her. "I've got an early start tomorrow morning. It was nice seeing you, Emilie. Take care of yourself."

"Yeah, thanks. You, too."

Emilie didn't know what to think as Ben wandered away from her and disappeared into the crowd. It seemed like an impossible coincidence that she would see him there that evening, but the universe often worked in mysterious ways.

Perhaps she should have asked Ben if he knew Ezra. Maybe there was gossip floating around about Ezra that rivaled Anderson's allegedly scandalous affairs.

Probably not, but maybe.

Before Emilie could think too much about it, Ezra appeared at her elbow. The drink she'd ordered was still untouched, but she no longer had the stomach for it.

Ezra was grinning at her, eyes full of leftover humor from whatever joke he must have just told a group of adoring gala guests.

"Hey, gorgeous," he said, sauntering up close and kissing her cheek. "Ready to go?"

"Yeah," she murmured, subtly slipping out of his grasp and leading the way to the exit. She never should have gone to the gala in the first place. She should have had the strength to put her foot down and say no to Ezra.

On top of that, Emilie was starting to wonder if she would be better off never accepting the job at Hudson Enterprises in the first place. She would still be working herself half to death for less money, but she wouldn't have run into Ezra and learned that he was living in the same city as her all along. If that never happened, then she also wouldn't have been tempted to accept his dinner invitation, nor would she have invited him into her home and given him the chance to weave his way deeper into her heart.

Ezra was a good man. She stuck by that. Despite his odd behavior about Anderson— which was largely justified—he gave her no reason to believe he was immoral or cruel. However, just because he was a good person didn't mean he was the right person for her.

When Henry pulled up in front of the venue, she slid into the backseat while Ezra held the door for her. Then she remembered, per their earlier agreement out on the balcony, they were headed for Soho rather than her place. She had to put a stop to that.

Emilie, sitting in the window seat rather than the middle spot to be closer to Ezra, reached out and placed her hand on his forearm.

"I'm not feeling very well," she lied. Was it a lie? Emotionally speaking, things weren't optimal. "I think I'm getting a migraine. I think I just want to go home."

Rather than allow himself to appear disappointed or annoyed, Ezra's expression instantly melted into one of pure, unquestionable concern. Instinctively, he lifted a hand to Emilie's forehead, the way her mother had done when she had checked her temperature as a child.

"I'm sorry you're ill," he murmured, then turned to address Henry. "Change of plans. Emilie needs to go home and get some rest."

Henry nodded in the rearview mirror, continuing down the avenue. They hadn't gone far enough yet to require him to completely change direction.

Ezra fussed over Emilie, making her feel even worse about lying to him, but knowing it was the right decision.

"Do you want to stop and get some medicine on the way? Do you want me to stay with you? Is it just your head or does anything else feel unwell?"

"It's okay," Emilie sighed, gently pushing his hands away. "I'll be fine. I think my busy week caught up to me and I just need to sleep it off."

Ezra nodded in understanding, but she could tell that he wanted to say more. It pained her to worm her way out of what would have been an incredibly blissful evening in his loft, especially since she was so eager for it less than an hour ago, but she reasoned that it might be a good thing for Ezra to think she was flaky and moody. Maybe that would be enough to dispel his feelings for her. Then she wouldn't have to work so hard fending him off, and she could sink back into her normal, Ezra-free life. No more CEOs in general would be preferable. Their domain wasn't meant for people like her, something she was aware of beforehand but chose to ignore.

Emilie belonged with someone like her. A struggling artist or musician. The type of person who didn't wear suits every day and who didn't pick her up in a shiny Bentley. That was the kind of man she was destined to end up with in the end—someone on her level.

It was fun while it lasted—which was barely a week—but Emilie couldn't keep fooling herself into thinking that she and Ezra would ever work out. If she didn't hurt herself now and subtly slip away from him, she was going to end up even more hurt further down the road.

Chapter Thirteen

Deep down, Ezra knew he would regret dragging Emilie to the gala. It wasn't that he wanted to show her off or brag about finally having a beautiful, down-to-earth date for that type of event—though that was definitely nice to enjoy for once. The reason he'd put so much effort into convincing her to go was because he wanted to prove to her that, even though he had a so-called glamorous lifestyle, he was still the same normal, humble guy that she'd met in London.

He didn't blame Emily for having a bias against wealthy people. Even he didn't like most of them. But he wanted her to be a part of his life, so it was important for her to see that he wasn't fake or shallow or ridiculous like so many others they met that evening.

He wasn't sure it had worked.

Ezra thought they were having a good time. Emilie was fending off prying questions with charm and grace. She was dazzling, drawing attention with her beauty. He remembered how gorgeous she'd looked in red at Pierre and Lena's was wedding, so there was no question he was going to get her a red dress to wear.

Was that the problem? Did she not like his dressing her up? It wasn't as if he had forced her to wear it—she was the one who claimed she didn't have anything to wear.

The gala was going so well that Emilie was finally interested in coming over to his place. He was convinced that, once they made it to Soho and he could make love to her again, she would be his once and for all. Perhaps it was childish, but Ezra was a romantic man. The intimate moment they'd shared on the balcony outside the ballroom had been hot and passionate.

Something must have happened the second he left her side. He regretted it. Who knew what Emilie had dealt with while she was on her own at the gala? Did someone make a rude comment?

Ezra wanted to believe Emilie was telling the truth when she changed her mind and claimed to be suffering from a migraine. Of course he did. He wasn't a paranoid man, and it wasn't as if he thought Emilie owed it to him to come over just because she said she wanted to in the heat of the moment. But something told him she was making an excuse to get out of spending the night with him. An excuse that wouldn't hurt his feelings, but also wouldn't be questioned.

Ezra let it slide. Whatever changed Emilie's mind was only his business if she chose to share it with him.

The next morning, he texted her to check in on how she was feeling. He offered to come over with medicine and to cook her a proper meal, but she replied with short, clipped sentences about how she appreciated the offer, but was fine.

When Monday rolled around, Ezra knew something wasn't right. She was at work, toiling away with the design team on the twenty-third floor, but she continued to dodge his text messages.

It went like that for the next week. He tried everything. He left more notes at her desk, more stupid poems and silly declarations. He sent another orchid to her apartment. She said thank you for everything, but her teasing and playfulness were gone.

Ezra feared that she had lost interest in him. Elegant balls and pretty dresses weren't a guaranteed way to hold every woman's attention. He tried to appeal to the special things he knew about her, the things that would surely make her want to jump back into his arms.

He called a friend for a favor and offered to take her on a private tour of the MET. She politely turned him down.

He invited her aboard his private jet for a weekend trip to Chicago for the world-famous art museum located there. She told him it was too last minute for her to accept, so Ezra offered to take her there next month. She replied that she would think about it.

Anyone could see that Emilie was purposefully avoiding him. If it had been anyone else, Ezra would have given up already. He'd never met a woman who was worth all his time and attention, but he understood how people could lose their minds in love after meeting Emilie.

At one point, he became so desperate that he bit the bullet and outright asked her for an explanation.

Em, he texted her. *Is everything okay? Did I do something wrong? Have I upset you? Whatever it is, tell me how I can make it up to you. I miss seeing you.*

His message went unanswered. It was Saturday. On Saturdays, he usually had a few work-related commitments to attend to—board meetings or projects seeking his approval. He ignored all of it. Given that he was perpetually single, and before Emilie, content about that, he didn't have many personal matters to attend to on the weekends.

In short, he was left with plenty of time to fret about where he had gone wrong when it came to Emilie. He couldn't let it go. It wasn't just that she was pretty and funny and miraculously unfazed by his status. For the first time in his life, Ezra was experiencing something that felt beautifully *real*. He couldn't let Emilie walk away from him that easily. It was his fault they never had the chance to explore their connection back in September. His stupid mistake—forgetting to leave his number behind in her hotel room—was the catalyst for the current strife he was suffering through.

What could he do? He'd lost his golden-haired girl once before. If it happened again, he wouldn't know what to do with himself.

***

Emilie felt terrible.

In her decade of adulthood, she had never had to deal with this situation before. Every breakup she'd gone through was desired and agreed upon by both parties involved. Ending a romance had never felt like this before. She felt like she was taking her heart out of her chest and throwing it onto the dirty sidewalk.

Could she even consider it a breakup? She and Ezra had gone on a couple of dates, and he had spent an evening at her house, but were they really dating? Was there anything between them to end?

Of course there was, she reasoned. There was something between her and Ezra that was so palpable and undeniable it terrified her. That was the problem. Their connection was so strong that it was taking up too much space inside her. She had to let it go before she lost everything she'd been working for in her career. As incredible as Ezra was, it was for the best that Emilie left her memories of him in the back of her mind. What had happened in London was wonderful, but it wasn't the beginning of a love story. It was just one special night. That was it.

Despite that, Emilie couldn't bear to say those things to Ezra. His last message to her was pleading, yearning for answers that she couldn't give him. He was determined, that much was obvious, and Emilie was too kind to ignore him. She hoped that if she continued to make it seem as if she were no longer interested, Ezra would eventually give up.

Until then, she would bide her time on the twenty-third floor of Hudson Enterprises and spend her evenings with her paint and brushes.

Things at the gallery were progressing well. Steven was excited about her work; several pieces were on display. Nothing else sold, but he was optimistic, so Emilie followed his lead. It was the opportunity she had waited a lifetime for and she wasn't going to risk screwing it up.

Instead of responding to Ezra's text in which he implored her to explain if he had done anything to upset her, Emilie turned off her phone and shoved it underneath her pillow. Then she lay on her stomach on the hardwood floor of her bedroom and painted tiny, delicate strokes of lavender onto a fresh canvas.

Emilie was on a roll. She hadn't painted this much since she was in college. Her newfound alone time coupled with the troubling whirl of emotions inside her offered her a stroke of ravenous inspiration that she attempted to quench. The second she got home from Hudson Enterprises, she changed into one of the tattered painting smocks hanging in her closet and dug her hands into whatever project was calling out to her.

She barely spoke to anyone. Emilie didn't have many friends; most of them having moved away after college. Annie was the only person she interacted with on a regular basis, but even her sister barely got a word out of her in the days that followed the charity gala.

One evening, Annie knocked on Emilie's door.

Emilie uttered a wordless grunt in response, which she knew Annie would understand as permission to open the door.

Her little sister poked her head into Emilie's bedroom and wrinkled her nose.

"It smells like turpentine in here," Annie complained.

"No, it smells like acrylic paint in here."

"You're going to poison yourself."

"I'm fine. The window is cracked. They're non-toxic anyway."

Annie sighed. "Is there a reason you refuse to open your door? Why are you avoiding me, too?"

Emilie paused her brushstrokes and glanced up at Annie from the floor.

"I'm not avoiding you," she countered. "I'm just in need of some solitude."

"Why? Because your hot, rich boyfriend keeps sending you flowers?"

"He's not my boyfriend."

"Emilie."

"Annie—"

Emilie's sister was used to her moody spells. They had been worse when Emilie was a teenager. Their mother used to say it was her artistic temperament rearing its dark side, but Emilie wasn't sure if that was true. In her eyes, it was perfectly normal for people to go through spells of joy and unhappiness. That was life.

Annie's opinion on the matter lay somewhere in the middle. Though she didn't make art, she knew a lot about it, so she understood that a large majority of artists were prone to introspective spells in which most people in their life were kept at a distance. But Annie was also an eternal optimistic. She believed that any bad mood could be cured with a show of support from a loved one.

Emilie resumed her painting while Annie invited herself inside the bedroom and plopped down on the end of Emilie's bed. If she was determined to stay, so be it. Emilie didn't have to listen to her.

"Emilie, I'm kind of worried about you."

"Why? I'm literally just laying on my floor and painting a flower," Emilie scoffed.

"Maybe because there's an entire greenhouse of floral arrangements out in the living room that you're completely ignoring?" Annie rebutted. "What did he do? He must be apologizing for something big."

For a few minutes, Emilie didn't answer. Unfortunately, Annie was unflinchingly patient. She lay back on Emilie's comforter and stared up at the ceiling quietly, waiting for Emilie to give in and explain what was going on.

Eventually, Emilie gave up. Annie would stay there all night, an immovable force that refused to budge until Emilie fessed up.

"He didn't do anything," Emilie told her. "It's just not going to work out. Once he understands that—"

"But you got all dressed up for the gala," Annie interrupted. "You've never done anything like that before. I thought it was a sign that you really liked him."

"I do really like him."

"Then what's the problem?"

With a huff of frustration, Emilie tossed her paintbrush aside and sat up.

"The problem is that he and I do not work together," she said. "There is no version of this life in which Ezra Hudson and I end up in a happily-ever-after scenario. Our life trajectories aren't compatible."

"What the hell does that mean? You sound kind of ridiculous," Annie argued lightly. "How can you be certain of that after spending, like, one week with him. I mean, I know you met him months ago, but you know what I mean."

Emilie frowned. "You should've seen those people at the gala, Annie. They were preening like tropical birds, squawking to be heard over each other. Do you know how many times I was asked who my family is or where I went to school? It's like all that income bracket cares about is pedigree and legacy. They don't actually give a damn if you're a decent person."

"Ezra didn't seem like that, though."

"Even if he isn't like that, those are the people he lives his life surrounded by," Emilie replied. "And maybe he's different, but he was so natural around them. I don't understand how he can be like that with them, but also be who he is when he's around me. It's too confusing. Plus, there's all this drama between him and his business competitor… it's not anything I ever wanted to get myself involved in."

Annie nodded thoughtfully as she absorbed her sister's words.

"So, if Ezra was poor, you would be with him?" she asked after a minute.

"No," Emilie answered.

"Why not?"

"Because his wealth isn't the issue. He, specifically, isn't the problem. It's just that I would rather spend my time on things other than dating. Love isn't my priority."

"Love should always be a priority," Annie countered.

"Well, then I love painting. Art is my true love, not some pretty boy who sends me flowers."

"You know that's not what I meant. The way your eyes light up when you talk about him tells me everything I need to know, Emilie. You're lying to yourself. I don't know why you're convinced that you can't have a flourishing art career *and* an amazing boyfriend at the same time, but I wish you would snap out of it."

"I don't want to balance those two things," Emilie said. "Sure, maybe I could have them both, but then I wouldn't be giving my all to either one of them."

"But—"

"I want to be a painter, Annie, not some rich guy's useless girlfriend."

Annie stood up and marched toward the door. She was well aware that she had reached the point in the discussion where she might as well have been talking to a brick wall, but she also knew that Emilie would think about the things she'd said. All she could do was hope that her words struck a chord somewhere deep inside of Emilie.

However, before she left her sister by herself once more, she had one last thing to say.

"I think you're being a little too black and white about things," Annie said to her from the doorway. "As a painter, you should know that things are never like that. There is no pure black or pure white. There's always a little bit of gray in them."

"Not true," Emilie quipped, holding up a tube of paint resting by her elbow. "The package right here says this color is literally called 'pure white.'"

"You're so annoying."

"I love you, too."

"You're stubborn, too."

"I think I get that from Mom," Emilie mused, already absorbed back into her painting as if Annie wasn't there anymore.

Annie sighed one more time, walking away without saying another word. She left the door open, but Emilie nudged it shut with her toe and carried on in her solitude.

I miss seeing you.

Whether he knew it or not, Ezra had a way with words. It was easy to say that you missed somebody, but to specifically state that the physical lack of them in your daily life was unbearable meant something entirely different.

Technically, Ezra could see her whenever he wanted to between the hours of nine in the morning and five in the evening within the walls of Hudson Enterprises. He could go for a stroll down to the marketing department under the guise of asking for an update on a project. He could even call her up to his office as he had on her first day. She was his subordinate, so it would be unwise for her to outright refuse.

Ezra didn't do any of those things, though. Emilie knew why. When he said he missed seeing her, he didn't mean in the context of their shared workplace. He meant that he missed seeing her outside of that hulking, glass-and-steel structure. He wanted to see her in the dim light of a dusty pub, in the cluttered spaces of her humble apartment, in the glittering candlelight outside a party full of important people who neither one of them gave a damn about.

She knew all of that because she felt the same way. She liked Ezra. She adored him. She could see herself falling deeply in love with him with shocking ease.

That's why it hurt so much. Letting go of someone who made you feel alive and electric and unstoppable was difficult.

There was another girl out there who was more perfect for Ezra than she was, Emilie told herself. One day, Ezra would go to another wedding—perhaps London again, or maybe Barcelona or Tokyo or Sydney—and meet another girl at the bar. They'd go to his room or hers and make love all night. Then, when he inevitably got a work call that dragged him away before sunrise, he would remember to leave his number behind.

Emilie had faith that he would be much happier with someone else.

And yet... the mere thought of him moving on with someone new made her feel like she was falling through the crust of the earth and crumbling into ash at the core of the cruel, unfair world.

Oh, well, Emilie thought.

Chapter Fourteen

"Ezra, you look like you haven't slept properly in days," Matt remarked one morning at work. The CFO of Hudson Enterprises was leaning against the doorframe of Ezra's office with his hands in his pockets.

"Then I suppose I look exactly how I feel," Ezra replied, flinching at how groggy his voice sounded.

"Everything all right?"

"Of course," Ezra answered, waving him off. "It's just stress. It'll pass. If Blackwell would get off our ass, I might remember what peace feels like."

"Amen to that. I'd like to personally punch that guy in the face for what he did to our Monaco contract," Matt replied.

"I didn't know you were a violent person," Ezra snorted.

"I'm not, but when it comes to Anderson Blackwell—"

"I get it. Me, too."

"Regardless, you really shouldn't be letting it keep you up at night, Ezra. Nobody is worth that."

"Yep. Thanks, Matt. I'll keep that in mind."

Satisfied with the advice he had provided, Matt wandered away toward his own office further down the hall.

Nobody is worth that. Matt was wrong, in Ezra's opinion. If he was going to screw up his sleep schedule for anyone, it was Emilie. Not that he was doing it on purpose. He wished he could get a night of restful sleep, but every time he closed his eyes, his mind replayed every single minute he'd ever spent with Emilie. Even though he was exhausted, Ezra's brain wouldn't give up searching for a clue as to why Emilie was icing him out.

She had never responded to the last text he sent, the one in which he admitted he missed her. Maybe she thought it was pathetic that he could be so hung up on her after such a short time. Whatever it was, Ezra decided to give it a rest for a couple of days. Emilie probably just needed space. He was smothering her. He had to try a different tactic.

Work was unbearable. All he could think about was the fact that Emilie was sitting at her desk seven floors below him. Did she like her job? Were her coworkers nice to her? Was she thinking about quitting?

When an email from Matt appeared in his inbox around mid-morning, he was grateful for the distraction.

Ez, check this out… This could be bigger than Monaco.

That was all the email said, but attached was a chain of emails exchanged between Matt and a man who didn't work for Hudson Enterprises, as well as a few documents about a contract bidding war that was currently underway.

Ezra read through the details, growing more intrigued by the second. As thoughts of Emilie drifted to the sidelines for the first time in days, his optimism skyrocketed.

This was the chance Ezra had been waiting for… the chance to put Blackwell in his place once and for all.

A satisfied smile crept onto Ezra's face as he typed out a reply to Matt, confirming he agreed they should go for it.

Blackwell will never live this down, he wrote to Matt.

Once he pressed *send*, he settled back in his desk chair and tried to hold on to the hope that was blooming inside of him. Optimism was infectious. If he could win this new contract, he would be on top of the world. Nothing could get in his way. It might even lead to him being enlightened on how to win Emilie back.

Ezra was so lost in his thoughts that he jumped when the landline telephone on his desk rang. It was his assistant calling from her desk.

"What's up, Jess?" he answered.

"There's someone calling for you from PG Bank," she replied. "He said his name is Ben Wang and he would *not* allow me to simply take a message and have you call back. He said it's urgent?"

"Huh? Ben… what?"

"Ben Wang. I already looked him up in PG's employee directory. He's an investment banker."

"I've never heard that name in my life."

"I think the only way I'm going to get rid of him is to hang up on him," Jess sighed.

"No worries. You can put him through. I'll humor him for a few minutes, I suppose."

"Okay, Boss."

Ezra waited with the receiver pressed to his ear, preparing himself to deal with whatever nonsense a random Wall Street banker wanted with him and his company. When the line opened up, Ezra spoke with an impatient tone to set the mood that he didn't appreciate people harassing Jess.

"This is Ezra Hudson," he said.

"Mr. Hudson," replied the friendly masculine tone on the other end. "This is Ben Wang at PG Bank. I was wondering if you had a few minutes to talk."

"I don't think you've given me or my assistant much of a choice," Ezra quipped.

"Right. Sorry about that," he said with a nervous chuckle. "It's just that I'm calling in regard to Emilie DeGaulle."

At the mention of her name, Ezra instantly straightened in his seat. Why was a banker calling him about Emilie? More importantly, was he calling about her because she was his employee or because she was his… well, what was she? His lover? His friend with benefits? Former, at least?

"Emilie? What about her?" Ezra asked. He cringed. He had given himself away with that question alone. Perhaps he should have referred to her as Miss DeGaulle or pretended not to know who Ben Wang was talking about at all. There couldn't be a good reason why someone from a major bank would be calling him to discuss her, though he couldn't come up with a legitimate reason on his own.

"She's an old friend of mine," answered Ben. "It's probably a bit strange for me to admit this, but I saw the two of you together at the youth art charity gala the weekend before last. Of course, I knew who you were right away."

One of Emilie's friends was a guest at the gala? He didn't realize she knew anyone there other than him. Why didn't she say anything? Is that who she'd spoken to when they parted ways for the brief period of time? Is that why she changed her mind about going to Ezra's place afterward?

Ezra sighed and pushed his chair back from his desk. "You'll have to pardon my rudeness, Mr. Wang, but what the hell is going on?"

There was a pause on the other end of the line followed by a quiet sigh.

"Listen, I think it might be better if we spoke face to face. I had a feeling I would fumble this phone call, so I came uptown and I'm currently standing outside your office building. Would it be possible to meet?"

"Right now? Are you joking? You haven't even told me what this is about," Ezra replied, growing more agitated by the second.

"Mr. Hudson, I'll cut to the chase," Ben responded, his tone somehow both resigned and determined. "I'm not a banker. I'm with the Federal Bureau of Investigation. And the matter I need to discuss with you is relevant to you, your company, and Emilie's safety. I apologize if I overstepped and misread the relationship, but if you'll tell your security to let me into the building, I can enter without flashing my badge and causing a stir. Then we can speak further."

Ezra didn't know what to think. His first instinct was to assume Ben was lying, that he was up to something and would do anything to convince Ezra to let him inside his office.

Then again, it wasn't as if anyone had to go so far as to say they worked for the FBI to gain access to the building. Signing in with the security desk and wearing a visitor nametag would get them up to the thirtieth floor without a hitch.

Still, Ezra was suspicious. He thought it was odd that Ben recognized him and Emilie together at the gala but hadn't introduced himself. Furthermore, he was being extremely vague, which the more paranoid side of Ezra's mind was taking as a sign that Ben didn't have good intentions.

But what could be the harm? There was heavy surveillance throughout the office and Ezra wasn't exactly small or weak. If Ben was trying to hurt him, why would he go to the trouble of inviting himself into Ezra's office where there would be a hundred other ears and eyes that could possibly intervene?

Realizing he was overthinking it—which was becoming a regular occurrence for him lately—Ezra decided it was pointless to call Ben's bluff.

"Sure," Ezra eventually replied. "I'll send a note down to security that you can come right up. I'm on the thirtieth floor—Jess at the front desk can point you in the right direction."

"Great. I appreciate it, Mr. Hudson. See you in a minute."

The second Ezra hung up, he stood and started pacing the room. While he waited for his unexpected visitor to make his way up, his thoughts ricocheted off the boundaries of his mind. He was so confused that even while using his usual threads of logic, he couldn't begin to explain what was going on. Ezra was a natural problem solver. Usually, he looked forward to the little conundrums that popped up here and there throughout the average workday; they kept him on top of his game.

This time, Ezra didn't know where to begin. There were too many separate puzzle pieces that couldn't sensibly work together. Ben Wang, a man he'd never met before, who was apparently a banker... and an FBI agent. Emilie, the girl he thought he'd never see again and whom he was now desperate to prove himself worthy of. Somehow, the two of them were friends. Did Emilie know that her friend worked for the FBI?

And what did any of this have to do with him other than the fact that he was romantically involved with Emilie? Formerly, at least.

It took Ben about ten minutes to get up to Ezra's office. When an unfamiliar figure appeared in the doorway with a polite smile, Ezra was surprised. He was handsome and incredibly well-dressed. Standing only an inch or two shorter than Ezra, Ben Wang also appeared to be of similar age. He wore an expensively tailored suit and his dark hair was combed off his forehead in a tasteful, business appropriate style.

This was a friend of Emilie's? How many other attractive men considered themselves friends of hers? Was that why she was giving him the cold shoulder? Had she already moved on to someone else?

"Mr. Hudson? I'm Ben Wang," he said, stepping into the office when Ezra waved for him to enter. Without being prompted to, he shut the door behind him and pulled a badge out of the inside pocket of his jacket. "Like I said, I'm with the FBI."

Ezra stepped forward to glance at the badge. He wasn't an expert, but he could tell that it was legitimate.

"Right. Okay," he said. "How about we sit down?"

Ben nodded. "Good idea."

"Should I call you... Agent Wang?" Ezra asked as he took a seat once again, watching as Ben unbuttoned his jacket and sat down in the chair across his desk. Even though he dealt with government officials and representatives on a regular basis, he'd never spoken with anyone from the FBI before.

"No need," Ben replied with a smile. "Ben will do."

"In that case, feel free to call me Ezra."

"Thanks, Ezra," he nodded. "I'm sure you're a little confused. Approaching you directly was never part of my original plan, but some recent developments have caused me to reevaluate the strategy."

"Okay—"

"How about I start at the beginning?"

"I think that would be a good idea."

Ben clasped his hands together and rested them in his lap. Ezra thought it was interesting that, somehow, Ben looked believably like both a banker and a secret agent. He supposed that was the point; idly, he wondered if Ben struggled to maintain his cover or keep track of his identities.

"I was placed in New York last spring," Ben began. "The Bureau has been investigating the suspicious behavior of a number of large companies based in the city, and in the case of one company in particular, they decided it would be beneficial to have someone go undercover."

Ezra tensed up. Once again, Ben's word choice was vague. Was Hudson Enterprises one of the companies the FBI was investigating? If so, they weren't going to find anything. Ezra ran a clean corporation. No funny business.

"The idea was for me to take on a role at a prestigious bank and worm my way into the same circles as New York's elite upper class," he explained. "I was supposed to play the role of a naïve, new-money guy. You know, the kind of person who might be easy to take advantage of."

"Sure," Ezra replied, still unsure where this explanation could possibly be going. He didn't know why he needed to know the details of Ben's mission.

"A couple of months into my placement here, I met a woman named Emilie DeGaulle," he said, instantly catching Ezra's attention again. "To be honest, this was a private, personal thing. I was undercover, but I still had the opportunity to date."

"So, you and Emilie—?"

"We dated very casually," Ben clarified. "She's a great girl but, unfortunately, there was some progress in the case that led to me having to prioritize work over her. Actually, it's embarrassing for me to mention this, but I was supposed to be her date to a friend's wedding in Europe last summer and I ended up having to leave her hanging because the Bureau needed me in the city that weekend."

Ezra's lips parted in shock.

"No way," he gasped.

Ben raised his eyebrows. "What?"

"A wedding last summer? In London?"

"Yeah, why?"

"That's where I first met her," Ezra said.

Ben shifted, raising his eyebrows even further. That was the only confirmation Ezra needed in order to know that *he* wasn't the one who was under investigation. Otherwise, Ben would already know how he was acquainted with Emilie. At least, that's what he assumed.

"At the wedding? You have a mutual friend?" Ben inquired.

Knowing that whatever details Ezra provided regarding the situation would go right into whatever FBI case file Ben was building, he tried to keep his answer vague for Emilie's sake. When he saw her sad and alone at the hotel bar, she'd told him she had been stood up by a guy. The fact that the culprit was sitting right in front of Ezra blew his mind. Part of him wanted to thank Ben. If Ben had gone to wedding with Emilie, Ezra never would have had the chance to meet her... and spend the night with her.

"I was a friend of the groom," Ezra said. "Emilie and I met at the reception, but never exchanged numbers, so we lost touch soon after. Her getting a position in my company was a complete coincidence, but I'm grateful for it."

"I see... so, you haven't been seeing each other long?"

Chatting with a stranger about the current state of his relationship with Emilie wasn't appealing. Especially now that he knew this man had also been romantically involved with her at some point.

"And how long has Emilie been acquainted with Anderson Blackwell?" Ben asked.

Understanding dawned on Ezra. How could he fail to catch on to the implications behind Ben's words? Although he'd never seen evidence, he'd heard rumors about Blackwell's ties to immoral business practices. It made sense. The way his rival played dirty hinted that Blackwell wasn't concerned about captaining a clean ship, merely about doing whatever it took to gain the upper hand.

"Honestly, I'm not sure," Ezra told Ben, no longer holding back. If Ben felt that Emilie's safety was a concern and Blackwell was involved, he wouldn't risk anything. In fact, he wanted to kick himself for not doing something earlier when Emilie told him Blackwell had bought one of her art pieces. "I was under the impression she was meeting him for the first time when we ended up at the same restaurant a couple of weeks ago, but I can't be certain."

Ben nodded thoughtfully. "And do you know the extent of their relationship?"

"I wasn't aware they had a relationship—"

"That was a poor choice of wording on my part," Ben quickly corrected himself. "I meant to say that I saw them speaking together at the gala. It was difficult to get a read on the exchange. It seemed neither friendly nor malicious, but Anderson Blackwell is known for being a very good conman."

"They—?" Ezra trailed off. That must have been it. Emilie had run into Blackwell at the gala who had said something ridiculous and untrue about Ezra, and it had scared her off. He wanted to kick something. That man would do anything to get under Ezra's skin, including getting involved in his personal life.

"I warned her that it wasn't in her best interests to continue communicating with him," Ben continued. "I believe she took the warning seriously."

That could be another reason why Emilie was avoiding Ezra. It was the best way to avoid getting involved further with Blackwell. God, he was so stupid. He never should have pulled her into this mess.

"So, are you implying that it's Blackwell Capital that is under investigation?" Ezra asked.

Ben blinked. "Yes. My apologies. I don't know how I skipped over that part. Yes, the Bureau has been monitoring the activity of Blackwell Capital for several years. By the way, please understand that everything I share with you in this room must remain confidential."

"Of course."

"We have concrete evidence of several instances of money laundering. However, the Bureau has found it difficult to uncover the reasons behind it. Is he smuggling goods? Is it drugs? Given who his father was, we assume it was the latter, but we need to gather more evidence before apprehending him."

"And what does this have to do with Emilie?"

Ben shrugged. "It seems that Blackwell has taken a liking to her. I assume it's disingenuous and more of a way to thwart his competition—you, of course—by any means necessary. He has clearly deduced that Emilie is special to you. There's really no guarantee that he's going to do anything truly harmful, but I do believe that his interest in her is legitimate cause for concern."

"Yes, I think that's a fair assumption," Ezra remarked. He could hardly believe this was happening. An old flame of Emilie's was an FBI agent, but the only thing that put her in true danger was meeting Ezra. It was his fault. Did Emilie blame him for bringing so much drama into her life or was she totally unaware?

"I want to—" Ben began, but Ezra cut him off.

"Does Emilie know about any of this?"

"I have good reason to believe she has no idea who I truly am, and therefore, is also unaware of how much she has become entwined in an FBI investigation."

"Right," Ezra sighed. "So, what can I do to help?"

Ben grinned. "I'm glad you asked. You will obviously benefit from the demise of Blackwell Capital, but you also seem like a good, honest man. Your cooperation with us will be very much appreciated, but please do know, you are under no obligation to assist us."

"I understand. Though I'd love to never have to deal with Blackwell again, my real concern is Emilie. I don't want her to get involved in anything that he's up to, so you can consider me cooperative," Ezra answered.

"That's great. Firstly, we'd really like to take a look at your version of the Monaco contracts that fell through—"

For next hour, Ezra shared the contents of the company hard drive with Ben. Not everything, of course. Just the things that involved Blackwell. Old communications, contracts that were won or lost, and any other physical documentation where Blackwell Capital might have been noted. It was grueling and Ezra knew they weren't done by the time Ben excused himself to allow Ezra to get on with other business matters, but he was satisfied that he might be one step closer to never having to deal with the frustrations caused by Blackwell ever again—in terms of Hudson Enterprises *and* Emilie.

Chapter Fifteen

Anderson… It was very nice to speak with you at the gala. I apologize once again for the delay in my response, but after giving it some thought, I must unfortunately inform you that I do not have the current bandwidth to take on such a large commission. However, should my circumstances change in the future, I will reach out immediately. Best regards, Emilie

Emilie sent her response to Anderson the Monday after the gala. She wondered if he would reply right away or respond at all. Would he be angry? Disappointed? Would he contact Steven at the gallery and demand his money back for the piece he'd purchased?

Anderson's response came a day later.

Emilie, I am disheartened to hear that your schedule won't allow for a commissioned project with me, but I am assuming it is because you are both a professional artist and working full-time for Hudson Enterprises. What can I do to convince you otherwise? Perhaps it is silly, but I am not inclined to settle for a different artist. Can I offer to pay you twice what you make at Hudson Enterprises? Triple? What would make it worth your time? Please let me know at your leisure. Yours, Anderson

Emilie didn't know how to respond. It sounded as if Anderson was asking her to either quit her job at Hudson Enterprises or take some time off. She was a new employee though, so the latter wouldn't be wise or practical. While the former would put more distance between Ezra and her, she was hesitant to do something so drastic just for one commission.

She still thought it was strange how Anderson knew that she worked for Ezra and had lied about how he found out. There was no way Ezra would have mentioned it to him in passing. The two competitors did not chat casually like that. They hardly spoke at all.

For a couple of days, Emilie thought about not answering Anderson's email, but she didn't want to risk building an unprofessional or flighty reputation. Anderson was a powerful man. In many ways, he could make or break her career as an artist.

Eventually, Emilie sat down and typed out what she hoped was a reasonable and polite response.

Anderson, that is a very generous offer, but I am afraid I cannot accept it. However, there are many more paintings of mine available for sale at the gallery on the LES, if you'd like to purchase more of my art. Please know that I am flattered by your insistence, but I am simply unable to do such a large commission in a timely fashion. Best, Emilie

Deep down, Emilie knew she hadn't heard the last of Anderson Blackwell. From what she'd learned about him from Ezra, her coworkers, and—of all people—Ben Wang, it was clear that Anderson was the kind of man who was used to getting his way and he would stop at nothing to do it.

Truthfully, if Emilie wanted to, she could find a way to make the commission project work. Anderson wanted a large mural, which would take at least a month for a full-time artist with no other professional commitments to create. If she could negotiate a longer deadline, she would be able to fit the project in on the weekends and after work on the weekdays. That is, if she didn't care about completely throwing away her free time for a couple of months.

She was used to working long hours, but it was Anderson himself that caused her to hesitate. Ben's warning about his alleged involvement with organized crime made Emilie nervous. She had no reason to believe Ben, nor did she understand how he could possibly know something like that about Anderson, but that wasn't the only thing that put her off. Even though she knew it was best for Ezra and her to put an end to whatever was going on between them, she still felt like she was betraying him by agreeing to do work for Anderson. Or rather, she was betraying the entire company. Sure, painting a mural had nothing to do with the actual work going on at Blackwell Capital, but she would still be doing something for Hudson Enterprises' biggest competitor in exchange for payment.

It took another day for Anderson to respond. Emilie saw his email slide into her personal inbox during her lunch break, but she didn't open it until she was home later that evening, sitting alone in her bedroom. Annie was on campus, so she was safe for the moment from another prying therapy session from her little sister.

Emilie, what if I told you that time is not an issue and that I would prefer it if you took as much time as you needed to get it done—even if that means a full calendar year? Furthermore, what if I tell you that I'm prepared to offer you a commission fee of $100,000.00 for the project? Would that change your mind? Name your price and any other stipulations you have… I will meet them. Yours, Anderson

She almost dropped her phone when she read his email. One hundred thousand dollars was astronomical for a mural, even a large one. Most muralists made a few thousand dollars per piece, depending on the size. Only the most famous artists in the world made six figures or more for a single mural.

Anderson was out of his mind. The fact that he was going to such extreme lengths to convince her to paint for him made her feel slightly uncomfortable. She knew she was talented, but she was also humble enough to acknowledge her work wasn't worth such a price. She was a nobody in the art world, and on top of that, had no experience doing murals. Clearly, Anderson had a lot of money at his disposal, but why was he so determined to spend it on her? Was he that taken with her? Or was this merely his method of stealing her away from Hudson Enterprises?

Emilie sighed and dropped her phone on top of the covers. She was agitated and restless. She wished she could go back in time and never accept the position at Hudson Enterprises in the first place. Then she never would have seen Ezra again, nor would she have met Anderson. She would still be waitressing, but at least her life would be blissfully normal. There wouldn't be two billionaires vying for her attention—both with different, yet confusing intentions.

A couple of days ago, Steven had called to let her know that one of her paintings had sold at the gallery. It was a small canvas, a simple abstract study of primary colors with delicate brushstrokes, but it sold for seven hundred dollars. That meant Emilie pocketed three hundred and fifty, which was not as much as she'd earned from the piece Anderson had bought, but it was still something.

If she could sell more, she would gain more recognition. Soon enough, she'd be able to get herself into more galleries across the city. She might even land a contract with a gallery in a wealthy neighborhood where art buyers were willing to pay premium prices for art, because in their eyes, high cost was equal to prestige.

If all those things went well, she could quit her job at Hudson Enterprises within a year. She could be free from it all, finally living her dream.

Emilie went to her closet and stared at the tiny space stuffed full of paint-splattered clothes and business attire alike. Hanging on the rack in the farthest back corner of the closet was a black garment bag. The red dress Ezra had bought for her was inside it, untouched since she had returned home from the gala and carefully pulled it off her body. She'd meant to return it to Ezra—to insist that he take it back to the designer and get a refund—but bringing up the topic felt more difficult than what it was worth.

Plus, Ezra had never asked for it back, even though it was fairly obvious at that point that Emilie wasn't going to give in to his endless invitations for a date. At least, she hoped it was obvious. He'd been quiet for the past couple of days, so she was taking it as a sign that he was finally giving up on her. It hurt her to do that to him, but she was adamant it was for the best.

She turned away from the garment bag and stared out her bedroom window, past the fire escape to the tree-lined street beyond. The branches were beginning to sprout with tiny blossoms. Soon enough, they would be full of lush green leaves and it would be summer again.

Where would she be in the summer? Would she still be working at Hudson Enterprises and fending off Anderson's commission inquiries? Would it still pain her to know that a man she felt herself falling head over heels for was only seven floors above her, yet they weren't meant to be? Or would she be over it by then?

With a sigh, Emilie knew she had a decision to make and she couldn't allow anyone else to make it for her. It was her life. What did it matter if Ezra and Anderson were business rivals? Who cared what Ben and others said about random rumors?

Emilie wanted to be an artist. A real one. An artist without a day job. She wanted art to be her day job.

If she accepted Anderson's ridiculous offer, she wouldn't have to give half of it to the gallery since it was an independent commission. It would be enough money for her to live off for at least two years—longer if she was frugal. With one hundred thousand dollars in her bank account, she could quit Hudson Enterprises immediately. She could buy a fresh stock of paints and canvasses and invest in a new set of brushes.

In truth, it was an opportunity she would be a fool to reject. Whatever Anderson did or didn't do in the backend of his own company wasn't her business nor was it her problem. Furthermore, whatever Ezra's business relations were with someone else was also not an issue that was her concern. She had a chance to boost her art career and she couldn't just let it go.

Emilie grabbed her phone, swallowed her pride, and started typing.

Anderson…Your offer is very generous. I truly appreciate your devoted interest in my art. After further consideration, I admit that I would be a fool to turn down this opportunity. When would you like to meet to discuss the specifics of the mural project? Warmest regards, Emilie

She wanted to roll her eyes at herself. She had been so opposed to doing the painting for Anderson for the past week, yet she was suddenly caving because he had offered her a large sum of money. He had no reason to suspect that she was desperate for cash, but he understood that money was the driving factor for most people's decision making. Emilie felt annoyed that she helped him confirm that, especially given her dislike and distrust of wealthy people, but it was true. Money made the world go round and people like Anderson had plenty of it to accomplish whatever they wanted.

People like Ezra, too.

Although it was none of his business anyway, Emilie found herself hoping that Ezra wouldn't find out what she was doing for Anderson. She couldn't help it. Thoughts of Ezra clung to her mind like sticky cobwebs.

It was difficult to move past him, but she would manage it in time.

***

When Emilie finished work the next day, she didn't head home to the lower east side. Instead, she took the subway all the way down to Tribeca to meet with Anderson at the Blackwell Capital headquarters. The rival company was located in a building similar in size and structure to Hudson Enterprises, though there were fewer floors and no security check-in once she entered the lobby.

Inside, Blackwell Capital was surprisingly plain. She had imagined an opulent interior with marble floors, Greek columns, and gold detailing, but it seemed Anderson's sense of fashion didn't translate to his company's décor. Of course, that was probably why he was so desperate for her to paint a mural in the lobby—at the moment, there was nothing but white tile and beige walls.

Emilie didn't have a chance to change out of her business clothing and into her artist attire, but she did have a sketchpad in her bag that she could use to draw up Anderson's vision.

He was waiting for her, smiling politely. Emilie felt a flicker of nervousness that she was making the wrong decision, but reminded herself of the paycheck she would get at the end of the journey.

"Emilie, it's so nice to see you again," Anderson said, shaking her hand. "I hope it wasn't too much of a pain to get downtown from all the hubbub of Hudson Enterprises' turf?"

"No, it was fine," she replied, shrugging off the gentle dig at Ezra's choice of location for his company's headquarters. This had nothing to do with Ezra, and yet it seemed like Anderson couldn't help bringing him up. The rivalry between them was strong; it ran deep.

"Well, good. Let's get started, shall we? I don't want to take up too much of your Friday evening," Anderson said, gesturing for her to follow him to the large expanse of dull beige wall that greeted all who entered the building with its glaring plainness.

Emilie took out her sketchpad and marked out the measurements of the wall, which Anderson had already gotten one of his contractors to calculate for him. She tried not to feel overwhelmed, but the thought of covering over one hundred square feet of wall space with a single painting was daunting. She'd worked with large canvasses before, but never to that extent.

Still, if Anderson was giving her all the time she needed to accomplish the task, she was confident she could do it.

"I was hoping you could do something similar to the drawing I purchased from you," Anderson told her, staring at the blank wall with a furrowed brow. He was acting different this evening. Less flirtatious; more professional. Emilie was shocked, but delighted. "The mission of Blackwell Capital is that we capture the spirit of New York City—the ambition, the industry, the constant thirst for something *more*. But I don't want another generic monochrome skyline like you see in doctor's offices and hotel lobbies. I want something special. I want an Emilie DeGaulle original."

Emilie smiled, feeling her cheeks warm slightly as she stepped back and tried to picture Anderson's vision on the wall in front of her. As she did so, her hand gripped a stick of charcoal tightly and danced across the page of her sketchbook.

"Do you have official company colors? Or a logo you'd like me to integrate?" she asked him.

"Silver and black," he answered. "I'd like to see those colors integrated, but they don't need to be the main palette. Oh, and let me email you a file with the logo. If you can find a way to place it subtly in the mural, that would be cool, but it's not necessary."

"Sounds good."

"You really do have a gift for this," Anderson remarked, stepping closer to watch over her shoulder as she drew. He didn't stand too close, though. Not the way he closed the proximity between them in the hallway at the gala. Emilie was so relieved that she wondered if she was just being paranoid the last time they had spoken in person. It could have been the general stress from being at the gala that caused her to think Anderson's vibes were off.

"Thank you," she replied. "But good art is rarely about natural talent. The greatest artists throughout history have merely put in the time and effort to master their technique."

"Even so, I don't think I could create the things you do even after decades of training. Do you really not believe that some people are simply born to be artists?"

Emilie glanced up at Anderson. She couldn't tell if it was a rhetorical question or not, so she merely shrugged.

"Perhaps it's possible," she replied. "But I doubt I'm one of them."

"Well, in that case, we disagree on at least one thing."

Ignoring the compliment with as much grace as she could muster, Emilie finished off her rough sketch and handed it to him. She explained how the basic lines would translate onto the wall and asked for his opinion of a variety of details. For the most part, Anderson didn't have many requests.

"I want you to take full artistic liberty," he told her. "At least, within reason."

"Understood," she responded. "I'll need a few days to draw up a solid blueprint and gather supplies, then I can come in after business hours on weekdays and the weekends so I can work on it without disturbing the majority of your staff."

"That sounds perfect," Anderson replied. He reached into the inside pocket of his jacket and produced a small envelope. "Here's an access card to the building and a check for the first half. It's customary to pay half at the start and the rest when it is finished, correct?"

Emilie blinked, trying to disguise the shock on her face when she realized she was holding fifty thousand dollars in her hand. She had no idea if that was customary for commissions, but it sounded fair enough to her.

"Y—yes. That works—that's definitely acceptable," she stuttered.

Anderson chuckled lightly. "Perfect. Well, I should get back up to my office. Unfortunately, I've got a call with some people on the west coast—that pesky time difference has kept me late at the office more times than I'm willing to admit! Feel free to stick around for as long as you need."

"Sure, thanks. Good luck with that call," Emilie replied somewhat lamely, watching with confusion as he shook her hand briefly and walked away.

What had changed? It wasn't that Anderson was being cold, but there was less warmth in his gaze and his mannerisms than the previous times they'd interacted. He was still speaking to her kindly and tossing flattery in her direction, but there was a difference in the delivery.

Perhaps Emilie was more egotistical than she wanted to admit. Perhaps Anderson was never interested in her in the first place.

She felt foolish for being disappointed. It wasn't that she enjoyed the blatant flirtations from the man, but was it so wrong to enjoy being desired?

Then again, being desired by a man was exactly what she was attempting to avoid at the moment. In that case, she supposed everything was going according to plan.

Chapter Sixteen

Things were not going according to plan.

Anderson thought he'd finally done it. He thought he'd finally managed to get a win over Ezra from which there was no recovery. Stealing the Monaco contract from him spelled disaster for Hudson Enterprises. On top of that, it was an embarrassment. The fact that the royal family had decided to pull out of the partnership because of Ezra's immorality—artificially constructed by Anderson, of course—was undoubtedly a huge blow to the man's ego and to employee morale in general.

Furthermore, the contract to upgrade and redesign the royal jets was a once in a lifetime opportunity. Winning government contracts wasn't unheard of, but they were usually domestic. Breaking out into the realm of working for international leaders meant that Hudson Enterprises could have been one of the greatest transportation engineering companies in the industry.

That is, until Blackwell Capital stole the contract out from under him.

Although it was a huge blow, Anderson wasn't satisfied with that alone. He wanted to go further. He wanted to earn a win over Ezra Hudson that was so devastating, he would never stand in his way ever again.

Miraculously, that opportunity came only a couple of weeks later.

Anderson had received word a few months ago that a transportation company based in Hong Kong was at risk of going under. The industry was saturated and competitive on that side of the world, and even the brightest engineers didn't always have what it took to stay afloat. It didn't take long for the Hong Kong company—which specialized in avian engineering—to be purchased by a larger corporation based in Singapore.

However, as the weeks progressed, it became clear that the Singaporean company wasn't prepared to handle the devastated Hong Kong company. They weren't stable enough. Anderson watched it closely, tracking the stock values and gathering intelligence from his contacts overseas.

Naturally, Ezra was doing the same thing. He wasn't an idiot. Though Ezra didn't have the kind of connections Anderson did, he wasn't totally at a loss.

When rumors began to spread that the Singapore company was looking for a purchaser, the entirety of East Asia pounced.

So did Ezra. Thus, so did Anderson.

It was a huge risk for both of their companies. Asia was a difficult market for a western corporation to break into. Understandably, they favored their own.

But Anderson was determined. It was the kind of opportunity he was dreaming of, the chance to expand Blackwell Capital onto another continent... and thereby expand the distribution of the various illicit substances his family dealt in. If he managed to win the contract with Singapore, he'd be one of the most powerful drug lords in the world and nobody would even know it.

After all, Anderson was smart. Smarter than his father, something he was only bold enough to admit now that the old man was in his grave. His father had run a strong drug supply chain, but didn't have the shrewd intelligence and unparalleled ambition to expand it overseas.

An engineering contract in Singapore—which would include threads in Hong Kong— would open up channels of movement that were otherwise inaccessible to him. He'd have barges and planes full of shipping containers exchanging materials with the East. It would be easy to smuggle in the drugs undetected.

It would have been a dream come true. It would have been perfect. It would have made all the long, grueling hours Anderson put into both sides of his job completely worth it.

And yet... Ezra had managed to steal it from him.

They played the bidding war, beating out the Asian companies easily and leaving nobody but themselves left to charm the Singapore company. Then they got into the cultural politics of it, appealing to the company's sensibilities and offering amendments to the original contract that would benefit Singapore immensely.

Anderson thought he had it in the bag. He had the capital, the connections, and the charm.

Unfortunately, Ezra had those things, too.

He didn't know the details. When his assistant told him the news, he was so angry he couldn't look anyone in the eyes for fear of lashing out against them. As cunning and merciless as Anderson knew he was, he wasn't keen to attack his own men. He locked himself in his office and paced back and forth for the better part of an hour.

Perhaps Ezra had a more solid connection in play, someone who was so close to the CEO of the Singapore company that it would be rude to deny the contract to Hudson Enterprises.

Maybe it was something else entirely. Perhaps Ezra had learned how to speak Chinese in a matter of days and wooed them with his wits.

Whatever it was, Anderson was so angry he felt murderous. He itched to destroy something, to kick a hole in the wall plaster or punch his fist through the computer screen. It took every ounce of willpower within him to refrain. He wasn't like his father. He would be powerful while keeping his temper in check.

In the midst of Anderson's agitated pacing, there was a knock on the door. He already knew it was Ivan, one of the Russian henchmen who used to serve his father. There were few people who dared to intrude into Anderson's office when bad news regarding Hudson Enterprises struck, and Ivan was one of them. Anderson was convinced there wasn't a single thing in the world that scared Ivan.

"What?" barked Anderson when he heard the knock.

Ivan let himself in, closing the door behind him.

"Boss," said the old, hulking Slavic man in lieu of hello. "I see you are processing the recent news well."

Anderson was used to the man's harmless sarcasm, so he shrugged it off. He had more worthwhile things to be angry about.

"No matter what I do, that brat always come out on top," Anderson spat. The two men stood across from his desk, staring at each other with opposite expressions on their faces. It always irked Anderson how Ivan remained calm no matter what, even when he had worked for the older Blackwell.

"I figured out how he managed to do it," Ivan reported.

"That quickly?"

"Yes, sir. It seems that Hudson Enterprises moved in with an unprecedented maneuver that the Singaporeans were extremely enthusiastic about."

"Go on—" growled Anderson, clenching his hands into fists to indicate that, despite Ivan's decades of loyalty to his family, it was best for him to not mince words at that moment.

"Instead of a complete and final purchase, Hudson Enterprises offered a merger contract," Ivan explained.

Anderson closed his eyes and pinched the bridge of his nose. Of course. He should have known. Mergers were complex and not always worth the trouble, but Ezra had one of the best attorneys in New York on his legal team. They had probably drawn up the new contract offer in under an hour.

"I see," murmured Anderson. The deadly calm in his tone didn't match the inferno of fury within him, but if he allowed himself to raise his voice a single octave, he was going to go ballistic.

"The Singapore company will not lose everything," Ivan continued. "Of course, the contract is less profitable for Hudson Enterprises than the original offer, but in the long run it's beneficial because it establishes a crucial sense of trust between the two—"

"I don't need a cost-benefit analysis," Anderson snapped, angrily yanking his chair back from the desk and sitting down with a sharp exhale. "I should've thought of it first. Why didn't anyone in *our* legal department consider proposing a merger? Fire every attorney on my payroll immediately."

"Yes, Boss."

Even though it was a clear dismissal, Ivan didn't budge. Anderson raised an eyebrow at him.

"Yes—?" he pressed.

"The girl is here."

The girl. Emilie. Foolish, pretty Emilie. Anderson knew she would take his six-figure bait the second he offered her such an astronomical amount for a stupid mural. At the gala, he could see how bright the stars were in her eyes. All starving artists had the same look about them. They exuded desperation.

Anderson managed a small smirk at Ivan's words.

"Of course she is," he replied. "She has a pretty little picture to paint for us."

"She is rather naïve," sighed Ivan. He shook his head in disapproval, as if it was a shame Emilie didn't know any better, but it was also therefore her fault for not making better decisions about whom she did business with. "Are you going to let her paint the entire thing?"

Anderson shrugged. "We'll see. We never really had a concrete plan with her, did we? Might as well get some decent aesthetic value out of her while she's here."

"And what if she catches on?"

"What is there to catch on to? Emilie DeGaulle has a clear, simple contract with Blackwell Capital to paint a mural in our lobby… and that is exactly what she's doing,"

Anderson argued. "I promise you, she's bright, but she's not intuitive. She slept with Ezra Hudson, after all."

"And what if *he* catches on?" Ivan asked. Despite the interrogation, his expression remained stoic and unbothered.

"My little spies tell me that Emilie and Ezra haven't spoken with each other in almost two weeks, though the cold shoulder has been one-sided," Anderson explained. "It seems that Emilie doesn't want anything to do with the CEO of the company where she's employed."

"So, she's a rule follower."

"It seems so."

"Where does her value lie if she and Mr. Hudson are no longer romantically involved?" Ivan asked, cocking his head to the side as if he were merely asking how Anderson took his coffee.

"Trust me," Anderson scoffed. "Ezra Hudson and I are not as different as he'd like to think. I understand him. Like me, he is a possessive man. He also likes shiny things and pretty girls. He especially likes Emilie. They have a history together that I think creates an important nuance that we might need to take advantage of."

"But why go through all these motions? Why literally pay her fifty thousand dollars?"

"Is this my company or yours?" snapped Anderson, becoming fed up with Ivan's prying.

Ivan bowed his head apologetically. "As you know, Boss, I was not only your father's main assistant, but also his closest advisor. I am only attempting to fulfill those duties with the next generation."

Anderson rolled his eyes. "Are you implying that I'm not handling things well?"

"I'm implying that your hesitation to leap at a chance to bring down Hudson Enterprises once and for all is right in front of you," Ivan countered. "If you bring down Mr. Hudson, there will be nothing standing in the way of you and the Singapore contract."

"You think I should take drastic measures," Anderson said. It wasn't a question.

Ivan nodded once. "I think you haven't been playing dirty enough, Boss. There is a naïve girl with her head in the clouds downstairs and a man who is desperately pining after her in midtown. Maybe he doesn't truly give a shit about her, but it's a worthy risk. Many people will do anything for love. Even given up their entire fortune."

Anderson rested his elbows on his desk.

He had a plan for Emilie. A real one. Before Ivan offered his opinion, Anderson was content with having her in Blackwell Capital headquarters nearly every day of the week. He liked the idea of having Ezra's lover—whether current or former—under his watchful eye while Ezra knew nothing about it. That alone was satisfying, but it was also useful to have Emilie around. He didn't have to send his spies out to hunt her down.

She was right there, down on the first floor. A sitting duck.

Emilie's fate wasn't written in stone, though. Anderson was a logical person, and he wasn't a fan of taking extreme measures unless necessary. However, he was prepared to act drastically at a moment's notice.

"I see where you're coming from," Anderson said to Ivan. "If anything was going to trigger an aggressive response, it would be the loss of this contract."

"But you might be able to win it back."

"I agree. I think this might be the moment we make the big move."

Ivan took a step toward the door. "Shall I prepare everything?"

"Yes, please."

His henchman left the office. Anderson sat still for a moment. He'd never attempted something like this before, but he'd been planning it down to the last detail since the moment he realized the perpetually single Ezra Hudson was seeing someone. Anyone who ran in the same circle as the two men knew Ezra wasn't often seen out and about in town with a date. It was a constant source of curiosity, given Ezra's good looks and notorious charm. Many wondered if he was permanently heartbroken or if he liked women at all, but Anderson knew patience would serve him well in this situation. As soon as Ezra showed affection for someone in public, Anderson could assume it would be the real deal.

And that was something he could use against him.

Ezra was a fool. He was stuck on morality and politeness. He didn't understand how to cement his place in the industry. He was too weak. Anderson was doing him a favor by taking him down this early in his career. Once he suffered his demise, he would have enough time to rebuild in a less competitive industry. Ezra could make a new name for himself somewhere completely different.

After all, Anderson wasn't heartless. He didn't want to ruin Ezra for the rest of his life. He just wanted to get him out of the way.

Anderson woke his sleeping computer and opened the software that allowed him to observe the live security footage. Blackwell Capital sprawled across eighteen floors, so there were many cameras keeping track of the comings and goings of individuals. He clicked around for a while, watching Ivan move from the top floor down to the so-called Operations Department, where the majority of Anderson's dirty money employees were employed. By day, they sat in cubicles and pretended to be hard at work on harmless spreadsheets. If he was ever audited by the IRS, there would be nothing to catch.

By night, those same men were the people he depended on most to oil the engine of the underground Blackwell drug trade.

In the grainy security footage, Ivan bent down to say something in the ear of a man sitting innocently at his desk. Anderson smiled to himself as the man's head nodded almost imperceptibly.

Perfect. Things were officially in motion.

Next, Anderson switched to the cameras positioned at equal intervals around the building's lobby. A portion of the space was cordoned off with a rope barrier. Within that space, canvas tarps were spread out to protect the imported stone tiles. There were various cans of paint scattered about and paintbrushes of all sizes. Emilie had only been working on the mural for a couple of days at that point, but she'd made a mess of the place. If Anderson was a different, softer man with different, softer goals, he might find Emilie somewhat adorable.

But he was who he was. He could only see her as a weak, gullible woman with foolish, dreamy goals that were only going to get her into trouble. He observed her, surprised to see her there. It was a Tuesday morning. Their agreement was that she would come downtown in the evenings after she finished her job at Hudson Enterprises and on the weekends for as long as she could. It was odd that she was there in the middle of the day on a weekday, but perhaps she decided to resign her position with Ezra's company. With a check for fifty thousand dollars, she no longer needed whatever salary he was offering her.

Emilie wore a loose-fitting jumpsuit, the kind of thing mechanics and janitors donned for their jobs. Her hair was pulled back, thick and tangled even when contained by a thick rubber band. She was a pretty girl. Quirky. Cute. Definitely Ezra's type.

He hoped Ezra was as enamored with her as his actions indicated, otherwise this wasn't going to work. Dan, one of Anderson's most skilled spies, reported that Emilie was the recipient of endless flower bouquets at her apartment. Whatever lover's quarrel Ezra and Emilie were going through, it seemed that Ezra was more invested in winning her back than she was interested in accepting him.

Anderson was going to give him the opportunity to play the hero. Even if Ezra wasn't as in love with Emilie as it appeared, he knew the goody-two-shoes wouldn't turn away from a damsel in distress. He was too chivalrous, too obsessed with doing the right thing.

He watched Emilie work for a little while longer. She was balanced on the top rung of the ladder, sketching the outline for the mural with a thick pencil on the wall. She worked with smooth, methodic strokes—a practiced hand. She was talented. Even though Anderson's patronization of her art was born from ulterior motives, her skill was undeniable.

He didn't regret what he was about to do. He was not delicate nor hesitant about the things that were going to get him further in his career goals.

No matter what it takes, son, his father used to tell him. Anderson had grown up hearing those words repeated to him over and over again.

No matter what it takes.

Regardless of his harsh attitude, Anderson genuinely hoped that all would go well for Emilie. He hoped Ezra would respond swiftly to the demands sent his way. If Ezra was cooperative, Anderson wouldn't have to hurt Emilie. The young couple could be reunited and in the process, Anderson would gain everything he wanted. Ezra was a smart man, but was he wise enough to acknowledge that?

Would his incurable morality be his downfall? Would he place justice above his affection for the girl downstairs? Would he be foolish enough to involve the authorities?

For Emilie's sake, Anderson hoped the answer to those questions would be *no.* But it was of no concern to him overall. He would do whatever he needed to in order to twist Ezra's arm and claim a final win over Hudson Enterprises once and for all. Whether Emilie lived or died didn't matter to Anderson, but it would be nice if he didn't have to get blood on his hands.

Blood stains were difficult to wash away.

Chapter Seventeen

Ezra was fed up. Ever since his meeting with Ben, the attention he paid to Emilie increased tenfold. He didn't think it was possible, but the fact that she could be in danger from Blackwell because of her involvement with him took up every spare inch of room in his mind.

He texted her. He left voicemails for her. He even sent emails and instant messages to her via the company software. She replied to a few of them with brief, one-word answers. She was barely humoring him.

She didn't even know that she was involved in one of the biggest FBI investigations to take place in the city in recent years. How was Ezra supposed to make sure she was okay if she was blowing him off?

One Tuesday morning, Ezra decided he had no choice but to confront her in a place where she couldn't avoid him. It was unfair of him to approach her so boldly at the company, but he was desperate. Ben advised him it was best if Emilie remained unaware of the investigation for the time being, but Ezra still felt it was important for him to at least provide a solid warning about Anderson Blackwell.

On top of that, Ezra was tired of her flightiness in the context of their budding relationship. How could she do this to him? Every minute they spent together was pure bliss. Their chemistry was unlike anything he'd experienced before and he knew he wasn't the only one who felt it. Feelings that strong couldn't be one-sided.

Ezra had always had a hard time giving his heart to others. After what happened to his father, he was afraid of losing another person he loved. To cope with that, he limited his circle. He kept his heart guarded.

But Emilie had snuck her way in. His heart belonged to her the first time she smiled at him at the bar in that posh London hotel. There was no going back. He couldn't give up on her. He had to have her.

He would do anything.

So, he decided to take a risk.

The second he was freed from a routine morning meeting with the rest of the executive staff on the thirtieth floor, Ezra told his assistant he would be unavailable for the next fifteen minutes or so, then stepped into the elevator and pushed the button marked with *23*.

As usual, the marketing floor was buzzing with activity. The large, separated offices of the top floor weren't a thing down there. Rather, everything was open and sprawling, a layout designed to foster creative collaboration.

Heads turned in his direction the second his presence downstairs was known. He didn't often pay visits to the marketing department, but he didn't have time to stop and chat with the various employees who were eager to great their CEO. Instead, he nodded politely left and right, picking up his pace on his way to the second cluster of cubicles reserved for the graphic design team.

Emilie's supervisor Yasmina was the first person to notice him.

"Mr. Hudson, what can I do for you?" she called out.

Ezra gave her a courteous smile and stepped past her, moving toward the cubicle that belonged to Emilie. He didn't know what he was going to say to her, but she would be unable to reject a private conversation with him if he confronted her in front of everyone. He hated resorting to such manipulation. It felt like something Blackwell would do.

However, sometimes such things were necessary.

Unfortunately, when Ezra rounded the corner, he saw that her cubicle was empty. Her computer and design tablet were powered off, her desk clean as if she had never showed up for work that day.

Yasmina hovered by Ezra's side, her petite figure hurrying after him when he bypassed her.

"Where is Em—Miss DeGaulle?" Ezra asked her, frowning at the empty cubicle. Was it possible the reason she hadn't responded to him that morning was because she'd quit? Ezra didn't know every single person who came and went from the company, especially on the lower levels, but he swore he would have noticed if Emilie quit without notice.

But no. That wasn't right. The longer he stared at her workspace, he noticed a cardigan left behind, draped across the back of her chair. There was also a strip of photos featuring her and her little sister tacked to the corkboard, as well as a creased, coffee-stained sketchbook. They were the kind of things Emilie wouldn't leave behind.

"Emilie? Why? Is there a problem?" Yasmina asked. She looked confused, and rightfully so. It didn't make any sense that Ezra was looking for Emilie, of all people.

"No, not at all," Ezra responded quickly. "I just wanted to follow up on our meeting from a few weeks ago."

"Oh, that's right! When she met with you on her first day!"

"Right."

"That's a really great new practice," Yasmina babbled. "I think it's going to make new employees feel very welcomed and comfortable here."

"Right," Ezra repeated. "So... where is she?"

"Emilie called out sick today," she replied. "She sounded really under the weather—must be a seasonal thing going around, don't you think? Probably a good thing she decided to keep her distance. A cold like that would sweep through these cubicles!"

"Yes, of course," Ezra nodded, already stepping away from Yasmina. "Thank you. I should get back upstairs. I'll just connect with her tomorrow."

"Sure thing, Mr. Hudson. Take care!"

Ezra lied. He wasn't going to wait until tomorrow to see Emilie. When he slipped inside the elevator, he didn't go back to the top floor, instead pressing the button for the lobby. Emilie was sick. So sick that her voice made it evident over the phone. Why didn't she say anything?

He texted Jess on his way down to tell her he needed to clear at least the next hour or so from his schedule. Luckily, he didn't have anything crucial on the books that day. The contract he'd won with Singapore was already signed, sealed, and delivered, but they had a few grace days to get their bearings before it was time to set things into motion. It was the calm before the storm and Ezra was going to take advantage of it.

Jess replied with an affirmative. She didn't ask any questions, which Ezra appreciated. He trusted her and she knew it. If he wanted her to know why he was doing something, he would tell her. If he didn't, he remained vague and she minded her business. He hoped he could keep Jess at his company for a long time. Even if she moved up the ladder and was no longer his assistant, he valued having her as an employee.

Ezra didn't bother calling Henry. Waiting for his chauffeur to make it uptown from Soho would take too long. He could get around without the ridiculous Bentley.

He stood on the busy street. New York City was warming up. Spring was settling in deep, coating the pavement in the dampness of melted snow as the snowbanks quickly disappeared into slush and puddles. The continuous stream of pedestrians wore lighter jackets than they had a few weeks before, their steps brighter and quicker as the embrace of winter loosened.

He stared around, past the fog of a manhole where a crowd of construction workers were milling around and through a line of corporate weekday warriors taking their morning smoke break. Across the street was a drugstore. Ezra waited for the pedestrian light to switch and made a beeline for it.

Inside the drugstore, Ezra grabbed a basket and hurried down the aisles. He took everything he could think of. Liquid medicine, cough drops, aspirin, green tea and honey, and canned soup. When he was sick as a kid, his father was usually too busy with work to care for him, and his mother never knew what to do beyond tossing a handful of pills at him. Despite that, Ezra knew how to take care of others. He was determined to nurse Emilie back to health just to prove that he wanted to be a part of her life, in sickness and in health.

Ezra tapped his foot impatiently while the apathetic teenager behind the checkout counter bagged up his purchase. When he was handed the bag, he snatched it quickly and hurried outside.

He stepped out of the stream of passersby and hesitated on the sidewalk again. He could hail a cab, but suddenly felt a need to prove himself to Emilie, even if she wasn't here to witness it. Whipping out his phone, he furrowed his brow at the digital map and typed in Emilie's home address. Thankfully, according to the map, it would only take one train with no transfers to get to her.

Satisfied with his progress so far, Ezra hurried down the steps of the nearest subway entrance and tried not to look completely lost as he navigated through the crowds to find the right platform. He triple-checked that the train pulling up was going in the right direction, not wanting to accidentally end up in Harlem instead of the lower east side.

The subway was cramped. There was nowhere to sit, so Ezra claimed a spot and held on to the pole, the bag of drugstore supplies weighing down his free arm. He felt nervous. It wasn't that he'd never taken the subway before, but the entire process seemed so complicated and daunting to him that he chose to favor his chauffeur, or in a pinch, a taxi.

The train screeched through the tunnel. It pierced his ears painfully, but nobody else around him flinched. They were used to the quirks of the city's rougher side. It caused Ezra to remember why he fell in love with New York in the first place. There was an incurable grunge that coated the city. Rats and roaches abounded. The possibility of random violence lurked in every shadow. And yet, some of the most glamorous people in the world called the city home. However, glamour or lack thereof, no one batted an eye at the grime. It wasn't a source of disgust, but rather a quintessentially New York City characteristic. There was a humility about the world-famous city that fascinated Ezra.

He felt closer to Emilie as he rode the subway. This was the New York she had grown up in. The one that she loved. The one she called home. She didn't have a chauffeur or an overpriced loft or any of the conveniences wealth afforded Ezra and his social circle. Emilie was a true New Yorker. She was humble and unshakeable, yet stunning and awe-inspiring at the same time.

When the subway train ground to a halt at the station closest to Emilie's apartment, Ezra battled his way out of the carriage and took the stairs two at a time up to the street. The buildings were shorter in this part of town, covered in colorful street art. There were artsy cafes and trendy pubs on every street corner. Fashionable twenty-somethings made their way up and down the avenue, paying no attention to the visibly disoriented man dressed in a suit.

With the help of the GPS on his phone, Ezra managed to locate Emilie's apartment. He hurried down the street, slowing only to glance down the alleyway where they had kissed on that first night after six months of separation. Ezra wished he could go back to that night and change everything. He never would have taken her to the Orange Rose. That alone would have solved so many problems. Not only would Emilie be spared the discomfort of the overpriced restaurant, but she also wouldn't have met Anderson Blackwell and caught his devious eye.

Furthermore, Ezra would probably still have the Monaco contract. The rumors he had to squash about Emilie being an expensive escort wouldn't have been created in the first place.

Oh, well, Ezra thought to himself as he dashed up the steps of Emilie's stoop. There was no use in dwelling in the past. All he could do was make up for his mistakes in the present.

He pressed the button for Emilie's apartment number on the intercom and waited. There was no response, so he pressed it again. She could have been asleep, dozing through her illness, in which case Ezra wanted to kick himself for waking her up. After a few seconds longer, Ezra sighed quietly when there was still no response. His arm was tired from lugging around the drugstore bag, but he ignored it and told himself to stop being such a privileged wuss.

Should he call her? Should he let her know that it was him and not some random person trying to get into the building?

If she knew it was him, she probably wouldn't let him in anyway.

Pressing the button again, impatiently tapping it multiple times, he considered pressing the other apartment buttons, too, on the off chance one of her neighbors would let him in without question. However, a crackling in the little speaker told him that such a deception wouldn't be necessary.

"Hello? Who the hell is it?" snapped an agitated voice through the intercom. It sounded somewhat like Emilie, but also different. The system was old, warping her voice into something almost unrecognizable.

Feeling foolish, Ezra started babbling at the speaker.

"It's me—it's Ezra. I heard you weren't feeling well, and I wanted to bring you some medicine," he spoke fast. "You don't have to see me or talk to me, but just let me drop it off at your door, Emilie—"

"What? Hello? I can't hear you—" warbled her staticky voice.

"It's Ezra! Ezra Hudson! I'm—"

His words were interrupted by a muted buzzing noise. He recognized it as the noise of the front door unlocking. His stomach swooped with relief as he quickly shoved the door open and practically ran down the hall and up the stairs to the third floor. When he made it to the door of her apartment, he was out of breath, but he didn't care. He'd made it this far. He wasn't going to turn around and let embarrassment win.

He knocked on the door frantically.

"Emilie?" he called. "Emilie, it's me. I just wanted to talk for a minute. You don't have to worry about getting me sick, too. I don't care."

Instead of the sound of her voice, Ezra was greeted by the sound of two locks clicking open and the chain bolt sliding out of place. The door opened a few seconds later, but Ezra didn't find himself face to face with Emilie.

It was Annie.

She stared at him, then let out a breath of laughter. "I was wondering when you would finally come knocking on our doorstep."

Wordlessly, Emilie's sister stepped aside and gestured for him to come in.

"I'm sorry for arriving unannounced," Ezra told her, placing the bag on the kitchen counter, which was only a few steps from the front door. "It's just that I heard she called out sick and I didn't know if she had any meds here at home. Is she in her room? Is she sleeping?"

Annie smiled at him sheepishly. "Actually... she's not home right now."

"What? Where is she? Did she have to go to the hospital? Is she—"

"No, no! She's fine! Jesus, sit down and take a chill pill, billionaire boy," sighed Annie. "You're making me nervous."

Obediently, Ezra followed Annie into the living room and flopped onto the couch.

"Sorry," he told her.

Annie crossed her arms against her chest. She was similar to Emilie in so many ways, but also very different. She was more fierce, her gaze more critical, and her speech more aggressive. Annie was outwardly tough, while Emilie's toughness flourished somewhere deeper inside her.

"She's going to kill me for telling you this, but she's not really sick," Annie told him. "She's really good at convincing people otherwise, though. She called out sick so she could spend the day working on some kind of commission she landed last week. I know you're not going to fire her for that but, like, please don't tell her I spilled the beans."

"No worries," Ezra replied, standing up once more. "What kind of commission?"

Ezra wasn't the least bit bothered that Emilie faked being sick to work on an art project. If her career was growing enough for her to be getting commissions, that was great news. Sure, it was unfair for her to lie to get out her job at Hudson Enterprises for the day, but it was a harmless choice. Emilie was a painter, not a graphic designer. If it were up to Ezra, he would commission her over and over just so she could quit her corporate marketing job and do art full-time. Emilie wouldn't allow that, though.

"It's a mural," Annie replied with a shrug. "Some company downtown. Blackworth, maybe? Black... something."

Ezra's stomach dropped. No. *No.*

"Blackwell?" he breathed. "Blackwell Capital?"

"Yeah! That! Do you know them?"

Ezra ignored her question. "She's there right now?"

"Yeah, and she probably won't be back until late, but you're welcome to hang around. I've got to head to campus, but you can make yourself at home—"

Ezra was already halfway to the door. "That's okay. Thank you, Annie. See you later."

"Wait, what are you—"

The rest of Annie's question was cut off when the apartment door closed behind Ezra. He sailed down the stairs, practically tripping over his own feet.

This couldn't be happening. He knew better than to assume Blackwell's commissioning Emilie for a mural in his company headquarters was purely innocent. Blackwell didn't do anything innocently.

Ezra didn't waste time with the subway. He hailed a cab the second he got to the main avenue and jumped in, barking out the address for Blackwell Capital.

"Step on the gas like your life depends on it and I'll throw in a few Benjamins," Ezra said. The driver nodded and zoomed through the narrow downtown streets as if they were in a high-speed chase. Ezra gripped the seat with one hand and dialed frantically on his phone with his other.

Please pick up. Please, please, please.

But Emilie's number went right to voicemail.

Ezra cursed out loud, causing the driver to glance at him nervously over his shoulder.

This wasn't good. Emilie was alone in Blackwell's lair. Who knew what his plan was? What if he was too late?

Ezra scrolled through his contacts and pressed the newest addition to the list.

Thankfully, Ben Wang picked up right away.

"Ez—"

"Ben," Ezra snapped, too anxious to mess with formalities. "Something's wrong. Emilie is at Blackwell Capital. Blackwell apparently commissioned her to do a painting, but something isn't right. It's too specific. I know he's up to something. He's probably pissed about Singapore—"

"Ezra, slow down," Ben replied calmly. "Where are you right now? Where can I meet you?"

Ezra spoke fast, not caring if the driver heard every word. The only thing that mattered was that he got to Emilie before Anderson Blackwell descended on her.

Chapter Eighteen

Emilie hummed to herself as she knelt on the canvas tarp and poured out a small puddle of paint into the plastic container she was using to mix the perfect shade of green for freshly cut grass. She'd spent all of yesterday evening and most of that morning sketching out the general outlines of the mural on the wall. Given that it was her first time as a professional muralist, she wasn't sure if she was supposed to start from the top or the bottom, but she figured there was nobody else with her qualifications who could judge her for doing something unorthodox.

So, she was going to start from the bottom. She had started her life that way, so it was fitting.

At first, she had been nervous to spend so much time at Blackwell Capital, but it didn't take long for her to ease into the routine of it. She came by in her paint-splattered jumpsuit and slipped under the rope barrier. No one bothered her. She rarely saw Anderson and when she did, it was only in passing as he waved to her casually on his way in and out of the building. Whatever flirtations he had attempted with her before, those intentions were long gone.

No other employees at Blackwell Capital spoke to her. Occasionally, a few people would pause for a few minutes to watch her work, then silently moved on to get back to work. Much like Hudson Enterprises, Anderson's employees were diligent and focused on their responsibilities.

She squeezed a tiny dollop of marigold yellow into the mixture and swirled it around, praying it was the last thing she needed to achieve the color she wanted. It was almost noon, but Emilie had no intention of stopping for lunch. She would eat later once she had made some progress with laying the groundwork of the mural on the wall.

It wasn't part of her original plan to call out of work that day, but when she woke up, all she could think about was the mural. Inspiration was itching at the corners of her mind, urging her to be creative. Sure, she was creative with the design team at Hudson Enterprises, but not to the degree that she was craving that morning. It was as if she would die if she didn't have a paintbrush in her hand immediately.

Emilie had faked a gravelly voice and called Yasmina, lying that she didn't feel well, and hopped on the subway heading west toward Tribeca. Maybe it was wrong of her to fib about something like that when she was still a new employee, but she had sick days that she could use at her discretion.

In short, it was none of their business.

But also, if she really wanted to be honest with herself, she *was* sick. She was sick of pining for the man who worked on the top floor while she toiled away in the marketing department. She was sick of how much it hurt to continue fending off his advances. The sooner she finished the Blackwell mural, the sooner she would have the second fifty-thousand-dollar check in her hand and could move on from Hudson Enterprises once and for all. Maybe one day she and Ezra could reconnect—for a third time—but for now she just didn't have room for that much passion in her life.

The first brush stroke Emilie made on the wall caused her heart to thump irregularly.

Here we go, she thought, sitting with her legs crossed like a pretzel on the floor as she dabbed spring green grass onto the beige wall. For some reason, painting a wall felt even more permanent than painting a canvas. You could discard a canvas that didn't turn out right, but if you messed up an entire wall, you'd have to go through the trouble of repainting the base coat over the large expanse and waiting for it to dry.

So far, it was turning out well. Plaster wasn't a totally unfamiliar medium to her, so she knew how to handle the paint and the brush to build the layers of color properly. As she got into the finer details on the very bottom edge of the wall, Emilie's back started to ache. She lay down on the floor, propping herself up on one elbow while she worked intricate details into the blades of grass with a thin brush.

She lost herself in her work. Many artists listened to music while they created their masterpieces, but Emilie preferred silence. There was enough going on inside her head without the added cacophony of music.

It was impossible to know how much time had passed. It could have been five minutes or five hours. Emilie was only vaguely aware of the world passing by around her.

Until a voice broke her out of her reverie.

"It's intriguing to watch an artistic genius at work."

Emilie jumped in surprise and looked over her shoulder to find Anderson standing beyond the boundary of the designated painting area, his hands in the pockets of his suit trousers.

"An artistic genius?" she responded. "Where?"

Anderson chuckled good-naturedly. "That's a lovely color. How did you mix that shade?"

Emilie wasn't sure how to explain color theory to someone who didn't have formal artistic training, so she shrugged her shoulders and said, "A series of very good guesses."

"I see," he grinned. "Well, according to my employees, you've been working for hours. I feel like it's my responsibility to ensure you stop for lunch."

She sat up but kept the brush in her hand.

"That's alright," she told him. "I'd rather work through lunch and eat something later on. I'm just a freelancer, so you don't have to worry about breaking any labor laws."

Anderson laughed again. "It's not the law I'm concerned about, but your wellbeing."

"There's no need," Emilie insisted. "I'm totally fine, I promise."

Anderson lifted the rope barrier and raised his eyebrows at her. "May I?"

Emilie nodded, not sure why he was waiting for permission to move freely around his own lobby. She was still baffled about his reserved politeness. It was the opposite of what she'd experienced the first few times they'd met and it was impossible to avoid wondering what had happened to change his demeanor. If she was bolder, she would ask him outright. Alas, she was not that brave.

Anderson carefully walked across the tarp, avoiding the wet splotches of paint that threatened to stain his leather loafers. They looked extremely expensive, though they had no obvious designer insignia on them; perhaps they were imported from a luxury cobbler in Milan.

Feeling awkward on the floor, Emilie stood up. She fidgeted with the mess of paint cans while Anderson stepped up to the wall and bent to examine it more closely. Despite the constant compliments he tossed in her direction, she was suddenly nervous that he was going to tell her that he hated it. She bit her lip when he straightened and faced her.

"It looks incredible," he told her.

She waved him off. "It's just grass."

"Incredible grass."

"I'm glad you like it," she murmured, fiddling with the brush in her hands. It was coated in deep forest green, a drop of which fell onto her well-worn boots.

"It's perfect," Anderson replied. "I'm not very good at eloquently explaining art, but there's something simultaneously realistic and surreal about your style. Do you do that on purpose?"

Emilie shrugged. "Sort of. In school, they really emphasized the importance of forming our own distinct rhythm in our art. I couldn't decide what I liked the most, so I adopted parts of my favorite art movements. My academic advisor called it a disaster, but he also said that I somehow made it work."

"I partially agree with him. It's not disastrous in the slightest and you definitely make it work."

"Thank you."

Anderson took a step closer to her. She had a brief flashback to his proximity at the gala when they were observing the children's art together, but swallowed down the bubble of unease that began to form in the pit of her stomach. Anderson had changed his tune since then. She had nothing to be afraid of.

"Pardon me, but you do look a bit pale. I really think you should eat something," he told her, his voice low. There was only one other person in the lobby: the security guard behind the front desk.

Emilie lifted the back of her hand to her forehead as if she could feel the paleness he was referring to. Admittedly, she did feel slightly lightheaded, but that was because she'd been breathing in the heavy-duty paint for the past few hours without a protective mask, hoping that the lobby was spacious enough to help dissipate any harmful fumes.

Clearly, it wasn't.

"Oh, but I'm in the middle of—" Emilie tried to protest.

"Nonsense," Anderson interrupted firmly. "Why don't you come rest in my office and I can send my assistant to pick up something for us to eat? Let's call it a business lunch. We can discuss what else in this boring building you can paint for me."

The thought of going to Anderson's office alone with him didn't sit right with her, even though she did the same thing with Ezra without fretting.

"I don't know… I'd rather just power through at least until the end of this paint color."

"I won't be able to live with myself if you start to feel ill, Emilie," Anderson said. He reached out to place a hand on her shoulder for the briefest of seconds. There was a flicker of something in his eyes that Emilie recognized. Her gut twisted.

Her instincts were trying to tell her something. Was his politeness for the past week all a ruse? Had he been attempting to lure her into a false sense of security?

Or was she just being paranoid?

She didn't know what to do. She had a feeling Anderson wasn't going to take no for an answer, nor could she think of a solid excuse to get him to leave her alone.

Perhaps there was no harm in accepting his offer. It wasn't as if the building were empty, or Anderson was going to be the only person on the executive floor. It was the middle of the day. What did she really think was going to happen? She was being ridiculous.

And yet, she couldn't help wondering what Ezra would think if he knew where she was at that moment. She hated how much she couldn't stop thinking about him. Her thoughts couldn't move an inch without bumping into him. It was ridiculous of her. She and Ezra weren't dating, not even before she cut him off. They'd slept together once and shared a few kisses here and there, but there was no good reason for her to be so stuck on him.

Frustrated with her mind's stubbornness, Emilie nodded at Anderson.

"Okay," she told him. "Sure."

Worst case scenario, he flirted with her and she extricated herself from the situation again just as she'd done at the gala. Best case scenario, he went back to being coolly polite and she got to enjoy a free lunch.

"Great," Anderson grinned.

He stepped off the tarp and waited patiently while she screwed the tops back onto the paint containers and gathered the brushes into a neat pile. When she ducked underneath the barrier, she glanced down at her outfit. Her oversized jumpsuit and creased leather boots looked horribly out of place amongst the suits that everyone else at Blackwell Capital wore. They had a much more formal dress code than Hudson Enterprises, Emilie noticed.

Feeling a bit like a car mechanic following her rich client to his overpriced luxury sports car, Emilie stepped into the elevator beside Anderson. While Anderson pressed the button for the top floor, Emilie leaned close to the highly reflective interior and fussed over her appearance. She had a streak of green paint in her hair and a delicate splatter of royal blue on her left cheek.

She knew better than to try to scrub it off with her bare hands. Removing it would require the water-based soap she kept at home for such messes.

The elevator doors slid shut, leaving Emilie alone with Anderson in the small space. She leaned against the opposite side as him, praying that she was subtle about the distance she was attempting to put between them.

"You must have paint somewhere on you at all times," he joked.

She forced a casual smile onto her face. "Pretty much. I don't mind, though."

Something didn't feel right. When the elevator lurched into motion, Emilie felt as if they were dropping rather than rising to an upper floor. That was strange. Anderson's office had to be on the top floor of the building, right? That was where most CEOs had their private spaces, at least according to Emilie's limited experience on the subject.

It wasn't impossible, but it would be weird if Anderson's office was below the ground floor of Blackwell Capital.

Except... that didn't make sense. She knew for a fact that the basement of the building was a private parking garage for senior employees. Anderson had told her so himself during their first meeting at the company.

As the realization dawned on her that Anderson was definitely not taking her where he said he would, his demeanor changed. His expression grew stony and cold, unlike anything she had witnessed from him before. Emilie's eyes flickered to the elevator buttons. His body was angled to conceal them, but she caught sight of them in the reflection that bounced around on the metallic walls.

Anderson hadn't pressed the button for the top floor. They were going to the basement level. Why would he try to hide that from her?

He met her gaze. A chill ran down her spine.

"What are you—" Emilie didn't know how to finish her question. What was he doing? Where were they going? Why would he lure her into the elevator under the pretense of kindness only to bring her down to the parking garage?

She had an inkling. It dawned on her that she had been foolishly blind. Too trusting. Naively willing to believe that everyone around her had good intentions.

"It would be in your best interest not to struggle," Anderson told her, taking a step toward her. Emilie flattened herself against the side of the elevator. "The idea of hurting you doesn't necessarily appeal to me, but I'll do it if I have to."

"What do you mean? What's going on?"

A pleasant *ding* met Emilie's ears. She racked her mind for escape options. Anderson was a large man and she was sorrowfully petite. Still, if she could be quicker than him, she might be able to slip away. She didn't have anything on her that could be used as a weapon. She didn't even have her phone; it was tucked away in the bottom of her tote bag, which she had stupidly left behind. There was a paint spatula with a slightly sharp edge back in the lobby; she wished she had thought to stick it in her pocket. Just in case.

Then again, how could she have known? What sane person would automatically think to bring a weapon with them when a handsome man invited them to share lunch?

Emilie took a deep breath.

"I don't understand," she whispered as the elevator doors slid open. Two hulking figures appeared in her peripheral vision, but she was too terrified to take her eyes off of Anderson.

"It's a shame you've found yourself in the crosswires of a heated competition between two companies," was all he said. "Truthfully, it's nothing personal."

He wrapped his hand around her forearm and yanked her out of the elevator.

No!

Emilie threw her weight into resisting him, but it was no use. She thought fast, remembering the wet paint smeared on the palms of her hands and reached out for the elevator buttons as she was dragged away. The least she could do was leave behind clues just in case anyone came looking for her. She smeared green paint across the button marked *LL* for lower level and prayed that her paint-covered boots had left tracks on the expensive tile of the lobby from the tarps to the elevator.

Of course, there was a chance no one would notice she was gone until it was too late. She had no idea what her fate was about to be, but as two large Slavic men—whom she immediately recognized as the men who were with Anderson at the Orange Rose—grabbed her and pulled her toward a waiting vehicle, she prayed there were enough people paying attention to her existence that someone would come to her rescue.

She screamed for help as one of the men roughly tossed her into the trunk. She couldn't see Anderson anymore, but she could hear him talking to someone as the doors of the sleek car opened and closed.

In response to her scream, the older man who leered above her merely snorted and rolled his eyes. From his view, she was pathetic for even trying. Maybe so, but it was an instinct that Emilie couldn't choke down in that moment. Her heart rate was rapid, pounding inside her skull as adrenaline flooded her blood stream.

She let out another scream, but the man slammed the trunk lid shut and effectively silenced her.

"This can't be happening," Emilie whispered to herself in the darkness engulfing her as she tried to fight back panicked sobs.

The humming engine echoed around her. Muffled voices from the passengers could be heard, but there was no way to kick through to the back seats of the vehicle. She fumbled around, searching for the emergency handle that would open the trunk from the inside. Years ago, she'd read an article about how most vehicle brands incorporated such handles in their newer models to prevent vehicular kidnappings. The handle was supposed to glow in the dark.

It seemed Anderson and his cronies were a step ahead of her, though. There was no way to open the trunk from the inside. Nothing but scratchy upholstery and her fear.

She couldn't believe it. She was being kidnapped. She knew it happened to children and adults alike, but it still seemed like the kind of thing that only occurred in action movies.

Emilie wanted to kick herself. Everyone had warned her. Her coworkers at Hudson Enterprises had told her that Blackwell Capital was known to go to extremes to outpace Ezra's company. Ezra himself implied from his body language that Anderson was not to be liked or trusted.

And Ben… Ben couldn't have been more clear. He had literally warned her about Anderson. He'd told her that Anderson had ties to organized crime, that he was rarely up to anything good. That alone should have been enough to delete the unanswered email in her inbox and never speak to him again.

Emilie had made so many bad decisions in the past few weeks. As the car pulled away and she involuntarily rolled toward the back of the trunk, she kicked the side of the interior in frustration.

She burst into tears as the engine's volume increased and the car sped up. Where were they taking her?

More importantly, would she ever find her way back?

Chapter Nineteen

The taxi driver screeched to a halt in front of the Blackwell Capital headquarters, but Ezra didn't wait for it to come to a complete stop before tossing a wad of large bills through the gap in the plexiglass barrier and flinging open the door.

Leaping onto the sidewalk, he ran into the lobby. He'd only been to Blackwell Capital once before. It was years ago, shortly after he'd launched Hudson Enterprises. Blackwell had invited him over for a business meeting between industry colleagues, but it quickly became obvious that the main purpose of the gathering had been intimidation. From the very beginning, Blackwell had made it clear that he was Ezra's competition, not his ally.

"Sir?" called out the security guy behind the front desk. "Can I help you?"

Ezra ignored him. The lobby was empty, but tarps and paint nearby confirmed that Emilie had been there. A section of the floor was cordoned off to make room for her workspace. Ezra stepped up to the edge of it and observed Emilie's progress. The space that the mural was meant to take up was large. There were lines sketched on the surface in pencil, implying a city scene in the quirky, somewhat fairytale-like style he immediately recognized. The only paint on the wall so far was a layer of bright green grass on the bottom edge.

He leaned forward and noticed that the paint was still wet. Emilie was there not long ago. Where did she go? Ezra checked his watch. It was around lunch time; perhaps she had stepped out to get something to eat.

But no… that couldn't be right. Emilie's tote bag was lying on the floor by the cans of paint. She wouldn't leave her wallet and everything else behind if she was leaving the building.

Feeling a sense of impending doom like never before, Ezra called Emilie's phone number again. As it rang in his ear, he heard the telltale buzzing of her phone laying abandoned in her bag on the floor. When the call rolled to voicemail, Ezra hung up and stared at the small collection of things she'd left behind.

At that point, the security guard had stepped around the desk and was approaching him.

"Sir, do you have an appointment with someone? If so, I need you to sign in at the desk," said the guard.

Ezra glanced at the man. They were roughly the same height, though the guard's muscles were noticeably bulkier than his. One look at the expression in his eyes told Ezra what he already knew. Blackwell wouldn't let anyone work at the security desk without ensuring they had Ezra's face memorized.

The guard knew exactly who he was, but he was playing dumb, nonetheless.

Ezra decided to join the game.

"Yes, I'm a client of Mr. Blackwell," Ezra lied, watching the guard's eyes flicker with annoyance at the obvious bluff. "This mural looks like it's going to be amazing. Do you know where the artist is? I'd love to get their information."

The security guard pursed his lips. "I think it's best if you leave. We both know that you are not a client of Mr. Blackwell's, Mr. Hudson."

"And we also both know that you know exactly where Emilie DeGaulle is right now."

The guard took a step toward Ezra, but he didn't lay hands on him.

"Actually, at the present moment, I have no idea where the girl is," he corrected Ezra.

Ezra's stomach dipped. There was an implication behind his words that terrified Ezra, a hidden meaning that indicated Emilie was no longer in the building. As in, Blackwell had taken her somewhere.

He tried sidestepping the guard and lunging toward the elevators, but a firm hand clamping down on his shoulder caused him to pause.

"I *said*, it's time to leave," growled the guard.

Ezra quickly glanced around. Despite the fact that it was midday on a weekday, there were no other employees milling around the lobby. That alone was a red flag, but it also meant no one would bear witness to what he was about to do.

Every once in a while, Ezra liked to dabble in boxing classes. He wasn't sure what kind of training the security guard had, but he hoped he could catch him by surprise and gain the upper hand just long enough to slip away.

Acting fast, Ezra turned to face the guard, shrugged off the hand on his shoulder, and swung his arm back. When his fist collided with the man's face, a sharp pain splintered up his forearm, but he ignored it. A splatter of blood spurted from the guard's nose and an audible *crack* indicated Ezra's punch had landed well. The guard grabbed his injury and stumbled back.

Ezra didn't hesitate. He ran toward the elevator bank, gasping in victory when he saw that one of the doors was already open and waiting for a passenger. Sensing that the guard was recovering from the hit quickly and pursuing him, Ezra punched the number for the top floor and frantically jammed his thumb against the *door close* button as the guard rounded the corner.

The guard reached out in an attempt to stop the elevator doors from closing, but he was a second too late. When the doors shut in his face and the elevator whirred upward, Ezra sunk against the cool metal interior and exhaled slowly. He flexed his fist. It ached from the broken nose he'd just given to the guard, but he didn't think anything was fractured on his end.

"Come on, come on," Ezra muttered under his breath as the elevator ascended leisurely to the executive suites on the top floor. He had to find Blackwell. Once he did, maybe he would discover that things weren't as dramatic as he feared. Perhaps Emilie was merely in Blackwell's office discussing the mural. Perhaps Blackwell truly had no idea where Emilie was and she really did step out for lunch. Maybe there was a logical reason for the fact she'd left her bag behind.

While he told himself all of those things, he knew they weren't true. One of the most important things Ezra had learned as a businessman was that trusting your gut instincts rarely led you astray. At that moment, Ezra's gut told him that something was very wrong.

When the elevator arrived on the executive floor, Ezra squeezed through the opening in the doors immediately. Just as it was at his company headquarters, there was a front desk with a young woman sitting behind it. Ezra jogged up to her as she stared at him over the rim of her glasses.

"Where is Anderson? Is he in his office?" Ezra demanded.

"I'm sorry? Mr. Blackwell is out—"

"Out where? *Where* is he?"

The girl frowned at Ezra, her eyes going wide with nervousness as she pushed her chair back away from the desk a few inches. He was scaring her, but Ezra didn't know how to tone down the raw panic that was clawing its way up his throat.

"Sir, Mr. Blackwell is out of the office for the rest of the afternoon," she told him. "He did not tell me where he was going, only that I needed to clear his schedule for the remainder of the day."

"So, he's not in his office?"

"No, sir."

"You'll forgive me for wanting to check for myself," Ezra told her, hurrying down the hall as a couple of employees stuck their heads out of their office doorways at the commotion he was causing.

As the girl called out after him, Ezra ran toward the closed door marked with a large, golden plaque. *Anderson M. Blackwell, CEO.* The similarities between Ezra and him were unending, but so were the differences. They were both CEOs in the same industry, based in the same city, and organized their headquarters with the same physical structure.

However, Ezra would never stoop to the levels Blackwell did to accomplish his goals. If it turned out that Blackwell managed to win the Singapore contract over him, his first instinct wouldn't be to hunt down the woman Blackwell loved—if Blackwell was even capable of love— and find a way to use her to get back at him. No way. Ezra would simply accept the loss and figure out how to do better next time. He wasn't a sore loser.

Ezra didn't bother knocking. He turned the knob and shoved open the door to Blackwell's office.

Empty. The lights were off, the computer screen dark and silent.

Ezra spun around. The female assistant and another unfamiliar man were walking toward him, but he took off at high speed and barreled past them back to the elevators. More shouts followed after him. It wouldn't be long until the entire building was alerted to the violent intruder. They might even call the police.

He had to find out where Blackwell had taken Emilie before he was stopped.

Once again, Ezra's pursuers weren't quick enough to catch him by the time the elevator doors slid shut. He pressed the button for a random lower floor, then an upper one, and then one more—he was stalling for time so he could think through his next maneuver. Pacing back and forth in the small space, Ezra pressed his fingertips to his temples.

He couldn't believe this was happening. All signs pointed to the reality that Blackwell had kidnapped Emilie. Either that, or he had gently coerced her into leaving with him and she still had no idea how much danger she was in.

Suddenly, something on the floor of the elevator caught his eye. He paused, staring at the tile with his lips parted in shock. It was a splatter of green paint. The same color green as the painted grass that was still drying on the lobby wall. Ezra looked around the rest of the floor and noticed a smear of yellow by the doors.

She had been here. Blackwell had taken Emilie into the elevator. Since she wasn't in the building, that must have been how he gotten her out. Did he take her to the roof? Did Blackwell even have a private helicopter?

What was he thinking? Of course he did. Blackwell Capital specialized in transportation engineering. Just like Ezra, Blackwell had pretty much every form of land, sea, and air vehicle at his disposal.

However, Ezra thought, a helicopter kidnapping was too conspicuous. Everyone in lower Manhattan would notice it coming and going from the rooftop, including Ezra when his taxi driver had sped through Tribeca.

So, if he hadn't taken her to the roof and he didn't drag her out the front doors, there had to be another way out of the building. Ezra glanced at the elevator buttons again, quickly punching the *door close* button again as it reached a new floor. Next to the button that would bring him back down the lobby was another option for a lower level, beside which was printed the universal logo for parking lot.

There was a parking garage in the basement. That had to be it.

As Ezra looked closer, he noticed there was a streak of green paint on the basement button. It was faint, but splattered, as if Emilie had reached for it quickly. Had she been trying to leave a clue behind? That was smart thinking on her part. In the end, while her chosen art medium wasn't an adequate weapon, it was still the thing that led him to her.

While he waited for the elevator to descend to the basement, he ran his fingers through his hair. The dark reality of the situation was settling in. Even if Ezra was right and Emilie had been taken away by Blackwell via a getaway car in the basement, chances were, she was long gone at that point.

But that didn't mean all hope was lost. Ezra wasn't a quitter. In fact, he was the complete opposite. Ezra didn't give up on anything.

When the doors opened once more, he expected a dozen Blackwell Capital employees in dark suits to be waiting for him on the other side, ready to pounce. Instead, he was met with nothing but concrete walls and floors. The parking garage was small; obviously private.

Ezra stepped out and ran a panicked lap around the underground space. There were only a handful of cars parked down there. They were all expensive, foreign models. All of them empty. There wasn't anyone down there other than Ezra, but there was another splatter of green paint on the floor nearby. Half a footprint, small and feminine, and smeared as if the wearer of the boot was struggling against her captor.

With a frustrated groan, Ezra crouched down on the concrete and dropped his head into his hands. He pictured Blackwell and his hulking henchmen tossing Emilie into a car and driving away. Did they let her have a seat or did they throw her into the trunk like soulless cargo?

"I'm so sorry," he whispered aloud, even though Emilie couldn't hear him.

This was his fault. She was in danger because of her involvement with him. Of course, he never knew Blackwell was this diabolical. He hadn't expected the man to play this dirty. If he'd known—if Ben had approached him sooner or if he'd just listened to the rumors that Blackwell was from a notorious crime family—he would have—

Well, what would he have done? Would he have chosen not to pursue Emilie? The thought of holding himself back from such a thing didn't sound possible, but if it was for the sake of her safety, Ezra could have done it.

He had probably made things worse for her these past couple of weeks. All the gifts and floral deliveries—if Blackwell had the resources to kidnap someone, he also had the resources to stalk them. His affection for Emilie would be evident to anyone who paid even the slightest bit of attention. Anyone with ill intentions would know that she was his weakness.

What was he going to do? What could he do?

Ezra stood up and glanced around. He was fairly certain he had reached the end of the road in terms of physical clues, but maybe there was something else that could tell him where Emilie was taken. Did Blackwell have a lair other than his penthouse along the Hudson River?

Suddenly, a loud trill caused Ezra to jump. It was his phone. He had forgotten he had switched it off of silent mode.

A rush of hope flooded through him when he saw it was Ben calling.

Of course. The FBI could do something. There was no way Blackwell could defend himself against one of the most powerful investigative agencies in the world.

Right?

"Ben," Ezra answered in lieu of hello. "I'm at Blackwell's. She's not here, but she left her bag behind with her phone and everything inside. She's—there's paint smeared everywhere. I think they grabbed her. They took her somewhere. They—"

"I see," Ben replied firmly. "A kidnapping attempt was always on the list of possible attacks. Don't worry, Ezra. I'm trained for this. The entire FBI is trained for this. We have a plan. I'm working on getting a warrant to gain access to Blackwell's security camera system."

"And how long is that going to take?" snapped Ezra, walking briskly up the sloping ramp leading to the street outside.

"Faster than you think. I should have it in about half an hour."

Ezra wanted to chuck his phone onto the ground and smash it under foot, instead clutching it tighter in his bruised fist and taking a deep breath. Half an hour was quick by most standards, but who knew what Blackwell might do to her in that small amount of time?

"And then?"

Ben sighed. Ezra could tell he was trying to remain patient in the face of Ezra's obvious agitation.

"And then we will track Emilie's movement through the building from the moment she arrived this morning to the second she left and go from there."

"That's all you can do?" snapped Ezra as he made it back to the street and stuck out a hand to hail the next cab coming down the avenue. He knew it wasn't right to take out his anger on Ben, but couldn't they do something more useful than merely watch the security cameras? Couldn't they call in the National Guard and comb through every single block of the city for Emilie?

He knew his wishes were impractical, but Ezra was desperate.

"Unless a ransom note is sent and we have something more substantial to track, this is currently all we can do," Ben replied. "I'm sorry, Ezra, but please take comfort in the fact that I'm an expert in this field. Kidnapping victims are taken for a reason. Until Blackwell has significant motivation, he won't hurt her. Remember, he's doing this because he wants something. Whatever it is, he wants that more than he wants to harm an innocent civilian."

"How can you be sure?" Ezra grumbled, sliding into the backseat of a taxi and signaling for the driver to head uptown.

"I can't," Ben admitted. "There are occasional outliers, but I am only trying to comfort you with the most common likelihood. Now, what's your current location?"

"I'm in a cab heading up Seventh from downtown," he sighed. "I'll be back in my office in about twenty-five minutes."

"I'll meet you there."

Ezra leaned his head back against the seat. The driver was barking into his phone in a foreign language he didn't recognize, not paying any attention to the tense conversation happening behind him.

"Sounds good," Ezra said.

He was about to end the call when Ben's voice caused him to hesitate.

"Ezra? I know this is frightening, but it's for the best if you try to stay positive for Emilie's sake," Ben told him. He sounded more like a real FBI agent than he had in any of their previous conversations. "We're going to find her and bring her back to safety. And we're also going to take Anderson Blackwell down once and for all."

Once and for all. He hoped so. Except for a few rare instances, defeating Blackwell came easily enough, but this time felt different. The stakes were higher. Someone's life was at risk.

All Ezra could do was swallow back his fear and force out an agreement that he didn't believe in.

"Got it," he said to Ben. "Thanks. See you soon."

"See you soon."

Ezra held his phone in his hands and stared out at Manhattan dancing past his window. Was she still on the little island? If not, Ezra knew he would exhaust every possible resource at his disposal to locate her. He would scour the earth for Emilie.

It was what he should have done for her six months ago.

Chapter Twenty

As the car drove on, Emilie paid attention to the changing sounds beneath her, like the purr of the engine and the hum of the tires on the ground. She could tell when they were driving over smooth pavement or rocky asphalt. Ever since she was little, she'd had a good ear. Maybe if she wasn't an artist, she could have become a musician.

If her ears were correct, the car had passed over two bridges since leaving the parking garage underneath Blackwell Capital. That was bad. Really bad. Manhattan was an island, and not only were there no bridges to drive over within the borough itself, but the only way to get out of Manhattan was to cross a bridge.

In short, they had left Manhattan, which meant they could be going anywhere. Brooklyn, Queens… they could even be going to Jersey. She tried to listen for any other sounds that might indicate where Anderson and his henchmen were taking her, but all she could hear were the engines of other vehicles around them.

She lay in the darkness, throwing desperate wishes out to the universe. She wished she had superpowers, that she had superstrength or could teleport. Perhaps it was childish, but it was pretty much the only thing keeping her sane. Because she didn't wear a watch and her phone was still sitting on the floor of the lobby, Emilie had no way to track the passing time, but she guessed that they had driven for approximately thirty minutes before the traffic quieted down. The road felt smooth and winding beneath the wheels, almost as if they were curving down peaceful country roads.

That wasn't possible. There was neither countryside nor calm lanes in any of the five boroughs of New York City, and unless she had completely lost her grip on reality, they hadn't been driving long enough to get beyond the city limits.

Unless… Anderson was rich. *Really* rich. There were neighborhoods in the quaint suburbs of Long Island full of massive stone mansions hidden behind towering walls. It was the perfect place for a villain to have a lair where he could keep his kidnapping victims.

It was the most probable conclusion, but it wasn't ideal. Emilie was about as familiar with the wealthy back roads of Long Island as the average tourist—meaning that escaping was going to be extremely difficult. There were no subways to hop on or taxis to hail.

All of a sudden, the smooth pavement turned into rough gravel as the car slowed to a crawl. The tires crunched loudly and Emilie flinched at the rough tread. She imagined they were in a driveway as the car curved in a tight circle before finally coming to a halt.

When the engine cut off, she could hear the muffled voices of Anderson and the two other men as they climbed out of the car. Footsteps dispersed in multiple directions. Two sets of feet maneuvered away from the vehicle, but the third came around to the back of the car. Emilie braced herself. She didn't know whether to be more afraid of Anderson or the other two men.

Instinctively, she prepared to fight. She was surprised by the automatic desire rising up inside of her. She'd never been in such a terrifying situation before. Apparently, when it came down to fight or flight, Emilie was inclined toward the latter. Regardless of that, she knew it wouldn't be wise of her to try to fight. She had no idea where she was, nor could she be certain that the man fumbling with the handle of the trunk wouldn't hurt her at the slightest sign of struggle.

In a matter of seconds, Emilie formulated a plan. She would be docile and cooperative for now, ideally lulling her kidnappers into a false sense of security until it became absolutely necessary to take a risk and fight back with all of her strength. Maybe it wouldn't even come to that. Maybe whatever they wanted with her was simple and by sunset she would be set free.

She knew it was naive to hope for something like that. People didn't kidnap others only to let them go hours later.

In that case, Emilie's best hope was that she could take care of herself until someone came to her rescue.

The trunk popped open. Instead of leaping up and clawing out the assailant's eyes or wrapping her hands around his neck as tightly as she could, she remained lying down and merely glared at him.

It wasn't Anderson. He must have been one of the people who walked away after getting out of the vehicle.

The man staring down at her was at least a decade older than her and twice—maybe even thrice—her size. Choosing not to fight was a good idea.

"Get up," he demanded from her. She noticed the subtlest hint of a tattoo peeking out over the edge of his shirt collar. The rest of his skin was covered by the suit he wore, but she imagined there was more where that came from.

Emilie didn't move, too shocked and terrified to make her limbs obey the instructions right away. The tattooed man reached under the hem of his jacket and pulled a pistol from a hidden holster on his belt. He aimed it at Emilie and she froze, staring down the barrel of the gun.

She expected her life to flash before her eyes, but all she felt was the icy chill of pure terror. Goosebumps erupted down her spine.

"Let's try this one more time," the man said. She detected an Eastern European accent in his voice. "*Get up.*"

This time, with the deadly weapon aimed right at her head, she sat up and awkwardly climbed out of the trunk, her limbs sore not only from being curled up during the journey but also from the morning she'd spent huddled on the floor painting that stupid mural.

She stood in the gravel and stared up at the man. He smirked down at her as if the entire situation was hilarious to him.

"Turn around and walk inside," he instructed her.

The last thing Emilie wanted to do was turn her back on a man with a gun, but she had no choice. Slowly, she turned around and found herself face to face with a hulking mansion boasting four stone columns and a grand, double-door entrance. In her peripheral vision, she noticed the hedges that encircled the property, stretching over ten feet high and undoubtedly fortified with steel fencing concealed by the leaves.

She took careful, measured steps toward the house and tried to take in as many details as possible as she went, but there wasn't much to see. There were no other vehicles in the driveway and there was no one else in sight. Anderson and his righthand man must have already gone inside the house.

"Hurry up, princess," snapped the man behind her, clicking the gun ominously.

She jumped and quickened her footsteps, not bothering to mention that she was the furthest thing from a princess any woman could get. From the look of the mansion, Emilie became more certain that they were on Long Island. It was colossal and flashy, the kind of monstrosity purchased by new money families flaunting their riches proudly. In college, her friend Lena dated a guy who had grown up on Long Island and the two girls had gone to a party at his place while his parents were gone for the weekend. The similarities between that house and this one were impossible to deny.

However, the moment Emilie made it up the front steps, past the roaring gargoyles, and into the grand foyer, she saw that this particular mansion was not a home. Rather, it was a ruse. The furniture was sparse and basic, just enough to make it appear as though someone could be in the process of settling in and not arouse suspicion.

This was Anderson's lair, a place to do his evil deeds outside the confines of the cramped city. What kind of things happened here behind the impenetrable hedges? At the gala, Ben hadn't mentioned what specific type of underground business Anderson was involved in, telling her only that the Blackwell family was well-known for their involvement with organized crime.

"Take a left down this hall," said the man with the tattooed neck, following close behind as she walked. She obeyed, turning down a marble-floored hallway lined with open archways that lead to an open sitting room and a blooming garden beyond on the left, and a series of closed doors on the right.

In the back of her mind, Emilie prayed that the kind of crime Anderson dabbled in was something not outwardly violent, such as drugs or smuggling counterfeit goods. Her blood ran cold with the thought that he might be running an undetectable, sophisticated sex trafficking ring.

She would fight to the death if that was the case.

Emilie didn't have to walk far down the hallway. Other than the sound of her boots and the man's shiny loafers echoing on the glossy floors, the house was silent. Where was Anderson? She thought it was rather cowardly of him to lure her into the parking garage, ride in the car with her to the destination, and not show his face again. She was under the impression that most villains wanted to personally keep an eye on their victims.

"Stop here."

Emilie halted, waiting by an unmarked door as the man reached past her and turned the knob. The hinges creaked as the door opened. Without ceremony, he pushed her roughly between her shoulders. Emilie stumbled into the room and tripped on the edge of a generic, antique-style rug. Unable to regain her balance, she sharply fell onto her hands and knees.

"Perfect," snickered the man. "That makes my job easier."

Emilie turned over and sat up, scrambling back from the man as he kicked the door shut behind them. There was nothing in the room except for the rug and two windows along the far wall that overlooked the sprawling back lawn and the continued barrier around the perimeter of the property.

The tattooed man, who was clearly not going to introduce himself, so in her head Emilie started referring to him as Tattoo, pulled out a small length of rope from inside his jacket pocket. How many nightmarish tools did he keep hidden under that thing?

"Wrists, please," he said to her in a disturbing sing-song tone.

Emilie glared up at him as he uncoiled the rope. Sensing her obvious hesitation to obey, Tattoo stepped close to her. She craned her neck to keep eye contact with him.

"I recommend behaving," Tattoo told her. "We've been given orders not to touch you, but if you make things difficult, I might just have an accidental lapse in my memory."

It was a threat if Emilie had ever heard one. She took note of the fact that the man wasn't supposed to lay hands on her, wondering why Anderson was bothering with respect in the first place. What kind of person was capable of picking and choosing morals like that? Was he a sociopath?

Knowing she had no other option, Emilie held out her wrists as Tattoo crouched down in front of her. No matter how hard she tried to conceal it, her hands were trembling as he wound the rope around her wrists, securing them with a complex knot that Emilie was confident she could never figure out how to do on her own.

She took stock of her wins and losses. At least her hands were tied in front of her instead of behind. At least her ankles were still free. At least she wasn't blindfolded or gagged.

At least she wasn't dead.

It was a pathetic list of positives, but she would accept whatever she got. Maybe they were being easy on her because they assumed a short woman with bony limbs couldn't fight for herself. They were underestimating her.

Emilie told herself that was a good thing. She'd be able to use it to her advantage when the time was right.

When Tattoo finished binding her hands together, he stepped back and admired his handiwork. He opened his mouth to say something to her, but the door creaked open before he could get a word out.

Finally, Anderson reappeared. Emilie huddled pathetically in the center of the bare room with her paint-splattered hands tied up in her lap. Anderson gazed at her as if he were observing an interesting piece of modern art on display at a museum, cocking his head to the side slightly as he took a few steps toward her.

Keeping his eyes on her, Anderson turned his face vaguely in Tattoo's direction.

"Go help Ivan upstairs." he said to Tattoo.

Emilie deduced that Ivan was the name of the other vaguely Slavic man who had helped kidnap her.

At Anderson's word, Tattoo nodded and ducked out of the room, throwing one last leering glance at Emilie before disappearing from sight.

When they were alone together, Anderson and Emilie stared at each other for a moment. His expression was unreadable, but one thing was clear: there wasn't an ounce of visible regret in his eyes. Emilie wondered what he was really like underneath the layers of fake charm, practiced politeness, and calculating cruelty. Did he have a family back in the city? A wife and kids? Did they know what he was up to when he wasn't home?

How could a man who was capable of building a family—something that required love, tenderness, and an ability to nurture—also be so manipulative and monstrous? Because of that perplexing question alone, Emilie assumed that Anderson was a solitary man. It didn't lead her to feel sorry for him, but it certainly explained at least some of his behaviors and actions.

Of course, psychoanalyzing the man who had abducted her wasn't the most productive use of her mental energy.

Anderson was the first to break the silence.

"I apologize for the manhandling earlier," he said to her. "You shouldn't take this whole situation personally. If it were up to me, I wouldn't have needed to bother you at all, but I have reason to believe that you're going to be very useful to me."

Emilie narrowed her eyes at him. "What might that reason be?"

"Ezra Hudson's infatuation with you, of course."

She easily caught on to the reason why she was being targeted. What else would lead to this other than the tense competition between Ezra and Anderson?

Emilie immediately thought Anderson was mistaken. Despite the magnetic pull between Ezra and her, they didn't have an unbreakable bond. They were nothing more than former lovers, a love story that ended before it could properly begin. The fact that Anderson saw her as an opportunity to gain leverage over Ezra baffled her. Did he really think Ezra was that fond of her?

The longer she puzzled over it, the more she realized Anderson had plenty of reasons to believe that Ezra was head over heels in love with her. He'd bought her a dress, taken her to a gala, and showed her off like a precious diamond. Deliveries of flowers flooded her apartment building, which Anderson could easily stake out with all of the devious resources at his fingertips. In his eyes, Ezra was enamored with her and would do anything to ensure her safety.

Emilie knew Ezra liked her. She liked him too, as much as she tried to deny it. However, she doubted he liked her *this* much. Whatever Anderson was about to ask of him, she couldn't help feeling as if her wellbeing wasn't a big enough price to pay. Anderson had lost to Ezra many times before. Emilie was convinced it was about to happen again.

"Surely you could have found a way to sort out your differences without involving me?" Emilie replied boldly. "I don't even know anything about engineering. I literally just draw pictures for a living."

"Well, Emilie, I wouldn't expect you to be aware of the contracts that pass through the offices of CEOs, but just know that I lost my last shred of patience today. I'm going to do whatever it takes to ensure Ezra Hudson never causes me trouble again."

He meant it. Whatever it takes... including kidnapping and threatening Emilie. She had no idea what had happened or what kind of contract Blackwell Capital just lost the battle for, but the wild darkness in Anderson's gaze proved he was truly at the end of his rope.

That wasn't good. Desperate people were the most dangerous.

"Ezra isn't the type of person who backs down easily," Emilie warned him.

Anderson cackled. "And don't I know it? I have a feeling I may have finally figured out how to hit him where it hurts. Honestly, when this all works out in the end, remind me to thank you. In the meantime, I need to take care of a few things. I've been gentle so far, but if you attempt a jailbreak, I won't hesitate to play dirty. Understood?"

Emilie didn't want to agree, but she was so scared, her body reacted automatically. She nodded, watching as Anderson backed out of the room and left her alone with a final *click* of the bolt. When he was gone, Emilie struggled onto her feet and tried the door. She discovered quickly that it was locked from the outside.

Despite what Anderson had just said to her, she had to try to save herself. She moved to the windows, using her bound hands to lift the bottoms of the panes with all her strength, but it was no use. They were secured shut. With a huff of frustration, Emilie turned around and scanned the room. The only vent was a tiny rectangle of slats in the floor barely big enough to fit her shoe in.

There were no other escape routes, no potential weapons, and no evidence to suggest she was going to make it out of there in one piece. Emilie's imagination spiraled to horrifying places as she thought about Anderson's use of the phrase *play dirty*.

How long would it take for someone to notice she was gone? It was early afternoon. Her boss and her coworkers thought she was at home sick. Her sister was probably studying on campus. If Ezra reached out to her, he would most likely think that she was simply ignoring him again. No one would start to question her disappearance for at least several more hours. Who knew what could happen to her by that time?

In short, Emilie was doomed. She was doomed and she might as well accept the fact.

With a sigh, she sat down on the floor and leaned her back against the wall. If only she'd guarded her heart from the beginning. She could have avoided all of this if she had never gotten involved with Ezra Hudson in the first place.

Chapter Twenty-One

Ezra was losing his mind. He paced back and forth in his office while Ben sat behind his desk and clicked around freely on Ezra's computer. When Ben arrived, he was no longer dressed in his banker attire, foregoing the undercover disguise due to the pressing circumstances.

He also didn't show up alone.

It was impossible to hide the arrival of several FBI agents at the company building, but Ezra did his best. Apparently, there were even more agents headed downtown toward Blackwell Capital, awaiting the pending search warrant. According to Ben, there were files upon files of evidence of "probable cause" in the FBI's possession that would earn them the warrant quickly, but Ezra felt like everything was moving too slowly. Every minute that Emilie was in Blackwell's possession was another minute her life was at risk.

Ezra couldn't decide which emotion to feel. He was worried about Emilie, terrified for her safety, furious at Blackwell, and embarrassed at what it might look like to outside observers to see the FBI van parked outside the headquarters of Hudson Enterprises. On top of that, he was annoyed by Ben's practiced calm, and frustrated that it had taken the FBI this long to pounce on Blackwell. If they claimed to have so much evidence, they could have taken him down ages ago.

If the FBI had acted in a timely matter instead of biding their time in hopes that they would uncover the breadth of Blackwell's underground network, Emilie would have never been caught in the crossfires of the stupid competition between their two companies.

Ezra could tell he was filling the room with nervous energy, but he couldn't help it. When Ben and his colleagues first arrived on the thirtieth floor, Matt and Jess both poked their heads in curiously. Before he could attempt to explain what was going on, Ben suggested shutting his office door and saving the explanations for later. Ezra was relieved, but offered apologies to his assistant and his CFO as he closed the door in their faces.

"Ezra, come here," Ben said. He hadn't said anything in several minutes and Ezra was too agitated to chat. At the sound of his voice, however, Ezra jumped into action and hurried over to his desk.

"What is it?" he asked, hovering over Ben's shoulder.

"You have a new email in your inbox and it looks suspicious. Would you like to open it, or do I have permission to—?"

Ezra gestured impatiently, signaling for Ben to click the notification that popped up at the corner of the screen. The message was from an unrecognizable email address. Both the description and the domain were a seemingly random series of numbers. Ezra had no idea how it managed to avoid being sorted into his spam folder.

Both men leaned forward to read the email.

This message is for Ezra Hudson. Emilie DeGaulle will be returned to you safely as soon as you agree to sign over ownership of Hudson Enterprises. Should you refuse, her demise will be swift and merciless. You have twenty-four hours.

While Ezra stared at the screen, frozen to the spot as he reread the email a dozen times, Ben leaped up from the chair and barked something into his phone. Seconds later, another agent came into the room and hurried over to the desk. She was a scrawny, bespectacled woman—barely in her mid-twenties if Ezra had to guess. She wasn't exactly the type of person Ezra pictured when he thought of a crime-fighting undercover agent.

He was so numb with fear from the message it was difficult to process what he was seeing. The girl bypassed a proper hello and introduction, helping herself to Ezra's keyboard.

"Luckily, I thought to bring Agent Lane with me," Ben explained. "She's one of the best hackers in the force."

Agent Lane paid no attention to her colleague's compliment. She plugged a digital tablet into the back of Ezra's monitor and he watched as rows upon rows of code filled the screen.

"Hacker?" Ezra asked. "You're hacking my computer?"

"No, she's—"

"I'm tracing the source of the ransom note," Agent Lane cut in with a brisk voice. Her eyes were glued to the screen as she spoke, her fingers flying across the keys seemingly of their own accord. "Every single domain can be tracked to a location, it's just a matter of how hard they've tried to cover it up."

"But what if the email wasn't sent from the same location where they're keeping her?" Ezra asked before he could hold himself back.

The young agent didn't even bat an eye at his question.

"Regardless, agents will swarm the location and either apprehend the suspect or gather evidence that will lead us further along the trail," she explained.

In short, Blackwell could lead the FBI on a wild goose chase all day and give himself the opportunity to get away with Emilie once and for all.

Twenty-four hours. Blackwell was giving him one day to sign away the rights to Hudson Enterprises. He would lose everything. The company he had built from nothing would belong to his greatest rival. Blackwell Capital would take over and absorb everything, all the trains, planes, busses, boats, and everything in between. Blackwell would get all of his employees, and be the one to decide their fates, too.

On top of that, Ezra would be handing over his hard-won contracts to Blackwell on a silver platter. After years of fighting him at every corner, the efforts would go down the drain with just a few signatures on a document.

If Ezra agreed to the demands in the email—which, although it was anonymous, was obviously written by Blackwell himself—Blackwell would gain a monopoly in the transportation engineering industry on this side of the world. There were few international competitors that could compare to Hudson Enterprises in the west, and now that Hudson Enterprises was merging with the Singapore company, they were going to have a foothold in the east, too.

Ezra would be giving Blackwell an empire.

...her demise will be swift and merciless.

Not once in all his time dealing with Blackwell did he imagine that he might have the potential to commit murder, but it certainly sounded like he was threatening to do it. Even if he was bluffing, how could Ezra dare to call him on it?

When Ezra said he would do anything to help Emilie, he'd meant it. His company and his wealth were nothing if he had the blood of an innocent woman on his hands. At least Blackwell was giving him a full day to respond, though he wasn't sure he trusted it. Blackwell wasn't known for being trustworthy or honest… at least when it came to his dealings with Ezra.

"Are we going to respond to the email?" Ezra asked.

Agent Lane continued typing, ignoring his question. Ben was staring down at his phone, reading a message with intense concentration. He glanced up when Ezra spoke.

"No," Ben replied. "At least, not right away. We have a procedure for handling ransom notes—"

"Plus," Agent Lane cut in. "The email's domain has already been destroyed. If we reply, it'll bounce back as undelivered."

Ben nodded, then glanced at Ezra, furrowing his brow with concern. Ezra could feel the panic written on his own face. It weighed him down.

"I know it doesn't seem like it, but receiving ransom notes is actually a good thing," he explained to Ezra. "When a kidnapper wants something, there's always room for negotiation. Also, when ransom is involved, the victim is usually kept fairly safe in the meantime."

"Fairly?" Ezra sighed.

"Come over here, Ezra," Ben replied, nodding his head for Ezra to follow him to the far side of the room. "Let's give Agent Lane some room to breathe while she works her magic. I've got an update from the team in Tribeca anyway."

"Really? Did they get the warrant?"

"They did," Ben confirmed. "They've got the building on lockdown and started combing through the security footage about five minutes ago. They have about four or five people on it, so they've already been able to confirm what you told us about her likely being transported via the parking garage in the basement."

Ezra nodded, waiting for more. When Ben pressed his lips together and looked back down at his phone, he realized that was it. For now, at least.

He started pacing again, lost in his own world as Ben communicated with the team in Tribeca, and Agent Lane continued to do God-knows-what to his computer. When his phone buzzed in his pocket, he yanked it out and paused by the windows that stretched from floor to ceiling along the entire back wall of the room.

It was Matt, texting from his personal number rather than messaging from the company software.

Ez, what the hell is going on? Don't keep me in the dark, man.

Ezra frowned. It was unfair of him to block Matt out of the situation. Blackwell kidnapping Emilie was personal, but it was also a professional issue because he had done it to attack Hudson Enterprises. Ezra and Matt had been business partners for a long time and friends for even longer. Ben suggested keeping the others in the dark for now, but Matt was going to have to be the exception.

He texted him back right away. *Come to my office, but don't let anyone else in with you.*

Matt must have been waiting right outside the door because there was a knock seconds later. Ezra hurried to answer it, ushering Matt inside quickly and checking to make sure the hallway behind him was clear.

Ben quirked an eyebrow at the visitor, but Ezra shook his head in a wordless gesture indicating that there was no point in protesting. Matt glanced at Ben, then noticed Agent Lane at the computer.

"So… what the hell?" he asked.

Ben stepped forward and shook Matt's hand. "Ben Wang. I'm with the Federal Bureau of Investigation."

Matt returned the handshake in kind, confusion written in the creases of his brow. "Is there a problem, sir?"

"I'll let him explain," Ben replied, nodding his head at Ezra and returning his attention to his phone.

Ezra sighed and faced his colleague. "It's a long story, but I'll try to keep it simple."

He told him everything as quickly as he could. He explained that he had been seeing someone named Emilie and that she was more than just a casual fling to him, then got into the dirty details of Blackwell's latest attempt to take down their company. When Ezra finally got to the part about the ransom note and how Blackwell wanted to buy Hudson Enterprises for the price of Emilie's life, Matt let out a long, low exhale and sank down into one of the leather chairs beside the desk.

Matt was silent for a minute, staring at the floor with wide eyes. Understandably, this wasn't how he had expected his Tuesday to go. Ezra didn't know what else to say, so he stood there and waited for his friend to process everything.

Finally, Matt glanced up.

"I knew it," he sighed, the barest hint of a smirk on his face. "I knew there was no other way to explain how you've been acting recently other than the possibility of you being madly in love. Shelby is going to be thrilled when I tell her."

Ezra groaned. "That's your takeaway from all of this?"

"Well, I'm sure everything is going to be fine if the FBI is on it," Matt shrugged. "Plus, you said he wasn't going to hurt her—"

"I've got an update coming in," Ben announced, coming over to interrupt their discussion. Ezra and Matt looked over at him expectantly.

"Yes?" Ezra prodded.

"The agents have been scanning the security cameras in the parking garage to catch a possible shot of the getaway car's license plate number, but Blackwell and his men were slick," Ben said, talking rapidly while he kept his eyes glued to his phone. "They operated only in blind spots, or maybe even changed the angle of the cameras beforehand. They did manage to get the make and model, though."

"And?"

"It's a Benz," Ben said. "S-Class. Black. Likely the most current model available on the market."

Ezra nodded. That sounded like the kind of car Blackwell would drive. The price was in the six figures, but it wasn't too flashy that it would draw unwanted eyes as he took Emilie away. Unfortunately, it was a common vehicle for many wealthy people in Manhattan.

"We're officially involving local law enforcement," Ben continued. "NYPD is combing all boroughs of the city for a vehicle that matches that description under the guise of random traffic stops. We're also in the process of tracking all toll highways leading off the island of Manhattan in hopes that we can catch a photo of the car."

It was progress, but it was still just a guessing game. Ezra fought the urge to kick the side of his desk. How could it be this hard to find someone? He always thought organizations like the FBI were unstoppable. Powerful. He thought they could do anything.

"Is that all you can do? NYPD pulling over every black Mercedes Benz they see?" snapped Ezra. "What about helicopters? What about boats monitoring the East and Hudson rivers? We've got pretty much every form of vehicle at our disposal here. Let me use them."

"It is the Bureau's opinion that calling in the agency's helicopter unit is not necessary at this moment," Ben replied sheepishly. "It has only been a few hours."

"Well, I'm not talking about your resources. I'm talking about mine. I've got a pilot license. I'll personally fly a helicopter over Manhattan to hunt down that vehicle," Ezra argued.

Ben nodded and began typing on his phone. "No need. We have a few pilots on call here. If you're volunteering the Hudson fleet, we can send a small team of agents up right away."

"Great. Let's do it," Ezra agreed. Matt nodded.

"We need—" Before Ben could finish his next command, Ezra's phone started ringing. It was a call from an unknown number.

He didn't hesitate, already knowing exactly who it would be. Ben leaped forward, thinking just as fast and signaling for Ezra to put the call on speaker as he used his own phone to record the call.

Ezra answered, letting every ounce of fear and anger inside him turn his voice cold with wrath.

"I swear to God, if you hurt even a single hair on her head—"

"Ezra? Hello? Ezra?"

Ezra stumbled and collapsed into the chair beneath him as Emilie's voice came through.

"Emilie? Emilie, are you okay? Where are you? Where did he take you?"

Ezra was vaguely aware of the fact that Agent Lane was no longer typing and clicking. She was stone still, listening to the panicked conversation with rapt focus.

"Ezra, you need to sign over the company," she whispered. "He's going to hurt me if you don't. He has a gun pointed at me—"

Emilie's terrified voice faded away. It was replaced by a shuffling sound and then Blackwell's voice crooned on the other end of the line.

"I know I said I'd give you twenty-four hours, but I have to admit that I'm an impatient man," Anderson murmured. "I thought you'd be a little faster to act than this, Ezra. What's the matter? Do you think I'm bluffing? Should I provide some motivation?"

"You better not touch her," Ezra hissed.

Anderson snorted. There was another shuffle of movement, followed quickly by a loud *thump*. Emilie cried out in pain in the background. Ezra's grip on the phone was so tight he wondered if he could crush it in his fist.

"Anderson Blackwell, I swear to God if you don't tell me where you've taken her—" Ezra warned, wondering why Ben wasn't inserting himself into the conversation. Maybe it wasn't proper protocol. He seemed like a stickler for the rules, but no amount of appropriate procedure was going to save Emilie.

Anderson cackled loudly. "Hurry up, friend. Every hour I'm kept waiting spells pain for her."

Then, just like that, he hung up.

Agent Lane stood up and held out her palm. "Give me your phone. Now."

Ezra was too shocked to move, so Ben grabbed the phone out of his hand and gave it to her.

"What are you doing?" Matt asked, his voice shaky as the true weight of the situation hit him.

"I'm tracing the call," Agent Lane snapped as if it were the most obvious thing in the world, plugging Ezra's phone into the tablet. Seconds later, she nodded as she watched a new series of code fill the screen. "It's not a landline. That's good. I can at least locate the service tower he connected to in order to make the call."

Ezra nodded numbly.

The world felt oddly still and silent as panic squeezed his lungs and twisted his gut. He tried to tell himself that they had more advantages on their side. They had police and federal agents on the ground, and soon enough, in the sky searching for Blackwell's car. They were tracking the email domain and the phone number. Plus, given how much traffic plagued the congested boroughs of New York City, it wasn't as if Blackwell could make it very far in the small amount of time that had passed.

There were reasons to be optimistic, but Ezra couldn't stomach them. All he could think about was the sound of Emilie's pain. It echoed inside his skull, replaying a hundred times a minute. Did he kick her? Slap her? She said he had a gun. Did he have any other weapons?

Surely he wouldn't torture her… he couldn't be *that* evil.

Ezra dropped his head into his hands. Agent Lane's and Ben's voices were muffled as if they were speaking from a different room. The unbearably heavy pounding of his heart was the loudest thing he could hear. He felt a large hand clamp down on his shoulder, but he didn't lift his head. Nausea was building in the pit of his stomach, and it was suddenly becoming a very real possibility for him to vomit.

If he'd known that starting his company and enjoying the successes that flooded his bank account over the years would lead to this… Ezra would have never pursued such goals. It wasn't supposed to be like this. This kind of drama was reserved for the movies. It didn't happen to real humans in real life. It didn't happen to innocent people like Emilie.

At least, it wasn't supposed to.

Matt squeezed Ezra's shoulder.

"Deep breaths, Ez," he muttered. "Everything is going to be okay."

Until he held Emilie in his arms once more, Ezra couldn't help thinking that Matt's comforting statement was nothing more than a desperate lie.

Chapter Twenty-Two

Emilie huddled on the floor of the room in Anderson's mansion, clutching her bound hands close to her side in an attempt to cradle the bruised ribs he'd just given her. He'd caught her off guard with the well-aimed kick to her ribcage. She'd done everything he asked her to. She had begged Ezra to sign over the rights to Hudson Enterprises, staring at the barrel of the pistol aimed at her forehead as she did so.

"You said you wouldn't hurt me," she groaned, the side of her face pressed to the rug as she willed the aching in her side to dissipate. She couldn't tell if anything was broken, but the pain was sharp and insistent.

Anderson shrugged, snapping in half the burner phone he had used to the make the call. "I lied. It served me in the moment. Nothing personal."

Emilie flinched as she sat up straight and glared at him.

"You should be ashamed of yourself," she hissed at him. "Kidnapping and abusing an innocent woman just because you aren't getting your way. Maybe if you were a better businessman, you wouldn't have to resort to such evil to get to the top."

Anderson's gaze narrowed, his dark eyes growing colder. The gun was still in his hand. Emilie stared at it nervously as he raised it vaguely in her direction.

"Keep talking and I'll shut you up myself," he threatened.

Emilie set her jaw. It was an empty threat. If he killed her right now, he wouldn't have any leverage. He would just be a tempestuous idiot with a dead body to bury and a murder on his criminal record.

"You won't kill me," she dared to say. "I'm all you have."

Anderson sneered. "Fair enough, but a bullet wound doesn't have to be fatal, gorgeous. I can get my point across without making too much of a mess."

Emilie's blood ran cold. She imagined how much it would hurt if he shot her in the foot or the arm, the kind of wound that would cause excruciating agony but not enough blood loss to kill her. Or, at least, not quickly.

She swallowed her fear, determined to keep him talking. If she could lull him into a chatty mood, she might be able to uncover a detail she could use to her advantage. Anderson was smart, but his intellect wasn't infallible. There had to be a way she could best him. How did Ezra do it?

Ezra had an entire corporation of people backing him up and providing assistance against Anderson's attacks. That's how he did it. Furthermore, he was the better person. He conducted his business morally, never searching for ways to cheat his competition. Emilie wanted to believe that being a good person was enough to ensure you would always win in life, but the current circumstances suggested that the phrase *nice guys finish last* might hold more truth to it than she was willing to admit.

She wasn't accustomed to using her wit to get out of sticky situations, but Emilie had to at least try to fight fire with fire—or rather, fight manipulation with cunning.

"I don't think you want to shoot me," she told him. "Have you shot anyone before? The way you're holding that gun tells me you usually let someone else do it for you."

Anderson pointed the gun at her feet. Within the close range, her thick-soled boots would do nothing to protect her from a bullet. She fought the urge to squirm away from his aim and held her ground.

"Are you calling my bluff?" he asked.

"No," she replied firmly. "I know it's true. You don't want me dead or injured. I'm too useful. But I'm not just useful as your captive. Did you ever stop to think that you could have used me to your advantage without going to such extreme measures?"

Anderson raised his eyebrows at her, humoring her as he cocked his head to the side curiously.

"How so?"

"Think about it," Emilie babbled, talking fast as her thoughts scrambled to produce a response that would hook him. "Until you intervened with your flirtations, I was the closest person to Ezra and his executives. At least, I was on my way there. He trusts me. Honestly, it's kind of insulting that you didn't consider I might be capable of helping you from the inside."

"Are you suggesting that I should've manipulated you into betraying your boyfriend?"

"Who knows? Maybe manipulation wouldn't have been necessary if you named a good enough price," Emilie fibbed. "You've made the mistake of assuming I'm innocent and harmless, but maybe I can change your mind. I don't think it's too late. Let me go and I'll say my disappearance was all a silly misunderstanding. I'll go back to Ezra. I'll convince him that you meant no harm and then I can help you take down Hudson Enterprises from the inside. Don't underestimate me."

Emilie hated every word that came out of her mouth. She wasn't that kind of person at all. She didn't lie and manipulate others, no matter what they offered her in return. But Anderson didn't have to know that. If she was convincing enough, he might believe she was telling the truth. The chances were slim, but it was worth a shot. Maybe Anderson was lonely for a partner in crime, a kindred spirit. She could pretend for the moment if it meant him letting her go.

Unfortunately, Anderson saw right through her charade. He was too good at reading people, too good at understanding their motives and goals. Anderson could see clearly that there wasn't a single malicious bone in Emilie's body.

He burst into laughter, throwing his head back with the sound and dropping the hand with the gun in it to his side. Emilie's stomach dropped. She had failed. She was too soft, and it was too obvious.

"I admit, that was incredible to listen to," Anderson chuckled. "Tell me, did you genuinely think I would fall for that? Emilie, dear, I knew the second I grabbed you that there was no going back from this. There's no letting you go, even when Ezra comes to his senses and gives in. Do you really think I'm going to let you go running off into the sunset so the two of you can tell the authorities what I've done?"

Emilie's lips parted in shock.

Of course.

The only possible conclusion hadn't occurred to her before because it was too terrible for her mind to entertain.

If Ezra gave Hudson Enterprises up to Anderson, there was no way she'd be released and allowed to go on living her life as normal. Neither would Ezra. Anderson wouldn't let them walk free after this. As soon as he had the rights to Ezra's company, he was going to go back on his word. The ransom note was a lie.

No matter what, Anderson was going to kill Emilie. He was going to kill Ezra, too, or at least get rid of him in the most permanent way possible.

They weren't going to survive this.

Emilie closed her eyes and pulled her knees close to her chest, her ribs aching as she rested her forehead on her knees. Anderson was pacing on the other side of the room, messing with another burner phone.

She was going to die. There was no way anyone would find Anderson. Ezra probably hadn't even realized she was gone until he received the ransom note and the phone call. How long would it take for Ezra to call the authorities? How long would it take for them to assemble and gather a legitimate lead? What if Anderson cleaned up after himself too well?

In the silence that followed, Emilie started to pray. She wasn't a religious person. Her mother didn't raise Annie and her under the guidance of a particular religion either, but merely taught them to be kind and generous people. She wasn't sure she believed in a higher power, but if there was one, it was a good opportunity to start pleading to them for help.

Please, she begged inside her mind. *Please take me back in time. Take me back to London in September. Take me back to Lena's wedding. Even if you can't change the fact that Ben will stand me up, that's okay. If you let me go back in time, I promise I won't leave the reception early. I'll stay the whole time and pretend to be happier than ever. I'll dance the night away and never go to the bar, never order a vodka, never meet Ezra Hudson. Please, please, please. Please let me go back and erase him from my life. I'll do anything.*

She didn't know how to end her pleading prayers. Saying *amen* didn't seem right.

Either way, she knew they wouldn't be answered. Nobody could help her. It was impossible to go back in time, even if she wanted it more than anything else in the world. All she had was the present moment... her last few minutes or hours or days on earth.

Her poor sister. Annie would be all alone in their cluttered apartment. She wouldn't be able to afford the rent on her own. She'd have to move back into their mother's place in Queens and go back to commuting two to three hours a day into Manhattan for school. Her mom would be glad for the house to not be so empty anymore, but Emilie's childhood bedroom would never be occupied again.

Oh, God. Her mom. She'd sacrificed everything for her daughters. It wasn't fair that she was about to lose one of them.

I'm sorry, mom, Emilie thought to herself. *I should've been careful. I should've listened when you told me to be careful whom I gave my heart to.*

Would her coworkers miss her? Would they know the truth about her death or would they be fed a lie by the replacement executives once Blackwell Capital took over the company? Maybe they would kill two birds with one stone and say that she and Ezra had died together in a tragic car accident. A common death that was easy to believe... that would be the best way for Anderson to go in terms of making up a story to cover up their respective disappearances.

Who else would miss her? Steven at the art gallery would be confused about her sudden radio silence, but hopefully Annie would remember to tie up that loose end once she had gotten over the bulk of her grief. Emilie wished there was a way she could thank the old man at the gallery one last time for giving her a chance.

He said she had potential. Maybe now that she was metaphorically marching toward her death, her career had more potential than ever before. The work of an artist who died tragically before the age of thirty was worth more than work done by yet another struggling painter who was alive and well. Perhaps Annie would use her half-finished museum curator degree to get her sister's paintings in the Whitney or the MoMA. Maybe even the Guggenheim would be interested in the melodrama of it all. The public ate up stories like that; talented people who died too young.

Why are you even thinking about that right now? Emilie chastised herself. She had a bad habit of letting her mind run away with itself. She wasn't even dead yet and she was already imagining what would happen to her legacy several years down the road. Like many artists, she was plagued by unchecked contemplation that bordered on pure delusion.

It was her mind's way of trying to escape the current reality.

Emilie was yanked out of her reverie by the sound of the door opening. She flinched and lifted her head as Tattoo and the other henchman—whom she was pretty sure was named Ivan—entered the room.

"All set?" Anderson asked them.

"All set, Boss," answered Ivan. "Boat's ready to go."

Boat? What boat?

The trio turned to smirk at Emilie. Her stomach swooped with a fresh wave of fear as she took in the sight of their hulking forms. They were a solid, impenetrable wall standing between her and the door. She'd never make it past them.

"Do you want to do this the hard way or the easy way?" Tattoo asked her, approaching with waggling eyebrows. "Doesn't matter to me."

"What do you mean?" she asked, glancing between Tattoo and Anderson. "Where are you taking me?"

"Apparently, the police are stopping any vehicle that matches the make and model of the one we brought you here in," Anderson sighed. "It's a pathetic attempt, but not a risk I'm willing to take. Thankfully, Long Island Sound is a perfectly normal place to sail a boat up the coast. Ideally, I'd like to transport you out of the state by nightfall."

"I bet we could get her up to Canada if necessary, Boss," Ivan added.

Emilie tried to make sense of the deluge of information. They weren't keeping her in the dark, further confirming the fact that they didn't intend for her survive much longer.

Taking her out of Manhattan wasn't enough. They were going to take her out of the state of New York… via the Atlantic Ocean instead of the highways.

They might even smuggle her off United States soil to elude the authorities.

Canada… Emilie couldn't die in Canada. Her family would never get her body back. She would simply disappear and never be seen again. She'd fade into nothingness, as if she'd never existed in the first place.

Tattoo stooped, hands outstretched as if to grab her and hoist her into his arms.

"No, wait," she protested. "I'll walk. I won't fight."

"Smart girl," he muttered.

Emilie struggled onto her feet while the three men watched. Her ribs hurt so badly, it was making her even more lightheaded than the lack of food and water. The injury from the heel of Anderson's shoe was also making it difficult for her to move in general. She let out an involuntary whimper of pain as she shifted onto her knees and attempted to lift herself onto her feet.

An odd noise sounded in the distance. For a moment, Emilie thought it sounded like a party, the dull thud of bass echoing from a loud sound system down the street. However, it was too consistent of a beat to be music. It was growing louder too, as if the source was moving closer.

If Emilie wasn't mistaken, the sound was coming from overhead. She frowned and looked out the windows toward the deep yellow sun creeping lazily toward the horizon. She didn't see anything in the sky, but she swore the odd thumping was coming from above the house.

"We don't have time for this," Anderson snapped. He stepped forward and grabbed the ropes binding Emilie's wrists together, roughly yanking her to her feet.

She cursed under her breath as the sharp movement caused her side to scream in protest. Anderson didn't pay attention to her visible pain, pulling her after him as Ivan opened the door and led the way down the hall. When Anderson jolted her arms forward, a jagged bolt of agony erupted in her ribs.

Emilie cried out and stumbled, her knees going weak. Something shifted in her ribcage, following by an audible *crack*. If her bones weren't broken before, they definitely were now.

The thudding noise was louder, so loud that it felt all-consuming. Or maybe that was her heartbeat, picking up pace as her heart frantically pumped adrenaline throughout her bloodstream, in response to the pain. Emilie couldn't tell. She felt faint, her vision blurring at the edges.

Anderson didn't care. He dragged her down the hallway.

"Get on your feet and walk or I'll shoot you right now!" he roared. Was it just her imagination or was there a sudden flicker of panic in his eyes?

Emilie thought his threat was a bit odd. She was in too much pain to move at the pace Anderson wanted her to, but she wouldn't be any faster if he put a bullet in her.

"We'll take the tunnel to the water," Ivan said from the front of the group, walking briskly across the marble foyer toward a dark doorway.

Emilie let out a choked sob as Anderson growled in resignation and lifted her into his arms. He wasn't gentle, squeezing her too roughly around the middle. She wriggled in his harsh cradle, yearning to be dragged like a useless ragdoll instead of being held in his cold embrace.

Anderson started jogging toward Ivan, Tattoo taking up the rear. Emilie was struggling to maintain consciousness as the fast pace jostled her body. Something else shifted just below her chest. Half a second later, white-hot pain ripped through her. She couldn't help it. She let out a scream.

"Shut up!" Anderson barked.

Emilie clung onto him, hot tears rolling down her face as she whimpered. It felt like her insides were being shredded apart.

Out of the corner of her eye, she caught sight of something strange. Colorful lights… red and blue… *almost like Christmas*, she thought dreamily. Was she already dying? Was her injury that bad? Had a broken rib plunged into her heart?

Was that even possible?

Before Emilie could come up with the answers to her questions, there was a deafening *boom* and a chorus of shouts erupted behind them. She craned her neck over Anderson's shoulder, but he was holding on to her too tightly for her to catch a glimpse of whatever was pursuing them.

"Freeze! It's the FBI!" shouted a loud, masculine voice.

An impossibly familiar voice.

That's how Emilie knew she was dying. There was no way she could be hearing Ben Wang's voice in that moment unless she was completely, hopelessly delirious.

It wasn't until a gunshot rang out that Emilie realized her delusion might have some truth to it.

"Emilie!" screamed another easily recognizable voice.

Ezra.

Emilie's body responded automatically, squirming toward the sound of his call as if it was the only thing she needed. She didn't understand how he could be inside Anderson's mansion, nor could she make sense of the symphony of heavy boots pounding across the floor.

Anderson clutched her tightly and lowered his lips to her ear.

"I'm going to kill you if it's the last thing I do," he whispered.

A chill raced down Emilie's aching spine.

Another gun shot rang out. Emilie gasped as the bullet made impact inches away from her skull… into Anderson's shoulder.

He shouted and dropped her, tripping over her and falling to his knees. Emilie landed hard on the marble, cracking her skull against the cool, smooth surface as warm blood spilled across her face.

Her body was made of pain, but she managed to turn her head just enough to see Ezra running toward her. Instinctively, she reasoned that she was hallucinating in her final moments, her mind searching for comfort as death descended upon her.

Before Ezra made it to her, Emilie's eyelids won the battle against her ability to stay awake and fell shut. After that, there was nothing but cold darkness and sweet silence.

Chapter Twenty-Three

Annie DeGaulle was ruthless, but for good reason. When Emilie was brought to the hospital from the bloody scene on Long Island, she barred Ezra from entering the room. He was under the impression that she liked him, that she wanted him to get back together with her sister. Despite that, it seemed that in the time span between his leaving the sisters' apartment earlier that morning and Annie receiving the call that Emilie was currently in an ambulance speeding to the closest hospital, she had reached the conclusion that every ounce of strife she was dealing with boiled down to a singular cause… Ezra.

So, she made it crystal clear he wasn't allowed to see Emilie.

He thought that was fair. It was his fault she was lying helplessly unconscious on a hospital cot.

But he couldn't bring himself to go home. He had recently stopped being good at following instructions.

For starters, Ezra wasn't supposed to go to Long Island, but when he stepped onto the private helicopter operated by an FBI pilot but owned by Hudson Enterprises, Ben Wang was too slow to stop him before they took off toward the location coordinates Agent Lane had managed to hunt down.

When the FBI learned there was a civilian on board, he had also been told that he wasn't supposed to leave the helicopter. He didn't listen to those instructions, either. He ran right into the chaos, side stepping agents and police officers alike to get to Emilie.

That moment had happened in slow motion. The piercing *crack* of a gunshot, a burst of red on the back of Anderson's suit jacket, and the way Emilie's body fell to the floor. She'd landed so hard on the marble, her skin splattered with Anderson's blood. Ezra knew instantly there was something wrong with her. She wasn't getting up. She wasn't moving at all.

All she could do was meet his gaze with wide emerald eyes for a fraction of a moment before she slipped away.

Ezra stayed with her, ignoring protests from everyone around him. Eventually, the authorities and medical staff gave up. It was clear that Ezra had no intention of leaving her side. They let him ride with her in the back of the ambulance. They even let him hover outside the operating room while they patched her up.

It was only when Annie arrived that Ezra finally met his match. She forced him out into the waiting room, claiming that their mother was on the way. The thought of meeting Emilie's mother like that—with Emilie's blood both physically and metaphorically on his hands—was enough to make him finally obey.

So, he waited. He bided his time. He watched the screen in the corner of the room showing the status of patients currently under operation, eyes glued to the *E. DeGaulle* as the minutes oozed by.

She was in surgery for over an hour until her name was moved to the column labeled *In Recovery*. He remembered letting out an exhale so forceful that he was halfway convinced he'd been holding his breath since he first saw her fall to the floor of the eerily empty mansion. She was okay.

Well, maybe not okay, but she was alive. *Alive.*

Twenty minutes after that, Annie reappeared. She sat down in the seat next to him in the waiting room.

"She has three broken ribs," she told him. "One of the fractures was so bad it punctured her spleen, but the surgery went well. They're worried about the extent of her internal bleeding, and she probably has a concussion, but that's the extent of the damage."

Ezra started crying. It was embarrassing, but the tears slipped out before he could blink them away. Annie didn't reach out to pat his shoulder or offer him a tissue, but her expression softened.

"It's my fault," he whispered, sniffling and wiping his eyes with the back of his hands. His jacket and tie were abandoned long ago, leaving him in wrinkled trousers and a shirt with the sleeves rolled up haphazardly. "I'm so sorry, Annie. I'm so sorry for all the trouble I've caused your family. I'll leave her alone, I promise. I just want to see that she's okay, and then you'll never have to see me again."

Much to his surprise, Annie cursed and tutted her tongue at him.

"Are you serious?" she hissed. "This is not your fault, Ezra. The reason Emilie is here right now is because a very bad person decided to hurt her. That was *his* decision and he's going to pay for it. I don't blame you. The only reason I shooed you out of there was because I didn't want you making a fool of yourself in front of our mom. You're a mess, man."

Ezra chuckled, gathering himself back together.

"Oh," he whispered. "Good to hear. At least one of you doesn't blame me."

"She's a nearly impenetrable fortress," Annie sighed, rolling her eyes playfully. "But she'll come around. Actually, you two have that in common. You're both unbearably stubborn."

"I'm not stubborn—"

"I have about a hundred silly take-me-back flower arrangements inside my apartment right now that suggest otherwise," Annie quipped. "Anyway, my mom and I are going to head downtown to pick up her things from Blackwell Capital and grab her a change of clothes. If she wakes up while we're gone, feel free to make your move."

"You're a really good sister, you know that?" Ezra said to her as she stood up again. Her eyes were red and raw, but it was the only evidence of her prior fear. If Emilie was brutally unyielding, Annie was remarkably resilient. Their strengths complimented each other. He was glad they had one another.

"Thanks," Annie shrugged. "But I'm not as good as she is."

With that, she scurried away.

Ezra waited a few minutes, allowing Emilie's sister and mother plenty of time to leave the hospital before he made his way back to her room. When he rounded the corner, a nurse was stepping out and closing the door behind her.

She recognized him from earlier and pursed her lips in annoyance. He expected her to tell him to get lost, but instead she nodded her head toward the room.

"She's awake," said the nurse. "But her stress levels need to stay low."

It was a warning. The nurse wouldn't hesitate to collect him and personally chuck him out of the hospital if he upset her and caused her vitals to go off the charts.

"Noted," Ezra murmured to her. "Thank you."

He slipped inside the room, closing the door quietly.

Ezra expected her to still be asleep from the anesthesia, but Emilie's eyes were open. She was staring out the window, gazing over the tops of the buildings that could be seen from their tenth-floor perspective. At the sound of the door clicking shut, she turned her head slowly and blinked at him.

She didn't say anything, but it was better than screaming for him to get out.

"Hi," Ezra whispered, cautiously approaching her bedside.

Emilie continued to gaze at him. The nurses had cleaned the blood off of her, and her surgery bandages were hidden by the blanket pulled up to her chest. Other than the IV in her arm and the bruise on her left temple, she looked relatively fine.

She swallowed hard, then parted her lips to speak.

"Were you really there?" she asked, her voice hoarse and shaky. "At the mansion? I thought I saw you before I—"

Ezra nodded when she trailed off. "Yes, that was me. I couldn't stay back and wait for news. I had to be there and make sure I saw that you were safe."

Emilie's brow furrowed. "I thought I heard someone else, too. A guy I used to date. But I wasn't in a very stable state of mind, so I don't know. I swear it was him, though."

The corner of Ezra's mouth curved into a crooked smile. The tangled web of connections was as amusing as it was unlikely.

"Ben Wang?" he asked, his smile growing more pronounced when Emilie became even more visibly confused on how he knew the name of someone she hadn't been involved with since last summer.

"How do you—?"

"Ben is actually Agent Wang. He works for the FBI. He's been in the city investigating Blackwell Capital for a while. He's the guy you were supposed to go to the wedding with, right? He'll probably explain this to you when he gets the chance, but the reason he stood you up was because he is an undercover agent."

Emilie blinked. "I see."

"He's pretty good at his job," Ezra continued. "He reached out to me when he realized we were… involved."

"That's right," Emilie mused. "He saw us at the gala."

Ezra nodded.

"How funny," she whispered.

Ezra's phone vibrated with a text. He pulled it out of his pocket as Emilie fell silent, claiming the plastic chair at her bedside. There were at least a hundred unread notifications on his phone, most of them messages from Matt—who was holding up the fort at Hudson Enterprises—and Ben—who was relaying minute-by-minute updates to him regarding the arrest of Anderson Blackwell. Mere hours had passed since Emilie had been saved from the scene, but

Blackwell was already handcuffed to a hospital bed on Long Island. The bullet wound was patched up and they were ready to book him first thing in the morning.

He wasn't sure if he should tell Emilie all of those things yet. Maybe she wasn't ready to hear about Blackwell after the trauma she'd gone through because of him. She probably needed time.

Ezra switched off his screen and glanced back at Emilie. She was watching him closely, but it was impossible to tell what she was thinking.

"What time is it?" she asked.

"A few minutes past midnight," he answered.

"It's been a long day."

"It sure has. You should get some sleep."

"I don't think I can sleep right now," she admitted. "The meds they gave me aren't working very well."

"Do you want me to find a nurse?" Ezra stood up halfway, but Emilie lifted a feeble hand to stop him.

"It's okay. I'm fine for now," Emilie whispered.

Ezra nodded and settled back down.

"Do you need anything else? Water? Are you allowed to eat yet?"

She ignored his doting questions. "Who are all those messages from? Where is… he? He was shot. Is he—?"

He obviously referred to Blackwell. Ezra was wrong. She did want to know.

"He's alive," Ezra told her. "The bullet wound is minor. He'll be officially arrested and moved to the federal prison's medical ward tomorrow."

"How long are kidnappers held in prison?" Emilie asked. "I'm sure he'll have an expensive lawyer."

Ezra bit his lip, tapping his phone. "I think the sentencing for that alone can be pretty intense, but that's not the only charge he's facing."

"What kind of charge do they give for attempting to steal another person's multinational conglomerate?" Emilie asked, the slightest hint of a joke in her voice. Ezra was relieved she was capable of humor after the events of the day. It was a good sign.

"Well, yeah. There's that…" he said, lowering his voice even though they were the only two people in the room. "But also, according to Ben, they raided the mansion on Long Island. They found an insane amount of drugs hidden in the walls, plus a secret tunnel that led to a hidden dock on the water. If it's true that the Blackwells are a crime family, I'd say that house has been used for their business dealings for generations."

"No way," she whispered. "Drugs?"

"Mhm, and now the FBI has all the probable cause they need to shut down Blackwell Capital and comb through their system for evidence of money laundering and other fraudulent activity. I think that's why Anderson was trying so hard to get rid of me and my company. He wanted to expand his crime network on an international scale. I mean, Ben said the FBI's been onto him for a while, but they were waiting for the ideal moment to pounce."

Emilie nodded slowly, her hands gently fluttering on top of the covers over her ribcage. She looked like she was in more pain than she was willing to admit. Ezra wasn't above bypassing her stubborn wishes and fetching a nurse, so he stood again.

He made it about two and half steps toward the door before she spoke.

"I quit, by the way," she said.

Ezra turned. "What?"

"My job," Emilie clarified. "I quit."

Even though it meant the loss of a talented employee, Ezra beamed.

"Really?"

"Why do you look so happy about it?"

"I understand why," he replied. "And anyway, you told me you were only planning to be there temporarily. Does this mean you're going to paint full-time? After you're healed, I mean?"

She attempted to shrug, but the maneuver was too painful, so she grew still again.

"Yes. That's the plan. I think life is too short for me to waste any more time."

Ezra thought about how scared she must have been when Blackwell had taken her. He was a conniving, untrustworthy man and, even though he made promises to keep her alive for at least twenty-four hours, Emilie was probably mentally preparing to die. Ezra couldn't imagine the trauma left behind by an experience like that, and was determined to do whatever it took to make sure Emilie knew she was safe from that point forward.

Anderson Blackwell was going to prison for the rest of his life. He was never going to see the light of day again. He was never going to hurt her again.

"That's amazing," Ezra told her, returning to her bedside. He took one of her hands. "I accept your resignation and would like to offer you twelve months of severance pay."

"That's ridiculous—"

"—and each time you try to fight me, I'll increase it."

"Ezra! Don't be so—"

"So *what*? Haven't you heard? I have a monopoly on the industry now. How about eighteen months of severance pay?"

"I don't need your—"

"—twenty-four months?"

Emilie shut her eyes and exhaled in defeat. "You're infuriating. You can't pay me for two years' worth of work when I worked at your company for a grand total of, like, three weeks."

"Consider it an apology for all the trouble I've brought into your life," Ezra offered. "A settlement of sorts."

"And what if I accept it, then donate it all to charity?" she challenged.

He shrugged. "Then I'll match your donation."

She let out a breath of laughter. "Whatever."

He squeezed her hand gently. "Hey, by the way, if you're not my employee anymore, does this mean we can go on another date?"

Emilie tugged her hand out of his grasp.

"I don't think that's a good idea," she told him.

He had expected the rejection. He was prepared. Instead of reaching for her hand again, he sank down onto his knees and pressed his palms together in a praying gesture. She let out a squeak of surprise, smirking down at him.

"Tell me what I have to do," he said, staring at her earnestly.

"What?"

"Tell me what I have to do in order to win back your heart," Ezra clarified. "Whatever it is, I'll do it. If you want me to walk barefoot across hot coals, fly to moon and bring you back a souvenir, and build you your own personal fleet of warships... I'll do it. If you want me to rip the sun out of the sky, I'll find a way to do that, too. Whatever you want, Emilie. Tell me."

The humor slowly faded from her expression until she was left staring at him with an impenetrable gaze. Ezra braced himself for another rejection. Here he was on his knees, literally begging a woman to give him another chance, and he wasn't confident that he was going to be successful. Emilie was unpredictable. It was one of the things he liked the most about her.

When she remained quiet for a beat too long, Ezra started babbling again.

"If you want me to build a time machine to go back to London last September and remember to leave my number behind, I'll find a way," he said. "I have some of the best engineers in the world at my disposal. I'm sure they can—"

"Ezra, for the love of God, get off the floor," chuckled Emilie.

She was laughing. Why was she laughing? Was it because she thought he was so ridiculous it was laughable or because she was endeared by his bold declarations?

Ezra obeyed, standing up and waiting for her verdict with a thudding heart.

"We have a long road ahead of us," she told him. "The police will probably want to talk to us a thousand times. They might even want us to testify in court. Plus, you're going to have to deal with a ton of PR stuff once everyone finds out about the Blackwell scandal. *And* just because I'm no longer working for Hudson Enterprises and painting part-time on top of it, doesn't mean I suddenly have a bunch of free time. Are either of us even going to have time to go on a date?"

"I'll make time," Ezra replied without hesitation. "You heard me. I'll do whatever it takes. Even if our date is just us holding hands on the way to Blackwell's trial or me sitting in silence watching you paint… I just want to be with you, Emilie. I've never been more sure of anything in my life. I was sure of it from the beginning."

"Since London?"

"Since London."

"We didn't even know each other's last names then."

Ezra shook his head. "I still knew. I wasn't aware of it, but deep down I knew you were the girl I was never going to forget. I spent months begging the universe for a chance to see you again. I'm not going to take that gift lightly."

"You're out of your mind, Ezra Hudson," she told him, shaking her head.

But she was smiling.

"Perhaps," he replied.

"Fine," she said. "I'll go on a date with you. But if I decide I don't want to go on another one after that, you can't turn my apartment into a greenhouse or write me adorable poems or offer to take me on a private tour of the Louvre. You have to promise you'll leave me alone if I ask you to."

"I promise," he told her, even though it pained him deeply.

"Good," Emilie replied, a delicate smile gracing her beautiful features. "It's settled. Now, can you please ignore what I said earlier and go fetch me someone with access to the gnarliest pain killers they have in this joint?"

Ezra punched the air in victory, grinning as the melodic sound of Emilie's laughter followed him when he darted out of the room in search of a nurse. The future wasn't set in stone, but if he could keep hearing her laugh and seeing her smile, he knew luck was on his side.

Epilogue: One Year Later

"It's closed," Emilie said to Ezra as they walked hand-in-hand along the Thames River on the cool, cloudless April night.

It was late, but London was still alive. It was only the second time in her life that Emilie had set foot in the city, but she remembered it as if she'd spent every weekend there. That was the thing about London. Once you set foot there, it followed you wherever you went afterward. The scent of fresh bread at Borough Market on Saturday mornings, the clink of glasses from inside a crowded pub, the stunning contradiction between the ancient stone buildings and modern glass structures... the familiarity of it comforted Emilie.

Even though she loved New York, she could picture herself living in London for a little while sometime in the future. She was a freelance painter; she could go wherever there were art galleries. Lena and Pierre had moved to Paris months ago, but they would still be closer than if she was in Manhattan. She could take the train across the channel to see them.

She and Ezra.

They were together in London again. After everything they had been through, it was the only conclusion that could be reached. Emilie eventually got over her stubbornness and acknowledged once and for all that she'd fallen for Ezra the first time she laid eyes on him.

"Ezra, it's closed," Emilie repeated.

Ezra ignored her protest, grinning as he squeezed her hand and tugged her toward the entrance of the Tate Modern Museum. The hour was half past ten. A sign on the door indicated that the museum closed hours ago.

And yet... there was a security guard waiting for them by one of the side doors.

"Good evening, Mr. Hudson," said the guard with a kind smile on her face. "Come inside."

Emilie chuckled quietly as Ezra shot her a wink over his shoulder. She should have known better. He was Ezra Hudson, CEO of Hudson Enterprises, after all. He could make anything happen, including gaining them access to one of London's most popular art museums.

Inside the massive, high-ceilinged entrance hall, Emilie paused and stared around in awe. The lights were dim, offering only enough illumination for the guards to make their rounds in the multitiered tower of priceless art.

"What are we doing here?" she asked him. "You do realize we can just come here during the daytime like normal people, right?"

"Ah, but if we aren't normal people, why should we pretend?" countered Ezra, using their entwined hands to pull her closer. He pressed a kiss to her temple. "Come on."

Still utterly confused but willing to humor him for at least another few minutes, Emilie followed Ezra through an archway to another section of the lobby, where yet another security guard was waiting for them by the elevators.

"Good evening," he said, gesturing for Ezra and Emilie to step into the waiting elevator. In hindsight, one would think Emilie might have a difficult time getting into unfamiliar elevators heading to undisclosed locations, but she felt completely safe with Ezra by her side.

As the doors slid shut she leaned into Ezra's warm embrace, wondering how much he had to pay to convince the Tate Modern to let him into the building after hours. Or perhaps he didn't have to pay anything at all. It was just as likely Ezra had made a connection in his dense network of international business transactions with someone at the Tate who happily agreed to let him in that evening free of charge.

Emilie learned not to ask how he earned the perks he enjoyed. Ezra was a good man with a pure heart. He was never up to anything suspicious and conducted himself with more morality than his former competition could even dream of possessing. Emilie trusted him; she was learning not to be so wary of the privileges that came with her relationship to Ezra.

For the first time in almost a year, Emilie thought about Anderson Blackwell as the elevator rose to the tenth floor—the top level of the museum. He had been sentenced to life in prison for a laundry list of crimes and Blackwell Capital, as well as the underground ring of crime operated by the Blackwell family, were completely dissolved. Ezra enjoyed being the unquestionable leader in the industry in their region, but he also welcomed healthy, productive competition.

In short, he would never let another Blackwell-esque villain rise again. Not if he could help it.

Emilie was surprised at how well she recovered from the kidnapping. Though her injuries were excruciating at the time, they were easily mended and quickly healed. On Ben's recommendation—who was, in fact, a real FBI agent—she saw a counselor to help her process the mental injuries caused by the event, but Emilie considered herself fully recovered ages ago.

She attributed it to the fact that she'd had an unbeatable support system. When Emilie was discharged from the hospital, her mother would accept nothing other than Emilie taking her bed rest in Queens so that she could dote on her. She had to practically battle her mother to let her leave and return to the lower east side. Emilie's brief stint back in her childhood home was also how Ezra eventually met her mom. She knew her mom would adore him, but the fact he was so nervous about the opposite was cute to witness. When Ezra brought Henry to drive them back to Manhattan, her mom acted as though her daughter was being whisked away in a royal carriage by a handsome prince.

The tiny apartment in downtown Manhattan was long gone at that point. A couple of months ago, Annie finished her master's degree and moved to Boston to start her first curator position at the Museum of Fine Arts. Shortly after, the lease ended and Emilie moved into Ezra's loft in Soho. Sure, they had barely known each other for a year at that point, but when things feel right—

And things did feel right. Every morning, she got to wake up beside the kindest, sexiest, nerdiest man in New York City. She kissed him while her coffee brewed and wore his t-shirts to bed and enjoyed the bliss of living intimately with someone she cared deeply about. Ezra designated a room in the loft as her private painting studio. He wouldn't admit it, but Emilie knew it was the best room in the house. Not only did it have perfect lighting, but it also featured a stunning view of the big, bright city around them. She had a feeling that it used to be his home office, but when she tried to say she could paint in the smaller room down the hall, Ezra wouldn't hear of it.

In terms of her art career, Emilie and Steven had built a close relationship that led to her meeting a proper art agent and other gallery owners with wall space to fill. Her paintings were available for purchase all over the city at that point, and when her agent learned she was going on vacation to London, he mentioned she could go international sooner rather than later.

But Emilie wasn't in a rush. She had a thriving career, a stable home, a wonderful family, and a boyfriend she loved.

Love. It was a simple thing, really. Love came easily to Emilie, and once the shadows of their shared past were securely locked away, she was ready to fall in love with Ezra Hudson. It didn't take her long to realize, at that point, she already was in love with him, but that wasn't the point.

The point was that life was full of surprises. Emilie had never expected to meet a man like Ezra. Never in her wildest dreams did she think their love story would play out the way it had, but she wasn't complaining.

Ezra hummed in her ear as the elevator rose languidly to the top of the museum. They were quiet, enjoying the peaceful shared solitude. It was their last night in London. After two weeks of exploring winding streets, tasting gin at little markets, getting caught in the rain on Primrose Hill, and making love in their suite on the riverside, they would return to New York to continue their lives together with fresh memories of the city where it all began.

When the elevator trilled and the doors slid open, Emilie gasped at the sight before her. She knew the tenth floor of the Tate Modern was not a series of galleries, but rather a public viewing platform of the entire city of London. What she didn't know was that Ezra had turned it into a romantic paradise for the two of them.

"Is this what you were doing earlier when you said you had to go meet a business colleague?" Emilie laughed.

A third security guard greeted them outside the elevators, then respectfully turned away to give them their privacy.

"You caught me," Ezra replied, a wide grin on his face.

As they stepped out onto the open-air viewing platform, a million twinkling lights greeted them. The multicolored windows of London's endlessly sprawling skyline glowed like fireflies. The Thames gurgled down below, splashing against the north and south riverbanks as a handful of pedestrians ambled across Millennium Bridge in the subtly glowing night.

That wasn't the most incredible thing Emilie beheld, though.

From the moment the museum closed, Ezra managed to coordinate an impressive amount of décor on the platform. Wisteria blooms dripped from the eaves of the roof, swaying in the gentle breeze. Lush ivy vines crawled along the barrier gate that kept visitors from falling to the street. Everywhere she looked was green. Even the dainty rose petals scattered on the concrete floor were dyed a delicate sage green. She knew it had been done on purpose.

Once upon a time, she'd told Ezra that green was her favorite color.

That was the thing about him. He never forgot a single thing she told him. He committed every part of her to memory as if she were the most important thing in the world.

Tucked amongst the foliage and flowers were hundreds of warm-toned fairy lights. They matched the city lights beyond, creating an overall image that was simultaneously cohesive and diverse. It was almost as if Ezra had brought one of her paintings to life.

"You are the most insanely romantic person I have ever met," Emilie whispered, walking slowly to the barrier and gazing out at the city of London. The golden dome of St. Paul's cathedral shone under the moonlight, reflecting the light it was given onto the world.

"So, you like it?" Ezra bit his lip, smiling down at her with giddy joy.

"I love it," she breathed, touching one of the delicate flowers on a nearby tendril of wisteria. "Are these real? How did you even manage this?"

"Pierre recommended a good florist," Ezra replied simply.

If Pierre knew about Ezra's stunt, Lena knew about it, too. How long had they been helping him plan this? And what on earth was the purpose? Sheer romance?

"I want to live up here," Emilie said, admiring the beautiful scenery Ezra had created with her in mind.

"It might get a bit cold in the winter," Ezra chuckled, waving his hand around at the lack of walls on the platform. "But, if that's what you want, I'll invest in a warm coat and join you up here."

Emilie giggled and reached up on her tip toes to press a kiss to his cheek. Just as she was about to pull away, Ezra turned his face toward hers and captured her lips in a kiss. Emilie smiled into it, wrapping her arms around his shoulders and leaning into him. His hands trailed up under the hem of her jacket and gripped her hips, digging into the fabric of her knit dress. She couldn't wait to get back to the hotel later that evening and get rid of the layers of clothing that separated them.

She pulled away from the kiss, smirking when Ezra pouted and followed her mouth with his to steal a simple, sweet peck from her.

"Seriously, though," she murmured. "What's all this for? It's very romantic, but I'm wondering why you didn't just bring the wisteria into our suite."

Ezra's eyes were sparkling brightly, but Emilie couldn't decipher the emotions whirling around inside his gaze.

"Well, I thought about that, but it didn't seem dramatic enough," he answered, hugging her close with his arms wrapped tightly around her waist while he spoke. "I also thought about renting out the entirety of the London Eye for the evening, but they weren't very accommodating. Oh, and for a minute I considered asking my contact with the Queen to let me use the Chelsea Gardens for tonight. In the end, I decided to go for something a little simpler."

Emilie laughed at that. Nothing about their surroundings was simple, but it was cute how Ezra thought decking out the top floor of a museum in flora and fairy lights was relatively basic.

"And why on earth would you need to go to the trouble of doing any of those things?" Emilie asked him.

"Because I wanted tonight to be special."

"Every night I spend with you is special."

Ezra kissed her forehead. "That's very sweet, but I meant that I wanted tonight to be *extra* special."

"—and why is that?"

Was she forgetting something? It wasn't his birthday, nor was it hers. Their anniversary wasn't until next month. Neither one of them had any outrageously incredible career wins to celebrate at the moment.

"Because I love you," Ezra replied. "And because I want to ask you something."

Awareness slowly trickled throughout Emilie's mind as Ezra let go and took a step away from her.

I want to ask you something—

No way. He couldn't be asking her *that*, could he?

Well, what else would he be asking? They already lived together. They were already on a lovely vacation together. They were already building a future together, day by day and brick by brick.

"Ezra—" Emilie whispered, her heart hammering so fast she feared it was about to burst out of her chest and rocket off into the night. She didn't know what to say. She could only watch as Ezra fumbled with the inside pocket of his jacket and then slipped whatever it was out of sight behind his back.

"Emilie DeGaulle," he murmured, staring deep into her eyes earnestly. "One year and seven months ago, I saw the most beautiful woman in the world sitting alone at a hotel bar. For some reason, I decided to do something completely out of character and sat down to speak with her. I didn't know it at the time, but it was a decision that would completely change my life for the better."

Emilie's throat tightened as tears pricked the corners of her eyes. She blinked rapidly and pressed her fingertips to her lips, the entire world beneath them completely forgotten.

"Maybe it sounds foolish, but I am a fool for love," Ezra continued. "I fell in love with you on that first night in London and I fell in love with you again six months later when you stumbled back into my life like a miracle. I fall in love with you every time I see you, every morning I wake up with you beside me, and every time I hear your voice and your laughter. I have London to thank for bringing us together, so what better place for me to do this than the city where we began?"

"Oh, Ezra," Emilie sighed as a single tear managed to escape and slip down her cheek.

Then, without hesitation, Ezra revealed the small black box he was holding behind his back and lowered himself onto one knee. He lifted up the box for Emilie to see and opened the cover, revealing a stunning emerald ring set in a crown of white diamonds on a delicate gold band.

An emerald, green like her eyes. Green like her favorite color. Green like the embrace of the lush plants that encircled them. It was beautiful.

"Emilie, I know it might seem like this is a little soon, but I know I love you with every cell inside my body," Ezra said, eyes shimmering with a hint of mistiness. "I want to spend the rest of my life with you. Will you marry me?"

A year ago, Emilie was dodging Ezra's calls and fending off his romantic declarations as if her life depended on it. A year ago, when she was kidnapped and didn't think she would live to see another day, she prayed for the ability to go back in time and erase Ezra from her history. She thought it was the only way to save herself, but it was a blessing that nobody answered her prayers. If there really was an all-knowing omniscient presence watching over her, they were adamant that Emilie and Ezra crossed paths.

They were meant to be together. Emilie was certain of that.

She was also certain that she loved him. She could picture their lives together. They would bicker over ostentatious displays of wealth, and five minutes later, make love on the kitchen floor. They would spend Sunday mornings at the farmer's market buying fresh flowers, go home and find the perfect patches of sunlight to display them in throughout the loft. Maybe she would teach Ezra how to paint. Maybe he would teach her how to fly a plane.

And maybe, just maybe, they would have a child with her eyes and his hair, her creativity and his ambition. Nothing felt truer than those visions of the future that didn't exist yet.

Therefore, without wasting another second, Emilie beamed and threw herself into Ezra's arms.

"Yes," she whispered into his ear. "Yes, I will marry you. I love you so much."

"I love you, too," he replied, lifting her off the ground and twirling her around with a wordless exclamation of joy.

When her feet touched the ground again, Ezra took her hand and slipped the ring onto her finger. It fit perfectly, as if it was meant to be there all along. Emilie admired the glittering emerald for a moment, then looked into the eyes of the man she loved. He grinned. In his smile, she saw a reflection of the happiness she felt deep in her bones. It was warm and radiant and full of hope.

And so, although it was the middle of the night, the sun shined brightly in London.

UP NEXT: Read Mary Jennings's premiere book *The Billionaire's Blind Date* included in the

Billionaire Rivals Series box set on Amazon: geni.us/blind-date

FREE NOVELLA: When my brother's cocky billionaire friend asked me to be his wife for the weekend, I never thought it'd be so hard to resist... Get *The Billionaire's Secret Wife* for FREE only at maryjenningsauthor.com/secrets

About the Author

My name is Mary Jennings.

I am a 34-year-old contemporary romance author living in upstate New York with my cat Pippa in our small cottage home.

Born and raised in upstate New York I realized at a young age that I loved fiction writing and sharing my stories with others.

This love turned into a passion of writing romance and a curiosity for traveling the world and experiencing everything life has to offer.

Now I spend most of my days writing new romance novels for others to enjoy. I hope to entertain you with my stories as much as I had fun making them!

I love all my readers dearly and I am thankful every day for those who get enjoyment and entertainment my books.

With Love,
Mary Jennings